A THOUSAND POINTS OF DARKNESS

ISBN: 978-1-62141-836-8
Library of Congress Control Number: 2012917880

Published by BookLocker.com, Inc., Bradenton, Florida.

The characters and events in this book are fictitious. Any similarity to real persons, living or dead, is coincidental and not intended by the author.

Printed in the United States of America on acid-free paper.

Booklocker.com, Inc.
2012

First Edition

"I'd Like to Teach the World to Sing" by B. Backer, B. Davis, R. Cook, and R. Greenway. "What Did I Do To Be So Black and Blue" by Fats Waller, Harry Brooks and Andy Razaf. "America" by Katherine Lee Bates and Samuel Ward.

Visit www.mymusicfriend.net
or www.athousandpointsofdarkness.com

Praise for *A Thousand Points of Darkness*

"An absorbing human struggle against the backdrop of a society consumed by its worst vices."

Able Greenspan - The Midwest Book Review

A THOUSAND POINTS
OF DARKNESS

For Suzanne,
for all
her support!

Adam Cole

Dedicated to Mike Shaffer,

World's Best Mailman.

Special thanks to my test-readers,
who made this book so much
better than it was:

Teresa, Louise, Vince, Suzanne,
Tom, Chris, Suzannah, Jason, Anna,
Milford and Eric.

IF ONLY

Some times I think to myself what
A beautiful world...
If only I could float on the
Blue wavy sea...if only I could
Fly in the beautiful sky like a
Bird...if only I could prance
Over the history of America.

Sophie Mumper

"Corporations are people, my friend."

Mitt Romney

Author's note: The name of the town in this book was chosen for its personal and literary significance. It is not meant to refer to the real town of Clear Point. The author has not been to any city of that name.

I love you...

Spots cover my eyes, like friends blocking out the light, gathering to look at me. But I have no friends. These spots are leeches that have always sucked the breath from my mouth and left me suffocated.

I brush them away and they scatter the way the images on the AVE scatter when you pass your hand through them, all the faces that chatter at you all day long 'til you get sick of the icons and force them to disperse like frightened fish in a pool.

I can see the outline of what might be a woman, blurry, soft skin, scent of a peach, it is both easier and more difficult to breathe near her. How old am I? Is this a memory, or what has been gone from my memory?

As I speak to her I hear a rumble from the grave, an older spirit that moans over my words and makes a mockery of them, tries to frighten the woman away.

She is not frightened and peers deeper into my face, the brown, wrinkled parched wreckage that contains the lines of where I've gone these last few...

Again I try to speak. Again the old man growls up from under the bed, cursing and rattling out my thoughts so that I get angry. I try and shout, but that just makes him angrier and he gets louder too. Through the blur I can see the woman's eyes open wide and she begins to back away, two steps, then three quick ones, turning and running as fast as she can from the room.

The anguished wail hurries after her out the door.

The Virgin

Just after his tenth birthday, in the first week after the thunderstorm season, Basil Ortega was waiting to catch a train to the Noke Company headquarters. It was going to be his job to provide drug entertainment to the executives at their party on behalf of the Drug Church on Glencrest. He stood on the platform wondering about the thirty minute ride that would make him a man.

Basil had ridden the train before, but never by himself. Never as the one in charge.

When Padre had told Basil he'd be going to Atlanta Proper, he had assumed it would be to help administer the drugs. He had been amazed when Padre had told him that he'd be going alone. He had never been to the heart of the Proper, much less to a big CUSA building. He wasn't even sure he'd be allowed in; he thought that somehow the embodied city would know who he was and prevent him.

But when he stuck his face into the holographic envelope, the sensation-generating AVE that produced it knew him and let him step on board.

Basil stepped back out of the pool of light, the dust-flecks flying inside it like fish in a fishbowl. Even though it was just a holographic space, it seemed to release him reluctantly, the light-ball in front of him closing like a disappointed pair of lips. He heard the doors coming together behind him, and he looked for a seat.

The first thing that occurred to him was how cool the air in the train was, a nice contrast from the searing November heat. Meanwhile, the acceleration was so smooth he hardly noticed the transition to flying at 100 kph towards the City Proper of Atlanta. The ramshackle buildings rocketing by him seemed to be fleeing from the mass of golden towers that made up the Proper. That mass, lying on the other side of Peachtree Forest, loomed larger and larger out his window.

This far out the train was generally empty. It only came to Atlanta's run-down outer neighborhoods to bring Shareholders who were making in-sight evaluations of real estate or other consultations in the land of the cricket-eaters. At least that's what Padre had told Basil. As the train got closer to the Proper it would pick up more veeps, some Uniforms. Would they be surprised to see the ten-year-old boy riding by himself? Maybe if they saw the canvas bag he carried over his shoulder, the bag of a Padre, they wouldn't think twice about it.

At the back of every seat was a site-based AVE, an Audio-Visual Envelope, which generated commercials all the time. If you had good number—that is, if you were rich—you could buy anything from them you wanted. All you had to do was speak to it or touch the pool of light, and it would respond like a budding flower. But Basil was ten and didn't have any number at all yet, and he wouldn't have been allowed to buy something if he had.

"Spikey, Spikey, so refressshhhing—"

A drink-can was hovering right in front of his hand, and if he moved through the image, he knew the AVE would go crazy trying to sell it to him. He kept his hand still while his thoughts spun backwards to the memory of his Padre's words.

"You're just a servant. As am I. Don't forget your sacred obligation, not to stand in the way of the Body and Blood, or I will beat you."

Basil had nodded quietly, even though the sound of Padre's voice was only in his imagination. He had been beaten several times before and was generally learning how to avoid it. You did a lot of nodding.

Coasting above the canopy of the forest, the train afforded an unobstructed view of the golden towers of the City Proper, wrapped in a loving network of alternate rail tubes. They loomed so large now that their shadows darkened the windows. On either side of the empty car the lush green alleys that had been planted full of briars with the bright red berries blurred into a messy brown. Basil opened his drowsy eyes to see a lone auto, over a hundred years old, lying on its side by some abandoned railroad tracks. The car was filled with dirt, and purple and yellow flowers sprouted out the windows. He passed it so fast that he couldn't believe he had really seen it. He jolted onto his knees and stared back the way he had come, hoping to get another glimpse, but the train had already gone around a curve and the car was lost to sight.

How did it get there? What was it? Old enough to be something from the last century? Honda? Volkswagen? The train ran on the old expressways heading in and out of the city, but the pavement had been wrecked years and years ago and no one could have driven on it. Had he really seen the car? No one would believe him if he told them. Padre wouldn't care. Maybe he'd tell Rosa about it if she wasn't being a pain.

A few minutes later the train pulled into the massive Five Points Terminal, where it became a local. As he stepped off, hundreds of suit- and skirt-clad Shareholders stepped on. A few gave him an odd stare, this little coffee-colored boy with his hemp shoulder-bag nearly as large as himself. Most just stepped around him, as though he were one of the vacumen gliding around sucking the dust off the pavement.

He didn't mind. He was too young to be in awe of Shareholders, young enough to be able to maintain a slight attitude of indifference. Besides, he had too much to think about. He had to remember what his Padre had told him. He had to remember the routine.

"We do not encourage the Indulgences of the unfaithful. But we are in no position to resist. They know we can arrange them and we are legally obligated to comply. That is why we take our duties even more seriously with the infidels than we do with our own flock. Who are the six who do not lock the gates?"

"Amphetamine," Basil answered. "Cocaine hydrochloride. Methamphetamine. Methylenedioxy-methamphetamine, methylphenidate, nicotine."

"Who are the three who sleep but do not die?"

"Benzodiazepine,   gamma-hydroxybutyrate, methaqualone."

"How is the lion brought to sleep with the lamb?"

"By the—" Basil paused. He could not remember.

He involuntarily winced and huddled towards the wall. He had been hit many times for forgetting that last one. *By the China Girl.* He could not forget it now. The words came to him along with a dull ache every time he moved his shoulder wrong.

Someone had decided to do more than stare at him or ignore him. A squat man in a grey charcoal suit and a matching cap approached him.

"Ortega?" he asked.

Basil nodded.

"I was expecting somebody older."

Basil shrugged. He waited patiently, and finally the man in the suit also shrugged and turned away. Basil followed him along the worn platform and up an escalator. In the stone façade of an ancient building buried in the tomb of the station, two bare-breasted women holding up laurels stared absently down over an old catwalk. Basil watched as the escalator slowly pulled the two sentinels past his view. At the end of the line, the escalator dropped him onto a sterling, scrubbed plaza. A glass roof filtered the sunlight pouring from above into a golden haze filled with bugs.

The man led Basil across the Elysian courtyard of Five Points Station to where his rickshaw was parked. Basil climbed into the back as the driver stepped behind the pedals. Leaning forward, the driver brought the carriage in motion and eased them into the light midmorning traffic.

Basil had never been to the Proper before and Padre had told him not to be seduced. But it was hard not to look as they glided past one after another of the colonnaded buildings of stone and glass, set off from the street by cultivated lawns with bright flower gardens and sleek plastic sculptures with brand names. Exterminators were everywhere, spraying to keep the endless bugs in check. A holographic band played commercials from a bandstand by the statue of Herman Talmadge. Basil's own world seemed drab by comparison; even the interior of the Church, which was beautiful and always clean, seemed ordinary in his memory. Everything here was *new*. Even the smoke-free air sparkled.

"Where do you live?" he asked the driver.

"In a coffin in the old Mariott Marquis," the driver said over his shoulder. "You ever been Proper?"

Basil shook his head. Then man, who did not see the gesture, looked back and said, "Eh?"

"No," Basil said loudly over the whistling wind.

"It's pretty, isn't it?"

Basil nodded. An immaculate woman, her skin glowing like a copper plate in the sun, led her two children and a perfectly groomed chow westward, balancing in her high heels on the marble sidewalk.

"Where do you live?"

"Sandy Springs."

"You really have drugs in that bag?"

Basil nodded.

The man did not see, but he asked a second question. "Anybody ever try and take that bag from you before?"

Basil did not reply. His Padre had never suggested that possibility. As far as he knew, no one would steal from a Padre in sight of an AVE. Uniforms would arrive to arrest anyone stupid enough to attempt it. Of course, he wasn't a real Padre. He folded his hands and looked away, across the lush expanse of Centennial Olympic Park. Happy *pequeños* could be seen screaming with delight as they romped naked in the squirting fountains.

The driver continued down Maynard Jackson for about ten minutes and then slowed at the base of a large pyramid. Before it floated a holographic sign that read *NokeCUSA LLP* in ornate Spanish letters. Smooth as a skateboarder, the driver swung the rickshaw around until it was parallel to the walkway neatly sheltered beneath the pyramid's base.

Basil got out, clutching his bag close to his side, and followed the driver through a revolving door and into a plush, spacious lobby bustling with prim, suited workers. They were lined up in rows before AVEs that sang the promise of various nutrition-bars and beverages. "Oooo, yes...*I never had anything like it before, Lotta. Spikey, Spikey...*"

Again, Basil noticed the perfectly manicured air of the place, filtered and cool, nothing like the drug-church with its sweet-smelling smoke and stifling, close atmosphere. An elevator shaft shot diagonally into that air, up the spine of the pyramid into the undersides of the office-homes that took up the bulk of the building's mass. Bypassing the curious receptionists with a sly nod, the driver took Basil across the lobby where a lift was waiting patiently for them. As they ascended Basil watched the floors collapsing beneath him, stacking like a deck of cards. For a moment, the elevator was enveloped by darkness as it reached the top floor.

The driver led Basil out the elevator and along a posh, carpeted hallway. The wall broke off after a short interval to reveal another level above and behind. Now

Basil could see the high ceiling coming to a point at the apex of an enormous area within which were hundreds of offices and apartments. Happy commercial music, cooing from a hidden source, suffused the whole enclosure.

The driver took Basil up a short escalator. Now he could see the expanse of the uppermost offices, the desks of the secretaries laid out like watch posts in front of the huge mirrored glass doors and walls of the execs. All the voices combined and floated up to the blue sky, which seemed to be trapped in the pyramid's ceiling-point.

"Wait here, okay?" the driver said to Basil.

He went on to one of the desks and exchanged words with the secretary behind it. She directed him with a transparent-nailed finger to a spiral crystal staircase a little way off. The driver nodded, turned around, and walked back to Basil.

"You sit here, *capitán*. He'll call you up when he's ready to see you. Dow!" With a cordial wave, the driver vaulted down the escalator and was gone.

The secretary, who was talking simultaneously to three holographic heads that floated in various places around her, did not seem to notice Basil. He sat down in a nearby chair. It molded to fit his bottom. Then it began to vibrate a little.

"They don't believe. They have no souls."

"They seek but they know not what."

"Little boy?" the secretary called down, standing over him. Basil had fallen asleep in the vibrating, form-fitting chair. Basil blinked, dazed. As if on cue, the chair ceased to shake. "You can go up." The secretary watched Basil get to his feet. He clutched his bag and plodded to the crystal stair.

Mr. Sattari's name was holographically projected on a door that dematerialized as Basil came within a foot of it. That door was the only executive door in the entire upper chamber that did not mirror the person in front of it. Instead it was opaque, black. Once the door had vanished, Basil could see that Mr. Sattari's office had two stories. Little boats floated in a small pool in the far left corner—real boats, real water, no holograph. Along the other corner sat what looked like a wide, squat armoire, its handleless doors closed tight at the bottom, its one drawer lying open in the middle, displaying a long row of black and white blocks arranged in a regular pattern of twos and threes. Leather-bound books, their spines decked in stately purples and forest greens, lined glass-enclosed shelves. Certain sections of the floor were transparent and revealed several stories below.

Three servants fluttered about the space. A woman in a black corset was removing the remains of a food tray to a hole in the back wall. A man in a tunic was busily dusting with an ion-sweeper.

Mr. Sattari's desk was on the upper level, accessible only by a short arching stairway of wide platforms, each of which seemed to have no visible support. The high plateau that was Sattari's work-space was crowded by a huge mahogany desk; a straight-backed chair facing it; a more comfortable chair behind it, in which Mr. Sattari sat; and a small sofa off to the side whose back was unprotected from the one-story drop. Just behind Sattari's left elbow, an unmoving servant with a solemn expression stood at the ready for anything he might desire.

Mr. Sattari, the *Siyo* of the Noke Corporation, was stern-faced, deep in concentration in the midst of his AVE. His fingers manipulated symbols made of light which floated around his head in a green halo, his eyes oblivious to the images blinking in the air before him as if he could see their characteristics without regarding them. To his right was a disregarded silver plate containing the remains of a meal. Basil gaped at the meat left on the plate. He had never seen *real* meat, only holographs of it in commercials.

Basil should have been in awe of the person rather than his dinner. This man with his green halo of faces and data was the *Siyo* of the Noke Company, one of the huge conglomerates that made up the Corporation of the United States of America.

Basil *should* have been overwhelmed. But, he reminded himself, he had a job to do. His position in the Drug Church kept him from losing himself. The *Siyo* would need him.

As the small boy ascended the platforms, Mr. Sattari's expression did not change; his brow did not unfurrow, nor did his eyes lose their concentrated focus. By the time Basil had mounted the lip of the last stair, the *Siyo* had returned his gaze to his fingers.

Basil stood uncomfortably for a second. "Sit down," Mr. Sattari dictated in a faraway voice. Basil took the straight-backed chair and waited.

After a while, Mr. Sattari looked up with the same distant expression and said, "I was expecting the Padre."

"He sent me, Mr. Sattari." Basil used his best Spanish.

Mr. Sattari regarded the boy critically up and down. "You're very young."

"I know the rites," Basil said, defending himself. "He sent me on my first assignment because I know them all."

Still, Mr. Sattari regarded him severely. "How old are you?"

"It doesn't matter, *señor*," Basil answered.

Surprised, Mr. Sattari started back in his chair. His eyebrows had exploded upwards, but his eyes remained crossed. Then he nodded, relaxed, sat forward. "You're right. You have the drugs, after all, don't you?" Now that Basil was closer, the *Siyo* looked very different. His brown face appeared much older, despite the absence of any grey in the bob of jet-black hair, tied in a pony-tail behind him. He sat stiffly, his body thin and erect under a white suit-blouse.

"The Body and Blood," Basil said, nodding.

Mr. Sattari barely heard him. He leaned back in his chair and regarded Basil more curiously. "How old are you?" he asked again, but this time the meaning of the question was different.

"Ten years."

"So young."

"Most boys start learning at four."

"Do all ten-year-olds make these trips?"

"My Padre's a stern man," said Basil with curious emphasis.

"So you really know what you're doing," Mr. Sattari answered, understanding his meaning.

Basil nodded.

"What about your mother?"

"Don't have a mother," Basil answered. "She died when I was little."

"Really?" asked the *Siyo*. "That's something we have something in common. I didn't have a mother either." Without pausing, the *Siyo* launched into a monologue. "I sometimes think I can remember her. Not her face, but everything else. Maybe she was there when I was a little child. I can almost see her in my mind, but then she backs out...fades away. Sometimes I feel her. She must have held me..." Mr. Sattari paused, his eyes distant again, no longer talking to the boy. Basil didn't reply. He had heard that sometimes before drug-parties the clients felt like sharing personal things.

"You know we're not worshippers," Mr. Sattari said abruptly.

Basil nodded.

"But you bring us the drugs anyway."

"We have to," Basil replied. Immediately he wondered if he should have said so in front of Mr. Sattari's servant, still standing obliquely behind the *Siyo*. Although anyone might have guessed how CUSA and the Drug Church were connected, no one was supposed to say it openly. CUSA liked to pretend that the Church, by offering free, limitless substances to its addicts, was evil. But the Corporation paid for everything. It was a compromise. The Church broke its rules, and the Corporation got its parties.

"It's a strange thing," Mr. Sattari said into his hand.

Basil didn't know what the *Siyo* meant. He sat in the straight-backed chair and waited.

"You give these drugs to addicts for free."

"Yes, *señor*." It was true. The addicts came and the Church provided. No questions were ever asked; no demands were ever made. Whatever means of worship addicts required, they got.

"Why?"

"They come, we serve."

"But they aren't happy," Mr. Sattari argued.

"Not until they use."

"But the drugs make them vomit. They turn them into slaves. They blindly roam CUSA like zombies. They don't even know how to feed themselves."

"We take care of them," Basil replied.

Mr. Sattari paused to consider. "Yes, but—" he began. "Why don't you help them quit?"

"That's their part," Basil said.

"What?"

"That's the burden placed upon them," Basil said, parroting his Padre.

"What do you mean."

"They have to quit. They take the drugs to go deep inside themselves. When they come out, they quit."

"But they never quit!" Mr. Sattari exclaimed, obviously irritated. "The drugs are so addictive!"

"It's up to them to quit," Basil said, simply.

Baffled, Mr. Sattari stared through Basil the same way he stared through his green halo. He leaned back, his hand on his mouth, his eyes pensive. After a while he straightened up. "Are you going to give my people addictive drugs?"

"No," Basil said. "We don't give those to nonbelievers."

Mr. Sattari nodded again through his hand. He seemed to have dismissed Basil with a thought. "Well," he said. "That's fine. Why don't you go down and wait by Ms. Sanchez's desk? The party won't start until this evening." By the time Basil had gotten to his feet, Mr. Sattari was immersed in his symbols again.

Basil descended the platform arc and exited into the lobby, hearing the door solidify behind him. He came down the stair to stand in front of the secretary's desk. Ms. Sanchez gestured to the chair where he had sat before. "You can sit there," she said.

Basil slid into the chair once more. It molded to fit his form. Then it began to vibrate again.

"We do not encourage the Indulgences of the Infidel..."

"Little boy?" The secretary, Ms. Sanchez, was standing over him, smiling. "It's time," she said.

Basil shook himself. The chair had once again gone still. The sky trapped in the apex of the pyramid was now black. Ms. Sanchez extended her hand. Basil took it and pulled himself out. He looked back at the chair suspiciously. "Usually clients aren't in there for more than forty-five minutes," she said. "You were in stasis for four hours. You can feel it." She sounded sympathetic. "You don't notice the time passing, but you can feel it." She nodded to affirm her own words. Basil had said nothing.

He felt naked, overly light. He looked himself over, and his breath caught in his throat. Trying to keep the trembling out of his voice, he said, "My bag." He was missing his drug-bag, with the sacred implements inside.

"We have it," said the secretary, reassuring him.

"Give it to me." He was quickly coming to himself as he looked directly into her eyes. The secretary frowned, unpleasantly surprised at the tone of Basil's voice. "Give it to me now!" Basil repeated, with more volume.

Put off by the intensity of his order, she found she could not answer him as she would have spoken to a child. She shook her shoulders a little as she turned.

"Follow me," she said. "I don't have it." Basil followed right at her heels, ready to overtake her at the moment he saw what was his.

"Oooo...yes..." came the voice from all directions, soft and sinuous. The AVEs were spaced every twelve meters along the wall, broadcasting at low volume. Voices came from everywhere, selling, tempting, accessible to anyone who came within reach of the spherical halo. Finally, after running the gauntlet of temptation, Basil and Ms. Sanchez arrived at an open doorway.

Several people were in a bare conference room, sitting around a low table on a sofa and chairs. The canvas bag was on the table.

Startling the occupants of the room, Basil sped towards his bag and grabbed it by the strap. They laughed, thinking him the child of an office-worker. "Hey, *amigo*, that's not yours," one of them said, rising.

Basil had gone into the corner with his back against the wall and glared at the man, who had begun moving towards him.

"It is," said the secretary quickly. "It is his. This is the dealer."

"Him?" the man asked, pointing at Basil. He seemed not to believe it.

The secretary nodded. Basil rummaged through his bag. It had been opened, but nothing was missing. He let out a barely audible sigh of relief.

"You'll be in here," the secretary said to Basil across the room. "You can start any time someone asks." Basil nodded at her curtly, to let her know he was ready for her to be gone. Making a funny shape with her mouth, the secretary turned on her heel and strode from the room.

The four people who had been sitting when he entered now regarded Basil. The one who was standing stepped towards him. "So, kid," he said. "You're the dealer."

Basil nodded, still holding his bag tight.

"We didn't go in it," he said, pointing at the bag. He was lying, but they were fortunate they hadn't opened anything. People had died at parties by ingesting unidentified powders and drinking liquids meant for syringes. If anyone at this party died, Basil would be held responsible.

"When can we start?" a woman asked him.

"Ms. Sanchez said we could start any time," a man interjected.

"Well, I want to start now," said the other woman in the room, getting to her feet. She moved towards Basil, who was still sitting on the floor in the corner. Coming near him, she slowed awkwardly. He watched her approach impassively but made no move to receive her.

"What do we do?" she asked, uncertain.

She had never taken before. "*White Lamb for the child*," Padre would have said. Basil opened his bag with a slow, practiced movement. He knew what to pull out without having to look, but he looked anyway, just for show. He removed a small pill, flexible like a sponge, with his fingertips.

She reached out her palm, but he shook his head. He signaled for her to get on her knees.

Smoothing her skirt, she knelt before him. As he held the pill before her mouth her eyes went soft. Like a child, she opened her lips, an expression on her face that was part surprise, part exultation, and solemnly he slipped the pill between them. "Don't chew," he instructed. "It has to sit beneath your tongue for thirty seconds. Then swallow it."

She nodded and closed her lips, remaining still. "In the name of the Holy Spirit," Basil said, making the sign of the cross over her. The other people in the room were getting to their feet. The man who had remained standing the whole time quickly knelt next to the woman, whose eyelids had begun to flutter.

"I want a Green Bus. Do you have a Green Bus?" he asked eagerly. "I had one last time." Basil nodded and reached for the capsule.

Next came a small man with wiry arms and weak eyes. He hardly looked at Basil as he knelt on the floor before him. Basil recognized the telltale expression of a Gamer. He was employed to play virtual scenarios in the AVE all day long. Basil knew about Gamers because they had to be blessed differently. Gamers rarely saw the world. Most of them had remained in full-time login since their school-days. Because they already lived in their own little world it was not helpful to give them certain kinds of substances. Basil had been instructed to make their forced sojourn in the physical world tolerable through mood-enhancers. Padre had told him that for Gamers this would suffice.

Just as the first woman was entering her convulsions, several other people came into the office. By the time her movements had stopped and her euphoria began, twenty people were lined up waiting for Basil's benediction.

It was always busiest at first, Padre had told him. The beginners rarely came back for seconds until near the end of the night, and the more experienced knew enough to wait before mixing effects. Those who didn't know how to be careful, Basil had to turn away for a while.

He had no trouble. By the end of the first hour, he was the only responsible person in the building; the rest of the occupants were engaged in drug-play. When things had finally slowed enough for him to take a break, he stood up, closed his bag, tucked it beneath his arm, and left to roam the top floors of the pyramid.

He had seen the effects of the sacred implements all his life, but only on the faithful, who used the addictive drugs. None of tonight's blessings would induce vomiting or generate hazardous delusions. As he walked around he saw some office workers leaping from table to table in a kind of line-dance, overtipping empty wine-glasses. A few sat in chairs and sofas in solitude and watched their own little mind-shows. Others talked back to the visions. They would not remember what they saw. As he passed the stasis chair he saw the secretary, Ms. Sanchez, sitting in it. She was trapped in an endless vision compounded by the technology of the chair.

Basil had not expected this situation, nor did he know how to handle it. The woman might be in real danger. Putting a hand on her arm, he brought the chair to its still state. She did not blink.

He pulled her gently from the chair by her arms. She came out easily. Laying her on the floor face down, he checked her pulse. It was slow but steady. He pulled a salve out of his pack, wetted two fingers, and applied a patch to the side of her neck. Then he left her. She would soon recover and come back for more.

He wandered past a couple who held each other without moving, like two mummies in a single coffin. Another pair just down the hall were trying to touch one another but seemed unable to do it. The faces approached one another again and again, only to be stopped when the lips were just centimeters apart. Each seemed perplexed by their inability to cross the space.

Standing next to them, three men watched the Denver Post at New England Kellogs game being broadcast by the AVE, not really knowing anymore what they were looking at. Instead of cheering, they stared, baffled, at the running men. Basil strolled past them, walking through the 3-D image of the players.

Finally, several people accosted him at the bottom of the crystal stair. "We want more," said a man in a black frilled shirt and matching vest. "I want the Rainpowder. Do you have the Rainpowder?"

Basil shook his head.

The man looked crossly at him. "I know you have it," he said. "I took it at a party once before. I know you guys keep it in your bags."

Basil shook his head, feeling a little nervous.

The man's expression darkened. "Give it to me *now*, you little shit," he said. He grabbed Basil by the lapel with a black fist.

"Leave him alone," said another man, interfering with his hand on the first man's arm. "He's just a kid."

"But this other stuff is candy," argued the accoster. "I want you to try the real thing, and I know he's got it." He glared at Basil. The boy returned the stare, outwardly keeping his calm over the panic that was making him tremble.

"*If you lose control, you've got to go,*" Padre had said. "*Don't let them see you're afraid or they'll take the bag.*" Basil kept control. He kept his gaze fixed on the man who was holding him. "*Remember, he's off balance,*" Padre told him. "*When he's on the light take, you're smarter and stronger than him.*"

The executive frowned down at Basil. Even in his current state he did not appear as if he would be intimidated by a ten-year-old. Basil began to be afraid that he'd given the man the wrong dosage or combination.

"Look," said a woman from behind. "He's just a little kid. Take him up to Mr. Sattari. He'll make him give it to you."

The accoster nodded. "You're right," he said. He grabbed Basil firmly by the wrist and began pulling him. The others followed, whooping, excitement surging behind them until, like a wave, they burst through the doorway and floated up the platform stair in Mr. Sattari's subdued, dark office.

The *Siyo* was still dancing through holograms with his fingers, though the servant had vanished. He did not look up at the stampede that had entered his office. Basil suddenly realized that Mr. Sattari was the only one who had not yet come to him. The *Siyo* was still attired in his work clothes, still penetrating the light-symbols with his fingertips.

"Mr. Sattari, why are you still workin-*guh*?" an older woman giggled like a child. Mr. Sattari looked up mildly, a patient expression in his eyes.

"Come on, sir," an older man said, moving to grab Mr. Sattari's arm. Irritably, Mr. Sattari pulled it away. It came easily from the rubber grip of his subordinate. He kept his voice mild. "Go on," he said to them. "Have fun."

"But Mr. Sattari, you're missing the party!" said the first worker.

"That's all right," he said, smiling a little. "I'll come down later. I'm sure the boy has lots of drugs still." He had not seen Basil.

He was pulled out roughly by the disgruntled employee. "Mr. Sattari, he's holding out on us! I asked him for some Rainpowder and he said no. I know he has—"

Upon seeing Basil, Mr. Sattari's expression changed dramatically. The *Siyo* surged to his feet. "Let him go! *Now!*"

Cowed and terrified, the man fell back into the shelter of his group. Everyone had fallen silent. They stood there like guilty children, looking away now, afraid to move.

Mr. Sattari swept his grave eyes over them for a long moment. "Go," he finally told them. "I'll handle our dealer. If any of you lay another *finger* on company property, your contracts will be terminated. Mr. Valazquez, you have had enough. Go to your office and go to bed."

The disgruntled employee nodded his head as if were sitting on a spring. Half backing, half tripping, the group of workers made their way down the platform-stair and out the door, a couple of them barely restraining a few giggles at last as they fell out of earshot.

Mr. Sattari cocked his finger in the air and the door became solid. He looked down at Basil. "I'm sorry," he said. "Did they hurt you?"

Basil shook his head. He was shaking a little, but he felt he had to keep himself under control. A Padre wouldn't cry.

Mr. Sattari sighed heavily and sat back down in his chair. For a while, he lost himself behind his hand, swimming in a wash of thoughts. Then his eyes flitted up to Basil.

"Here," he said, gesturing in the air with his finger. The air lit up where his finger was for a second. Instantly a servant emerged from the wall bearing a frosted metal dish of chocolate ice-cream.

Basil looked at it, stunned. Sattari nodded once, and Basil seized it greedily. He had never had ice-cream, but had seen it in commercials.

"Why didn't you give him the Rainpowder? Is that what it was?"

"I'm not allowed," Basil answered quietly, shoveling the chocolate in as quickly as he could. The metal spoon slid cold and wonderful through his mouth.

"Do you have it?"

Basil nodded yes. "I'm supposed to carry it in case I meet an addict. But I'm not allowed to give it to you." He paused to consider his response. "It's for the faithful." Mr. Sattari considered for a moment. Then, as if he had been thinking about it since their earlier conversation that afternoon, he said, "It's the mission of your believers to quit."

"Yes," Basil nodded, his mouth full.

"How can they quit when you keep giving them drugs?"

Swallowing, Basil answered, "We support them so they don't have any excuse."

"What?" Mr. Sattari seemed baffled.

"Only they can quit," Basil insisted. Still vexed, Mr. Sattari frowned at Basil. "Padre could explain it to you," Basil said. He was scraping the remains of the chocolate off the bowl with the spoon, trying to get the last dregs. "They take the drugs to see. We make sure nothing gets in the way."

"What do they see?" Mr. Sattari wondered aloud.

Basil hesitated. "I don't know," he replied. "We're not allowed to take the dru—the Body and the Blood."

"You've never taken them!" Mr. Sattari repeated, astonished. Basil shook his head no. "Why?"

"We're not allowed," Basil repeated simply. At first, Basil appeared as though he either would not or could not explain. "Sometimes they see demons," he said.

"Demons," Mr. Sattari's voice sounded hoarse, as if the word was heavy on his throat.

"Sometimes they see angels, too," Basil said quickly. "They scream and carry on, or they sit for hours, sometimes days; some of them, they don't eat unless we feed 'em, don't drink unless we give 'em water. They just see and see." Basil was examining his bowl carefully to see if there was anything left in it.

"And do they ever quit?" Mr. Sattari asked.

Basil shrugged, putting the bowl on Sattari's desk. "Not when they're with us. They come and go, they move from Church to Church. One day, maybe, they stop coming. We never see that part."

"What do you suppose they see that makes them stop coming?" Mr. Sattari asked.

Basil shrugged.

The secretary's face appeared. "Siyo," said the face. "Your wife wants to talk to you, but you've got her blocked. Do you want me to open a link?"

Mr. Sattari hesitated. Basil watched him curiously.

With a sideways jiggle of his head, Mr. Sattari shut his AVE off. The faces babbling around him vanished. Now only Basil and the *Siyo* were in the room.

Shifting, as though the weight of the light had been a huge burden on his head, the Siyo leaned sideways and cocked his neck to look at Basil. He seemed to be trying to decide something.

Abruptly, he spoke. "I want to quit," the *Siyo* said.

Basil jumped, quite taken aback by the words and tone of the Sattari's voice. "What did you say?"

"You heard me," said the *Siyo*. "I hate this place. I hate what it stands for, and all the people who help it along. Every day I do my job and I despise myself." Mr. Sattari paused to regard Basil's reaction. "Does that surprise you?"

Basil shook his head quickly, emphatically. He thought it best to agree with the *Siyo*.

"I want to see," Mr. Sattari said.

Basil pretended he didn't understand. His eyes fell upon the objects on Mr. Sattari's desk. Holographic projections were organized and stacked upon each other. One of the papers blinked.

"I want to see," Mr. Sattari repeated.

Basil looked up at him as the dealer again. "You want to escape?"

Mr. Sattari's brow wrinkled. "No," he clarified. "I don't want any party drugs. I want to see like the faithful see. I want the real drugs."

"You can't take those," Basil said.

"Why not?"

"You're not a believer."

"I want to believe."

Basil's face wrinkled in surprise. Padre had never spoken to him about this. Nobody joined the Church. Addicts simply appeared, already lost, looking for a fix. Basil wavered. "I don't—"

"You have them with you. You said you did."

Basil began to be afraid again. He remembered the locked door behind him.

Mr. Sattari went on. "I have demons I need to see. I have to talk to my demons."

"I can't," Basil said. "I—"

"You must," Mr. Sattari growled.

"I don't know how. I'm not a Padre."

"You have them. Just give them to me."

"I can't!"

"Give...them...to...me..." said Mr. Sattari sternly, standing up again to his full height.

"I can't!" Basil's voice was strained and anxious. Clutching his bag, he retreated from Mr. Sattari. The executive glared, but not directly at Basil.

"You don't understand," Sattari said gruffly, trying to explain to Basil as if the child were his colleague. "It's not sane here. You see? I've got to become insane to think clearly."

Basil regarded Mr. Sattari carefully from the edge of the platform. The *Siyo* was standing behind his desk looking down at the glass floor, as if reading the words that came out of his mouth on the polished transparent surface.

"I need—" he began. Stopping, he brought his hand to his mouth to consider. "I need absolution...to be released from my responsibility, if only for a minute. I need...*absolution*," he said again. The *Siyo* looked at Basil now, his questioning eyes soft and pliant like a dog's. "Aren't you supposed to give that?"

Basil nodded. Then he shook his head. He didn't know. "To the faithful," he stammered.

"I want to join," Mr. Sattari said again.

Basil shook his head. He could still taste the ice-cream on his tongue.

"I said *I want to join!*" Mr. Sattari's palm slammed onto the surface of the desk. Virtual documents flew into the air and quickly reorganized themselves in a blinking pattern.

Basil backed up a step, though there was nowhere to run. "You going to hurt me?" he asked.

That stopped the *Siyo*. But it didn't shock him. He seemed to be considering, his face taking on the familiar glassy, distantly rational expression. He lowered himself slowly into his chair once more, moving forward a little. Its springs adjusted with a groan to his weight. It was an old-fashioned chair, not resting on a magnet or an air-cushion. "Do you play your history?" Sattari asked.

Basil paused for a moment before answering. "I play a little."

Mr. Sattari held the boy in his gaze, unblinking. "Have you ever played *The Sword of Hendrix*?"

Basil shook his head, no.

Sattari's eyes lit up. "It's brilliant!" he said. "If you ever really want to understand CUSA, you must play it. Do you log on to school? Do you know who Hendrix was?"

Basil hesitated. Quickly, Sattari spoke up. "He was the man who, seventy-five years ago, created the Corporation in order to rescue the old USA from its waste and dissent." Sattari looked away and swallowed. "In the game, you become Hendrix. You are trying to end the Correction. You must make the decisions which will defeat your rivals and satisfy the American People, all the while keeping the Sino Conglomerate from buying us. It's a difficult game. But in facing his demons, you come to recognize his brilliance, the impossible ideas he was able to spin.

"We had to pay off our debt, do you see?" The *Siyo* gazed intently at Basil, trying to ascertain whether the boy could understand. "To China, to Japan. By seizing all of this country's assets, making all of us employees of one great nation, he saved us!"

Mr. Sattari's eyes looked off to the left. "It's really stirring," he said, "to walk the flooded streets of old Washington. To be there for the Kansas Famines, the Armageddon Swindle, the Sterility Incentive." Mr. Sattari breathed deeply.

He looked back at Basil. "Do you know what 'budget' is?"

Basil shrugged.

"Well, you need to know," said the *Siyo* kindly. "Let me explain it to you. Have you ever run out of number?"

Basil nodded rapidly. Yes, he knew what it was like to have nothing.

"Well," Mr. Sattari said, "If you're CUSA, you have to make lots of decisions every day. How much to spend, how much to keep, because lots of people are depending on you to stay alive.

"One of the most difficult decisions Hendrix had to make was how to keep the climate steady. We're in a delicate, constant negotiation with the Sino Conglomerate, MexIran, all the corporations of the world. Enough number has to be flowing in to keep CUSA healthy, but if we get that number from too much of the wrong sources, it can affect the environment. Our planet." Mr. Sattari placed his hands on his desk and looked at Basil.

"We're consuming too much," Mr. Sattari whispered. "The Canadian farm-reports are indicating a record low yield. There's too much carbon in the air again. The floods and famines are coming back."

"What?" Basil cried. "Can't you do something?"

"No, no..." Mr. Sattari said, shaking his head. "Our revenue stream depends on a delicate balance of burning the right amount to keep the economy stable. It's my task to make sure that we only use as much as the environment can stand." Mr. Sattari sat back and laced his fingers behind his head.

Basil waited a moment, then asked, "What happens next?"

"Well!" said Mr. Sattari with a nod, approving of the question. "We don't know, do we? We have to find a solution or the entire world falls apart. Then where are we? What do *you* think we should do?"

Basil shrugged. "Use less energy?"

Mr. Sattari shook his head. "Yes, but how? CUSA relies on a certain amount of revenue to keep the economy stable. If we curb that revenue, we risk sending many, many people into poverty." Mr. Sattari's eyes seemed to cross as he looked away from Basil. "They might rise up again. Become violent. You wouldn't want that, would you?"

Again, Basil shrugged.

"I have to eliminate some of our demand in the right way. Just enough to keep us under the carbon threshold, but not so much that revenues will be disrupted." Mr. Sattari paused. "One million one-hundred-fifty thousand and nine." he finally said.

When Basil showed no sign of understanding, the *Siyo* went on. "You see, we can't simply ask people to stop consuming. That wouldn't be fair. We could terminate their employment, make them poorer, but once those people stop working, they would become even more of a burden on the economy.'" He stopped again. "You know what I'm talking about?"

Basil nodded slowly, beginning to understand. The *Siyo* was supposed to order a million people to be killed.

The *Siyo* continued speaking. "Basil, I've just told you a lot of state secrets. I wanted you to understand what my life is like, why I need absolution."

Basil's throat seized like his arms, clutching the bag before him like a shield that could protect him from the information he knew was coming. "You see," said Mr. Sattari, "a man like me, he has to make extremely difficult decisions.

For the last time, Mr. Sattari rose solemnly to his feet. "You have to make a difficult decision, too. Right now."

"You can stand there and watch while I order the early termination of a million people, or you can give me the drugs I want, which will surely incapacitate me and possibly make me forget you. Then you can get out the door and run to your Padre." Mr. Sattari clucked his tongue.

Basil didn't want to hear. He wavered on the edge of the platform, rocking from side to side.

Mr. Sattari put his finger over one floating button near his desk. "This symbol," he said, moving the icon over a little, "begins a process which will solve CUSA's problem. Executives will make adjustments and give orders. Termination centers will open for 24-hour service. Young Guns will come around to peoples' houses and begin taking families away. More than a million of them." The *Siyo* moved his finger. "*This* symbol," he said, "opens the door and lets you out."

Mr. Sattari looked expectantly at him. "Make a choice."

Basil did not answer. His eyes searched the room, the little glass ceiling raised to a point above them, the distant lights of the buildings beyond, the desk, Mr. Sattari's face, Mr. Sattari's fingers.

"I don't want to," said Basil.

"I don't want to either," said Mr. Sattari. "Isn't that awful? We all have to make awful decisions...I'll give you ten seconds," said Mr. Sattari.

Basil looked at the door, which was obviously locked. He wanted to run, to get out. "One," came the *Siyo's* voice. He looked up at Mr. Sattari, who was watching him with his finger over the death button. What if Mr. Sattari slipped and his finger fell through it? "*Two,*" continued Mr. Sattari ominously. "Three. Four..."

Basil could smell the sweat of the man, now. Mr. Sattari looked calm as stains grew around his armpits and his hand began to shake a little.

Basil looked through his bag, going over the possible choices. What would Padre suggest? A stimulant; the *Siyo* would feel it much sooner. He was asking for a hallucinogen, but that would take too long. Basil's hands found a syringe and a phial with a rubber membrane sealing it. He pulled them out. Leaving his bag on the floor, he rose to his feet and held the implements up to Mr. Sattari. "This is what you want," he said.

Mr. Sattari gazed in wonder at the phial and syringe. "That will make me a...believer?" he asked in a surprisingly small voice.

Basil nodded. Mr. Sattari reached for them, but Basil held them back. "Take off your blouse," he instructed.

Immediately Mr. Sattari did so. He fell back into his chair with a thump of flesh against leather. Basil looked at the executive's virgin forearm. The veins were large and easily defined.

As Basil came around the desk, Mr. Sattari's body lurched forward. Basil jumped back, but Mr. Sattari was only reaching for the symbol that unlocked the door. Falling into his chair again, he looked up at Basil. "I've ordered a rickshaw to drive you home," he said. He offered up his soft forearm to Basil.

His heart beating wildly now, Basil applied a tourniquet to Mr. Sattari's triceps. Returning to his bag,

Basil took the syringe, expelled the air, and inserted it into the membrane. He drew all the fluid out of the phial.

Smoothly Basil injected the needle into Mr. Sattari's forearm. " 'He was crucified'"—he gave the syringe a slow, steady push—"'under Pontius Pilate, suffered, and died.'" Fascinated, Mr. Sattari watched the fluid leave the syringe and enter his vein. "'And on the third day he rose.'" Now the drug was completely gone and was coursing through Mr. Sattari's system.

The *Siyo* leaped to his feet. An obscene grimace stretched his face so far it could have pulled the skin from the bone. He began to shake triumphantly. "Go," he whispered to Basil.

But Basil was already gone.

I turn away from the door to face the window where blackness reigns beyond the glass. I feel as if I have known this room for some time, have spoken to the glass and the man in the glass, but I have no memory of anything except not sleeping, not sleeping for the longest time, tossing and turning, feeling the ache in my hands, the burning inside each knuckle, angry wasps trapped in my joints, a commercial of hornets humming in their incessant, throbbing drone. Only sleep could set them free, but I never sleep. I only vomit into a great and coated bucket by my bed on the hard wooden floor and then I feel a little better and lie on my back and rest.

Now I am turning to the window. Beyond the glass is the image of a little boy. He peers through at my face. I roll towards his image and fall into a tangled mess on the hardwood, my shoulder throbbing, my head hitting the bed frame. I moan and I try to reorient myself, try to find the window. I don't want to lose the little boy. I need him. Without him, I can't escape.

I roll for ten minutes until I can get my skinny legs under me and I shove sloppy against the floor and somehow I rise, I get my head six feet in the air and I float across the room because I am not walking, could never balance on feet I no longer feel. Fortunately I float towards the window and there is the face of the boy, still peering, unbelievably curious about me, and I see myself now.

Haggard, wrecked, bloodshot, my face is not as black as the inkiness beyond, but it shows the wear of the time I have forgotten, the stories I have created, some which were real and others...I get closer and my own face gets larger, so that I can see the lines I have followed to get me here to this place, this room I don't know with the hardwood floor and the dresser against the far wall, the bed with the bloody sheets and the pail in a puddle of vomit on the floor.

But the boy's face doesn't get larger, and it doesn't get clearer, and he doesn't look afraid as I approach. I only realize that his face is a reflection when I finally reach the glass and smash through it with my hands.

The American

Executives lived in crystal chandeliers, upside-down earrings, champagne glasses. Drivers lived in corrugated boxes. As a driver, Vam preferred the chandeliers, but drivers couldn't live and work in the same place. That was a luxury for the citizens on the upper end of the rubber ball.

Maids, street sweep operators, repair ops, and waste recyclers, born to their tasks, went to school for six years to learn the rules, then hit their stride mopping green slime off the reactor floor. Vam had inherited his position from his dad, who had passed up a higher bid for the position in order to bequeath to his son a way of life that was at least human.

But his father had miscalculated the effects of his deed, for Vam as a driver got to see the inside of the palaces, the work-play centers that were the world for the lucky few, those money-trading heroes of the City

Proper who were the hum in CUSA's hive. Vam's father had died in a Euthanasia Center at age sixty-five before he could recognize the dissatisfaction in Vam's expression. His mother, ten years shy of her Discount Death Option, stood over the body of her husband and looked at her son with eyes sunken like trails in a canyon. She saw. Those maid's eyes had also been in the palaces and she knew the look of envy, and of self-disgust.

"Son," she said. "Your father died a happy man."

"Sure, Mamma," he answered. Sarcasm was merely a choice of repertoire at that age, not yet the habit it would soon become.

"Don't desire more than you can get," she warned him, her comment sizzling like a quickly drawn machete. He did not answer her, still not sure in his own mind of what he had already seen.

The programming had still been fresh on him, barely dry. *In America you got what you deserved.* "You could be anybody in America," they said, meaning that it didn't matter what race you were, what sex, where your family was from. There was fundamentally no difference between you and anyone else in CUSA, except your circumstances. So you needed to be happy with the position you found yourself in and never be bitter or sad, because you were supporting the way of life of your equals, even if they lived in a palace and you lived in a coffin.

That was the idea everyone was taught. But Vam had begun to see through this philosophy. Having been privy to the nicer places, he had seen where his education ended and true opportunities began. He knew there had to be a way to get more than your allotted share, have comforts of the palace in your corrugated box, be someone else for a while, or forever.

That's what he always wanted, to be *somebody else*. One Halloween, when he was just a child, one of his neighbors, an old woman living in the coffin next to theirs, had taken him in her lap to tell him scary stories. She had said that in the old days people could change who they were just by working hard. An office boy could become President.

That had scared Vam and made him cry. The woman nodded like she understood. She agreed that they were evil times. You had never known who was running the show. You might end up with an office boy as President. She told him he should always be grateful to the Corporation, where only the worthy served. She told him never to strive or dream, but always to stay focused on the President.

The woman had meant well, but the story had the opposite effect on him. As he got a little older the memory of the story began to appeal to him. More and more he began to dream of an escape from his life, although he knew that was impossible. Even when he learned about identity theft, he knew he could never afford it, couldn't even buy a night in an executive's living room with a girlfriend. It would have exceeded his debt limit.

Still, the commercials coming out of the AVE made friends with him. Deep in their thirty-minute stories and three-minute tunes were the smiles of the people he might have been, holding out a sweet drink to him, vacationing in the view-resort, encouraging him to spend his account on trifles by telling him that the products would transform him, make him someone else. No one ever came out and said it, but the advertisers used the programs, the little holo dramas, to play on the one void in his soul like a drummer on a stretched skin. Each blast to his eyes, ears, and nose shook him. He bought product after product with what little credit he had, depleted himself until he had to work like a dog just to get back out of the debt cycle long enough to get up enough number to cover his coffin, some macaroni and cheese, a cotton blanket.

But he stayed barely negative most of the time, his number taken out by his modest expenses, the food, the cost of his living tube, treading number like an exhausted swimmer, a lucky day's tip putting him on top for a few hours. Then he'd succumb to temptation, buy a stim and go under once more.

It had gotten worse lately. His negative was deeper, the warnings on his brand coming more and more often. He might lose his coffin, have to sleep in his rickshaw. He could eat every other day maybe?

Then, one day, he'd forgotten himself and gone from negative to super negative, spending number he didn't have on a bottle of wine and a stim. It had been a mistake, but there was no going back.

So he was here on 285, the neighborhood that circled the city, full of bug-filled tin corridors called homes full of people. The old expressway, I-285, long since blocked off from cars and taken over by teeming filthy squint-eyes living close together like rats, some without even walls to divide them. There, among the faceless, he could pretend he was anybody. He could dream he had a spare dozen on his account, he could gamble his number and get it up to forty-eight. Then he might buy an hour in the company of a perfumed call-girl, dressed in a business suit, bowing to him and telling him he was so clever in the privacy of a noisy tent. Or maybe he could see the circus, watch the acrobats and tight-rope walker tottering twelve meters above the ground. Lots of executives in that crowd. In the dark he could be one of them.

But he wasn't here to dream. He was looking for Son.

It took about a half-hour to find the man. He was always harder to find when you were looking for him. Son San, the Freeway Baker, who could be relied on to get your number up, somehow, for a little while.

A man with a five-o-clock shadow of dirt on his lip whispered to Vam that the Baker was in Xiu Xiu Alley. So to Xiu Xiu Vam went, and there was the Baker, hunched over some woman or other. Vam approached cautiously.

"Sonny," he managed, like a weak greeting.

The Baker half turned, his eyebrow up. "Vam, chic, how you doin'?"

Spoken in Spank—half Spanish, half black English—a smooth voice, slick like the train rails. Oily hair, combed smooth to a stylish point, cross-stitched leggings under a pleather vest, light build, arms with veins like branches.

"You bein' taken care of?" he asked.

"Yeah, guess so."

"You *guess* so?" Son repeated.

"Yeah."

"You guess so." Son's body stood at a profile, buckled, and a wave ran through him like the breeze through a corn stalk.

"Yeah," Vam said lamely.

"What's wrong?"

"Nothin'."

"What's *wrong*?" Son approached, hovered around Vam like a bat. "Ex-mas coming. Life too short not to be happy *all* the time."

"I'm negative."

"Ah knew it," said Son, nodding. "What you want from me?"

"*You* know."

Son's smile vanished. "You want me to take care of it for you. You want little Sonny to make it go away."

A string of fireworks went off behind some stalls. The smell of flat smoke suggested a cave behind his sinuses.

"Don't want to lose my house," he said.

Son nodded, his lip twitching. "What you gon' do for me?"

Vam shrugged. "What you want?"

Son smiled for the first time. "Now you talking. That's what I got to hear." He put his hands in his oil-slick pockets. "I tell you what. This you lucky day. I got me this situation, and you the duckie can take care, take care. I got this game, it's a sucka's swim, and I can put you on top. Three veeps looking to get some 285 ass showing off round the table, they play with these sweepies on they arm, all the numbers flow like fine wine."

Vam's interest was piqued. He smiled just a little bit. Son seemed not to notice and roiled on. "These guys play so bad at card, you feel like you could walk on they heads."

"Son, I got *no* number," Vam insisted. "What I got on my tattoo isn't enough to get me kicked off my own wagon."

"Puppydawg, I spot you a dollah. You top the game, we good."

"Payday, then?"

"Payday, Mayday," Son said, waving. "It's so nice. You want to play?"

Vam nodded gamely. "Thanks, chic!"

"Sweet and Lovely, you gonna smile for me just one time." He had already taken Vam by the arm and led him to a wall-terminal. Vam pulled open the flap on his left shoulder, exposing his brand through the manufactured flaps. Son pulled him gently back towards the scanner.

"You good," Son said, beaming, after the transfer had taken place. "You good. Your number 26, mine that much lower."

"Son, thanks," Vam said.

Son had not answered. Vam still felt his hand on his arm, but it was a ghost of a sensation, which changed when he turned around to find Son gone.

"Sonny?"

Two children knelt at the base of a stall, looking for still-edible vegetables and scrap parts. A cat crept across the top of a dumpster, her nose bouncing off the rubber. Son was nowhere to be found. No footsteps, no wild talking in the distance.

"Son, where's the *game?*" Vam asked, like his friend was invisible. Of course, there was no answer, none even apparent, none likely to follow.

He heard a scuffling, and the cat and the kids were gone. Vam blinked instinctively before it occurred to him who was about to appear around the corner.

Two Uniforms arrived in blue, silhouetted against the glare of the floodlight hanging from a nearby stall. They were out of breath from walking fast. Vam's eyes looked them up and down, suspicious, as any law-abiding citizen would be.

Strangely enough, he knew one of them. The officer was the same height as Vam, with putty cheeks that were permanently pulled out, giving his face a fat quality that his body lacked. He generally kept a beat near Fairlie-Poplar where Vam did most of his driving.

"Yo," Vam said smiling a little. "Arni."

"What you say, Vam?" Arni replied, but his eyes did not look at Vam. They continued to scan the alley behind him. His partner, a lean, bony woman Vam had never seen before, kept busy looking around at other things.

"What's doing?" Vam asked. "You a long way from your beat."

"They got a hundred of us looking for someone," Arni said. Now his eyes fell on Vam. "Anything interesting just happen around here?"

"No," Vam said shrinking.

"We gotta go," Arni said, looking around a final time. He thumped his partner on her arm. "Dow," he said to Vam

"Okay," Vam replied, nodding.

The two officers moved on. Vam remained behind, his thoughts returning to Son and his disappearing act. What had just happened? Son had generously given Vam an advance on his number. Out of the goodness of his heart.

Huh.

Vam turned around to face the numbers machine against the wall of the alley. He figured Son had taken a temporary loan off of him, putting him in the red. He slipped into the caring arm of the reader and let it infiltrate the flap on his shoulder. It blinked.

The number that came up was so ridiculously high it was too long for the screen. The only thing familiar about the readout were the words "DO YOU WANT TO GAMBLE?" blinking a little faster than normal underneath the Ex-mas shopping countdown, as if nothing was wrong. His water-ration pie-chart was completely full, instead of a little sliver.

He never even gave it a second thought: the reader was broken. Maybe it was blinked when Son had touched him. He set off to find another reader.

Down the street, he checked again at a machine hovering by an overpass over the distant orange, rain-swelled Chattahoochee River. The high number flashed by a second time, with the standard queries beneath. This time he decided that his brand was obscured. Maybe a mole had grown over it or something.

Automatically he headed for Julia Villanhueva. He didn't want to wait in line at an official brand center, have them ask all sorts of irrelevant and time-wasting questions, be probed, dressed down, reminded, then charged for the service. Julia would fix it for nothing.

Her shop was a little massage hut on Xien Wen. She had a customer when he arrived, because the curtain was closed, and behind it a man was moaning.

She came out in short order, businesslike air about her, wiping the oil off her hands with a white cloth. When she spotted Vam she smiled and mouthed a "hi." Her former customer came out from behind the curtain and slunk away. After a few seconds, she wheeled around and swept the curtain aside. Her battered table waited patiently.

"Yo, Vam!" she said, coming over and putting an arm around him. "Detox!"

"No slice," he said, smiling back.

"You want some coffee?" She turned back to her table and was heading for a hot-pot. She looked over her shoulder at him.

"No, I need a favor," he said.

"A *favor*," she repeated heavily. "Whatchu want?" She scowled. Then she beamed to let him know she was joking.

"Can you check to make sure my tattoo is okay?"

"What wrong with it?"

"I can't get it to read right."

"What happen?"

"Number I get is way high," he said.

She looked at him cross-eyed. "Boy! You crazy! You got a high number by accident, you spread it now! Fore they fix it!"

"No, it's *really* high," he clarified.

She eased him onto the table, which, despite its age, was sturdy under him and did not rock as he got on his stomach. Her expert hands entered his flap and found the tattoo.

"I don't see nothing on it," she said. "No hairs—you as hairless as you ever was!" She laughed. "Perimeter looks good. No pock marks." Clicking her tongue, she found a portable reader and brought it over to the brand.

"Whoa," she said, her voice lead-heavy. She stared at the number, having never seen one so large before. She read the number off to him. He confirmed it.

"Then it ain't my batteries," she said. Another pause. "Oh my God," she said.

"What?" he asked, lifting his head.

"Oh my God," she said again, backing away from him.

"What?" he insisted, flipping over to his side. The flap dropped into place.

"What you been doing?" she asked, eyeing him from the corner.

He squirmed a little. "Nothing," he said. "Do you know Son?"

"I've heard of him, I think. Trickster, pretty boy."

"Hangs around Bankhead arc," Vam said. "That's him. He offered to spot me a loan."

"So you let him alter your brand," she finished for him.

"Yeah."

"Look," she said, handing him the reader. All he saw was the number. He look it back and forth, trying to ferret out whatever hidden meaning she had seen in it.

"No," she said, pointing a short, shiny, glitter-red fingernail at the screen. He followed it and saw, where his name usually was, the word SATTARI.

"Who's that" he asked.

"It's *you* now," she said. "That guy just made you a new name."

He sat on the table for a moment, his mind wandering. "What?" he asked absently.

"You just became the proud owner of an executive's identity. Buddha's butt," she cursed, looking over the screen. "A *Siyo*. This guy...you...a *Siyo* at Noke."

"Noke," he repeated, still not registering what had happened. "I deliver there all the time."

"Well, now you *live* there," she said, tossing her reader on the side table like it was hot.

They both sat there blinking for a minute. Then she said, "Vam, you got to go. I'm gonna have this reader wiped."

"But wait," he said, still stunned.

She wasn't listening to him. She was packing her things. "Wait," he said, getting to his feet.

"You an accomplice to some bad shit," she said. "IDing is a risky business anyway, but nobody's crazy enough to traffic a *Siyo*."

"What should I do?" he asked, but Julia didn't answer. She was too busy packing. "What should I do?" he demanded, taking hold of her arm.

She shook him off like a bad itch. In seconds, she had zipped her flap, folded her table, and moved away.

"Julia! What I do?"

"Turn your ass in, I guess," she said from far away. Then she was gone.

He stood there awhile at the empty tent and listened to the wind blow the old curtain. He had to find Son and make that crazy sumbitch put him back the way he was.

It wasn't as easy as usual. Ordinarily, Son was so vain and noisy you could just about put your ear to the ground or your nose in the air and follow your best guess. This time there wasn't any sign. Even the people who knew him didn't know him today.

But someone like Son was too conspicuous to stay hidden forever. Vam spotted him on the overpass at Cascade. He pushed his way towards the exit and sprinted up its long incline.

At first, Son didn't turn. He was talking in a low voice to someone standing in front of him, and Vam began to wonder if he had the wrong man. He stopped just shy of jumping on the pretty boy, panting heavily at his back.

Slowly, Son turned. He regarded Vam casually. "What's up, slice?" he muttered conversationally, then smoothly returned to his present business.

Vam stood there, stupid. His chest ached. Son's refusal to run or look guilty eroded his assurance that he had been wronged.

Son finished his conversation. The other person walked away a piece, then hung out by the rail, leaning over 285. Son wheeled around once again to face Vam.

"What's the word, deal?" Son said to him.

"'Cope, what you do to me?" Vam demanded.

"What you mean?"

"You messed with my—"

"Keep your voice down," Son instructed, stooping and raising his eyes.

"My number—" Vam tried to begin again.

"Yeah, baby, I'm sorry to pull the wool," Son said, pulling Vam close and putting an arm around his shoulders. "I needed to do something quick. But I make it worth your while."

"What?"

"Baby, you in paradise now," Son said, smiling. "You all the way to the top. You can do anything! How you like it?"

"Chicope, you *crazy?"* Van exploded. "Anything I do they gonna nail me for IDing."

"No, sweet, no. Look, you just gotta slow down. I wouldn't put you in that kind of jam! Slice, we go way back! I love you."

"You gotta take this brand off me," Vam said, panicked.

"No, no!" Son reassured him, stroking his back. "Look, now, we can make some number on this. We play this right, you get some nice spiffy, get out squeaky free."

Vam stared at Son, incredulous. Son responded as if hurt. "Why you eye me, child? Look, I got the medicine for everybody's boo-boo. You just listen here.

"You *is Siyo* Sattari now, you zon? No imposter, you the real steal. Anything you want come straight out of that sweet little tattoo."

"I don't want—"

"And let me tell you what you want," Son went on. "You want to go to his little *cuna* in the Noke building."

"Why I want that?"

"'Cause, sweet, you gonna get on his eyes-only AVE and pick up some goodies for us."

"Son, you out of your mind."

"Child, you gonna pass up an opportunity *this* good?"

"But—"

"I ain't gonna make you go it alone. See that lovely right there?" He turned his body aside to reveal the woman he had been talking to, looking out over the railing into space. "She know AVE better'n AVEinc. She gonna piggyback with you and get what we need."

"What?"

"Beauty, never you worry!" Son scolded gently. "I can use it, and you gon' get some."

Van worked his mouth. He squirmed under Son's light arm. "No thanks, Son," he finally said. "You find somebody else. Fix me back."

"*Ain't* nobody else!" Son cried. "You it! Sattari! The man!"

"Make somebody else Sattari," Vam begged. "Trick them like you tricked me."

"No no, slice, no no!" Son soothed him. "Listen, I need you because I know what you want."

"What I want?"

"You want to be somebody else."

Vam did not reply. He kept working his mouth and squirming. "Sure, baby, you talk about it all the time. I don't blame you. Nobody wants to stay where they is. That ain't America."

Vam looked up suddenly. "What you mean?"

"America about movin' up," Son went on. "In old days, before CUSA, you could be anybody you want. Sweep a store one day, work your way up to President." Vam blinked, watching Son with quiet, childlike eyes. "That's the way it *s'posed* to be!" Son expounded. "Nowadays, you want to move up, you gotta steal your way up."

"But Son, I can't be the *Siyo*," Vam pleaded.

"No, baby, you can't," Son agreed. "But look here." He reached under his arm and pulled out a portable scanner. Flipping a button, he displayed a list of names. "I got lots of people, child. Dead, sick...Some that went ahead and stole up themselves, left they old self behind. You want to be one of them?"

Vam pored over the list with greedy eyes. Son saw the look and smiled.

"Sure, baby, what's your pleasure," he said. "You want to be a Uniform? A comptroller? Accountant? How about a small-time associate living at the GM Plant? He was retired, so you could take him on and keep to yourself. Nobody know."

"Nobody?"

"Sweet sweet, ain' no way I risk the well-being of my best customer, that'd be you, once you help me through my raspberry jam!"

Vam lowered his head and took on a thinking pose, but he had made his decision before breaking eye contact with the bakerman. His look of contemplation was just a show, and Son knew it. Son was waiting patiently for Vam to look up with agreement on his features, and sure enough Vam did.

"God bless America," Son said. Vam didn't know what that meant, but he believed it.

Vam left his rickshaw somewhere on 285 for Son to take care of. Meantime, he and the woman with whom Son had been talking, a short, bullish figure named Sance with a stiff tuft of hair covering her wide scalp, made their way to the station.

Vam was petrified when Sance told him to let the station scan his brand, but he did as he was told, and the train came impossibly fast to pick him up. The only door that opened was the one on the front car, so they moved through into a plush cabin with deep-piled sofas, a stim table, and a 360 HoloAVE.

"Nice," Sance muttered, nodding.

There wasn't anyone else in that car, so Vam nervously made his way over to one of the couches and slumped down into it. As the door slid shut he saw two blue-uniformed officers running through the scanstiles. He slumped down to the floor as far as he could, and the train pulled away from the station, leaving the Uniforms behind. Sance had not seen them. She was observing the HoloAVE.

"Come over here," she said. "I want you to turn this thing."

Obediently, Vam rose to his feet. The train seemed to be moving faster than usual towards the City Proper, probably geared into an express mode for the sake of its all-important passenger. He walked over to the 360 and sat in the revolving chair. It roared to life like a gas flame, surrounding him with images of available merchandise and services that danced to tunes he had never heard. All his favorite commercials had been for low-grade snacks, the lotto, or shoes. These were for stock options, collectibles, gourmet foods, and air passage to other countries. The singers chanted numbers he couldn't have found if he'd looked ten years through his accounts.

"See if you can direct it," Sance said. "If you got access to Sattari's personals here, it'll save us a trip."

Vam tried to access higher channels. He was able to get nearly everything he wanted: realporn images of lower-class citizens having sex in their homes, dogfights at the Stone Mountain Ice Skating Rink, the Quarterly Earnings Report.

Sance ignored everything but the earnings report. "That's not bad," she said. "See if you have access to deeper info." She directed his hand towards certain symbols but did not touch the interface herself. He followed her lead, and streams of data came through. Sance devoured the readouts eagerly, but it became apparent after a minute that she didn't see what she was looking for.

The train had slowed appreciably. All of a sudden it stopped, and looking around Vam realized with a sick feeling that they were not yet at City Proper.

The door slid open and two executives stepped on board. Van froze on the spot, not knowing if he should run, explain, try to turn himself in. Sance watched the new arrivals casually.

They glanced at Vam and Sance for only a second, their eyes taking in the sight. Then they continued their conversation and wandered to the other end of the car.

Vam said. "What—"

Sance shrugged. "If you got in," Sance said, "you must be somebody. They don't want to do the Uniform's job."

"But aren't they going to tell someone?"

"I doubt it," Sance said. "When you're in, you're in. You are who your tattoo says you are, Mr. Sattari."

Vam blinked, hardly even seeing the images on the AVE anymore, forgetting the tunes, not even smelling the artificial scents wafting out of the little grate by his foot.

"This doesn't have it," Sance said quietly. "Apparently, Sattari kept his information very private. Unusual, but not surprising."

"So we have to go all the way in?" he asked her.

Sance nodded.

At the next station, the other executives got off without a backwards look. The train glided a little farther on until it penetrated the bowels of the Noke building. Following Sance's prodding, Vam left the safety of the train and made his way to a row of elevator doors. One of them opened up especially for him as he approached. The others remained closed.

"That's us, baby," Sance said.

"Just a minute," someone called out from across the dark basement. The woman who approached was tall, thin, and muscular. The hat that covered up her dyed blonde hair pegged her as building security. Vam had seen and spoken to this woman many times from his rickshaw. She was sure to recognize him. Vam froze, knowing it was game over. Sance tensed, looking ready to bolt or make excuses or whatever she had as an out.

Yet, the guard seemed to place little credence in what she saw. Vam and his companion had just come off the executives-only train and were heading towards a special elevator that had opened for them. These facts seemed to give her more pause than the presence of two foreign faces in the basement.

"Uh...Sir, I'm sorry to have to detain you," she said cautiously.

"That's all right," muttered Vam. But his companion in crime was not so easily cowed. Seeing their advantage, she spoke up.

"Actually, it's a problem," she said. "Mr. Sattari has to hurry up and get to his suite. He has a meeting at six o'clock with a number of very important people. You can see he's not himself right now."

Vam quailed at the bad joke, but the guard seemed a little put off by Sance's confidence. "Who are *you*?" she asked Sance, trying to sound menacing.

Speaking up quickly, Vam said, "This is my associate. She's with me." He swallowed hard and pressed the guard. "Do you have a *problem* with that?"

"No, sir," the guard replied, trying to keep control of the situation.

"Good," Vam said, shaking inside. "I can either enter a commendation for you for doing your job or I can put in a request that you be dismissed for detaining me." His heart was pounding very loudly in his ears.

The guard held his gaze for a moment, but now even Vam could see that she was scared. Again, she looked at the train from which they had just emerged and at the elevator door that was unquestionably waiting for them. Finally, her gaze dropped. "Sorry, sir; yes, sir."

Vam nodded and quickly made his way past her to the elevator, meeting no resistance. Sance followed along.

"That was nice," Sance said after the door shut.

"I can't believe it. They're willing to pretend I'm Sattari!" Vam exclaimed.

Sance nodded. "I've seen it before. Nobody wants to take accountability. It'll work for a day or so...this has got to be the *nicest* elevator."

The executive elevator was a class affair all by itself. Even the AVE in it was nicer than one usually saw in such places, with a little glass pitcher of water and two crystal goblets next to it.

"Ooo...yes...*Spikey, Spikey...I tell you, Lotta, I've never had anything like it...*" As the elevator climbed through the heart of the great pyramid whose exterior he had approached on his little rickshaw time and time again, Vam helped himself to the cold, filtered water. The elevator door opened again just as he set the glass back on the counter by the AVE, which was now playing a commercial about the water he had been drinking.

They stepped into a palatial apartment. Elegant furniture was arranged comfortably around a crystal staircase in the center, which led up to a raised platform. The servants whom Vam would have expected were all elsewhere in the building.

"Niiizzze," Sance said, dancing around the room. "Where's his desk?"

"Up there." Vam pointed. "I think that's the one you want."

It was. As Sance practically fell up the staircase in her eagerness, Vam strolled about the room, touching the fine furniture and gazing longingly out the window. The view across the Park was spectacular. Far below, people were dancing in the waters of the five-ring symbol. Beyond it were miles of office-dwellings, the recreation centers, the CUSA-Westin City Hall Tower, and, still farther away, the more modest blocks where people like him kept their tiny rooms.

No, where people who *used* to be like him kept their tiny rooms. He lived *here!*

He moved towards a large piece of furniture unlike anything he'd ever seen before. It resembled a wide armoire though it lacked any doors on its face and contained only one drawer, which already seemed to be pulled out. But the drawer was covered with some kind of wooden sheath. He brought his hand towards the small yellow metal button that protruded from its front, and lifted. The sheath rose easily and, as if it were pulling his hand, slid gently back into the armoire, revealing a huge row of black and white teeth, spaced evenly in some kind of regular pattern, the fewer black teeth raised higher than the more numerous white. His fingers reached towards the teeth and made to touch them when a sound like a tinkling bell made him freeze.

He and Sance both looked up and back at the large door. From up on the platform Sance said, "That's his front door. Do we answer it?"

"I don't know!" Vam cried.

Whoever had rung the bell answered the question, because the door vanished and a small, stout man strolled in. He was youngish, about Vam's age, but his hair and his skin would have suggested someone much older. He was dressed in the suit of an executive.

"Oh Dow," he said, startled, seeing the two of them. Again, Vam winced, fearing the worst. But the executive paused for only a second, put off far less than the guard had been.

"I'm sorry, Mr. Sattari," he said, trying not to look at Vam. "Vana said you were back, but I didn't believe it, and I wanted to check on something."

Vam still did not answer, still incredulous at having one of Sattari's own colleagues call him by that name. Sance looked down at him and smiled.

"That's all right, Mr. —" He faltered, wishing he had not said anything.

"Tran," finished the executive. "Come on, Mr. Sattari, I know you've got a lot of people to manage, but after ten years I'd hope you'd recognize my face!" He laughed, and Vam laughed with him. Vam scanned the man carefully. Now he could see that the executive was hardly looking at him at all. His eyes were glazed, because he was just barely using them, having obviously decided that the image they were receiving was unreliable. No one else but Sattari could have been in Sattari's apartment, so Vam must be Sattari, no doubt about it.

"It's not that," Vam said, chuckling. "I'm just not good with names."

"All right, sir," said Tran with relief. "All right. Sir, I came to talk about the Freodone Campaign, I actually came to ask about some information which you know by heart and—"

"Not now, Tran," Vam said, quickly. "All right? I'm very tired."

The executive glanced up at Sance. Then he got a knowing look in his eye. "Oh, I see, Mr. Sattari. All right. Sorry to bother you. I'll tell everyone you've returned. There's a board meeting scheduled at four. Will you come in person or holo? It's only just down the hall."

"I'll see you later," Vam said, dismissively.

Tran nodded quickly. He backed out of the room.

"You want me to lock that door?" Sance asked, when it had reappeared. "I guess it was set to open for him in your absence."

"No," Vam replied, climbing the crystal stair. "What's the problem? They all think I'm Sattari!" He was elated, felt lighter than air, half believed he was floating up the stair and could have continued right through the window to drift over Centennial Park.

Sance scowled. "I wouldn't push it."

"What do you mean?"

"You may be honorary Sattari for a day, but if anybody asks you any questions about his business, you aren't going to be able to answer. That'll wake them up."

"So maybe you could stay and help me," Vam suggested.

"What?" Sance looked confused.

"What did you find in his desk?"

"As a matter of fact," Sance said, snapping out of her confusion, "I need you to come over here and see if we can activate your halo. There's an extra security precaution here, probably set up just in case this sort of thing happens. But that ID of yours is foolproof, so I'm not worried about it. Get over here and let me scan your shoulder."

He did as he was told, took a seat in the chair, and let her bare his shoulder with its now-sterling brand. A gentle wash of light came and bathed his back, then disappeared into the nook from which it had come. "I was only thinking," Vam said.

"What?" Sance said, a little annoyed. Words and symbols were floating around his head, and she was hungrily reading them.

"Look," he said. "We're in—you get it? You've got the brains, and I've got the tattoo. Everybody thinks I'm Sattari!"

"Of course," Sance muttered, shaking her head. She was absorbed in her work.

"Well, if you can get any kind of information out of that thing, you can tell me what's going on. Between the two of us, we should be able to convince other people that I'm really him. Think about it! We'd have the best life in the whole world."

Sance pulled out her portable and interfaced it with his halo. "That's it," she said. "I got what I need. Now let's get out of here."

"No, *listen!*" Vam said, grabbing her by the upper arm. "We could make this work. I had no idea it was so easy to fool all these people. All we have to do is take a retreat in one of this guy's hideaways for awhile, get up to speed. What's Son paying you? I swear it'll look like decimals compared to the kind of life we could have up here."

She pulled free of him, but for a moment she wavered. Then she looked up at him. "Are you coming?" she asked.

"No!" he exclaimed. "Don't you get it? I'm somebody else now! Somebody worth *being*." Sance did not respond. Vam scowled. "If you won't help me, then to hell with you. I'll hire me somebody who will. Someone to tell me what to do, someone who won't ask questions. I'm going to run this little slice of heaven, and the first thing I'll do when I figure it all out is invite Son up here for a party. You got it?"

Sance shook her head a little and made her way towards the elevator. "Open it up for me," she told him. "It's that symbol on the upper left, in the corner."

He found it and put his finger through it. The elevator door obeyed him and slid wide for her. "Why?" he demanded as she made her way towards it. "Why won't you help me?"

She turned back to consider. She shrugged. "I like who I am," she said. Then she entered the elevator and vanished.

He let her go, didn't give her a second thought. He spun around in the chair and looked through the green light of his halo at the beautiful sunset that was pouring across the roofs of the buildings in the panorama in front of him. The chair felt so nice, he'd have traded his whole life just to sit in it.

"Wait!" said a voice from below and behind the door.

He spun around in his chair, and his eyes flew open. Two Uniforms were walking towards the staircase, Mr. Tran running behind them. "What's this all about?" he cried. "You can't just barge in on the *Siyo!*"

They mounted the stairs, and as their faces crested the platform, Vam saw the same two Uniforms he had met on 285 not two hours ago—one of them his friend Arni, with the putty cheeks—advancing on the table.

"Whoa...Arni!" he began. "I can explain!"

Arni did not stop, but he slowed down. For a moment, he gazed, confused, at Vam sitting in Mr. Sattari's chair. Of all the faces Vam had seen, his registered the most indecision, the most bewilderment.

"Sorry, sir," he said finally. "You'll have to come with us."

"Arni, no," Vam protested, getting to his feet. "Look, I didn't mean to take the guy's brand. It was stuck to me, and I had to do this to get out of it."

"I'm sorry, Mr. Sattari," Arni said sadly, coming over to Vam and placing his gloves on Vam's upper arms. Vam felt the stasis field overcoming him. He lost control over his upper body and most of his lower, so that he had to be held up by Arni and the other Uniform. "I've been instructed to arrest you for dereliction of duty. You're to be held pending auditing by the authority of NokeCUSA."

"*Arni!*" Vam exclaimed. He missed a beat, but no one said anything to interrupt him. "I'm not Sattari! I'm *not!*"

"It'd be better if you weren't, sir," the other Uniform said. "We've been tracking you for a month. As clever a runner as you are, your brand is just too easy to spot."

"But I—" he cried. "I—" Exhausted by the stasis, he let surrender overtake him and fell into the caress of the Uniforms.

The elevator glided down the shaft. He watched NokeCUSA build itself up in front of him, level by level, his mind slowly drifting. He dreamed of a cozy little coffin with his name on it, now occupied by whomever would be fool enough to buy his name from Son. His last coherent thought was wondering if his mother would feed that person when they showed up at her coffin on Ex-mas.

There is a man holding me down in the bed, a white man in a black outfit. I am too sore and too weak to resist him. I have been screaming and my hands are cut and bloody.

"We'll get through this," he whispers in my ear. "We'll get through this together, me and you."

Then his face dissolves into an enormously charismatic face, a man with patchy brown skin and dark circles under his dark eyes, sweat stains under his arms. This is a man whom I love.

He holds the gun pointed at me and smiles.

"Me or you," he says. "Me, or you."

Abruptly and without my consent I feel my bowels push and smell my feces.

I have been in the bed for some time and the lights have been out. I don't feel like I can move. I simply lie there in the smell, wondering what it reminds me of.

The woman appears by my side from out of the darkness. As if I am a baby, she turns me sideways upon the bed. My pajamas are pulled down to my ankles and removed. I feel a cool, wet cloth probing carefully between my butt cheeks as she cleans me. I am too out of it to be humiliated, though my bottom is relieved and I am grateful in a distant part of my mind.

A new, cleaner pair of pajamas is fitted on me, stiff and cool. I have just enough strength to follow her impetus as she ushers me back between the sheets. She smells like sweet little flowers.

She gets in bed next to me and, though I am larger than her, she wraps her arms around me in the darkness. My face turns to rest against her breast, soft behind a satin blouse. Quietly, she begins to hum, and then to sing, and though I haven't really slept since I can recall, I drift in and out. Each time I come to she is still there, holding me, singing strange commercials I have never heard.

The One-Way Trip

Like most twelve-year-olds, Rosa hated school. Every morning and every afternoon she'd sit at her AVE in her bedroom and stare for three hours at a time, playing some dumb game with hundreds of thousands of other kids she didn't know. The game was always boring, and anyway it was so hard to concentrate when the commercials popped up on the side.

But Rosa had figured out that if you stay logged on to your game you could actually leave your AVE and nobody would ever notice. So many kids were logged in that the Administrator never actually talked to you, and if he did he'd probably think you were just shy or something.

Mamma was always working on her own AVE in the next room, and she kept so busy that she never checked on Rosa 'til lunch. Daddy was usually sitting next to Mama on his own AVE, trying for hours every day to figure out what form the City of Atlanta wanted him to fill out so they could finally get a funeral stipend for Rosa's little brother who died last year, and get his body out of frozen storage. But today Daddy was out fixing somebody's roof. So if Rosa just turned her AVE a little louder than usual, Mamma would think she was being a good girl and staying in front of it instead of sneaking off.

They lived with a million roaches in the dining room of a three-floor McMansion on Randall Court. That room, their living space, was divided in two by a big piece of splintery plywood. The plywood separated the front half of the dining room which they used as a kitchen from the back half where they slept, and there was a little curtain between her parents' bedroom and hers.

Rosa's room was farthest from the kitchen so she couldn't sneak out the front door without her parents' hearing. But she had a window which opened up on a weedy backyard lawn. It was a risky place to go because Mamma could see the lawn too. But there was a big broken fountain out there with a huge crack in it, and as long as she could get to that fountain without Mamma seeing, she could hide behind it until she knew the coast was clear. Then she could slip down the hillside and go around the side of the house next door.

The window was supposed to be locked to keep the burglars out, but Rosa had broken the lock a year ago, and nobody ever bothered to fix it. There were bars on the outside, but they were loose. Rosa had sprayed some lubricant on them one time, and now they swung without squeaking, far enough for her to get out.

Everything went pretty smoothly this time. She got out the window and to the fountain and didn't hear anything except her heart beating really loud. She ducked down under the clothes line, the clothes still smelling of disinfectant, and slid down the grass into the woods behind her house. She didn't want any of the other parents to see her either because she knew they'd tell her Mamma. She had to be careful 'til she got all the way around the ratty, condemned house next door. After that, it was a straight shot out to the street.

Randall Court was a cul-de-sac and didn't have a lot of traffic, but once you got onto Mt. Paran it was pretty crowded. Lots of bikes, a few city workers with electric carts, some rickshaws pulling Landlords around, every once in a while a bunch of kids playing tennis with nappy balls across the center line. And squirrels --- squirrels everywhere, running around like they owned the place.

When she got out there she had to stand where everyone could see her. She was scared to death her Mom would spot her, but she couldn't leave now. She was waiting for Basil.

Basil was her boyfriend. Mamma said she was too young to have a boyfriend, but she was almost twelve, and most of her friends had already Chinese kissed, so she figured she was old enough. Anyway, Basil wasn't *really* Rosa's boyfriend; he was just *sorta* her boyfriend.

Even if her Mamma had let her go out with a boy, she wouldn't have been allowed to see Basil. Basil was apprenticed to the Pastor of a Drug Church. Rosa's family were *chuseno* and hated the Drug Church. Sometimes her Daddy didn't come home nights because he was rocking with a crowd in front of one of the Churches, yelling at the addicts as they filed past. If Rosa's Daddy had known she had even looked in the direction of a Church he would have had a *chuseno* cow.

Rosa was getting mad at Basil now because he still hadn't showed up, and she was really worried somebody would see her, but then he finally came round the corner on his bike. He did this little wheelie thing and spun out in front of her, and she smiled.

"Sup slice," he said.

"Sup!"

"You ready?"

"Ahite!"

Rosa hopped up behind him and hung on tight to him, 'cause the seat wasn't very big in back. She didn't mind holding around his tight little waist, and she didn't think he minded either. He started pumping with his muscular legs. He was strong for a boy his size. That was a good thing, because they had to take Lake Forrest to avoid all the gang gunfights on Roswell Road, and there were a lot of hills between Rosa's house and the place they were going.

They started moving into the traffic, which always kept pretty slow on Mt. Paran, and dodged around a stalled exterminator vehicle. The old public AVEs hanging from the telephone poles looked like they were going to fall on them as they moved along the curvy street. Most of them out there in the 'burbs were broken. Once in a while one of them would be kinda working, and Rosa and Basil would cash in on a commercial or something as they passed.

"You sure you want to do this?" Basil asked Rosa over his shoulder.

"Yeah, I'm sure!" she said, though she didn't really know. She hadn't ever been inside a Drug Church before. None of her friends had, either, not even the ones who weren't *chuseno*. Only addicts and drug-clergy were allowed.

Basil hung a left on Lake Forrest, and the road dipped way down way fast. Rosa held on tight as Basil let the bike pick up speed. Not too far ahead, she could see the black asphalt swooping swiftly up again like a wall. Basil wanted to get enough momentum so that they'd make it to the top. When the bike hit top speed Rosa screamed because of the feeling in her stomach.

Suddenly there was a goat on the street right in front of them. In order to miss it, Basil swerved so hard that Rosa knew they were going to wipe out, and she braced herself against his back. But Basil saved them somehow. He pedaled away as the goat's owner came running out, shaking her fist at them, swearing at them in Vietnamese.

The swerve had taken out his momentum, and his legs were obviously starting to hurt halfway up the other hill. So they got off and walked the rest of the way. After a few minutes the bugs caught up with them in the stifling April heat.

"You sure Padre ain' gon' catch us?" she asked him, wiping the sweat out of her eyes.

"No!" he wheezed. He was still out of breath. They were nearly at the top, and Rosa's legs were screaming now just from climbing this thing. But when they got up there she was glad they had walked, 'cause the downhill on the other side was way steeper than the one they had just left, and she wouldn't have wanted to ride down it on the back of Basil's bike. She didn't think Basil would have wanted that, either, but he didn't say anything. They just shuffled down with the bike in between them.

"If he catch us, what happen?"

"Nothing, to you," Basil said. "I get hit."

"Then why you doing it?"

Basil shrugged. "I ain' afraid," he said.

Rosa knew he was. He just said that to impress her. It worked.

They passed under 285. Some of the mongrel kids who lived up there were dropping rat-shit on them. Basil grabbed a rock and threw it at the kids, and they ran back to their tents or whatever they lived in.

They got back on the bike. Basil merged onto Mount Vernon and cut across Roswell Road. From there it wasn't far to Basil's Church. It was a little grey stone building on Glencrest. Couldn't have been more than two rooms inside of it, or maybe three. There were some ruins behind it, some old shell of a building that used to be part of the Church but now wasn't anything but a place for grass to grow. The Church building was old, probably been there since before Rosa's grandparents were kids.

In front of it was a cemetery with faded gravestones. Rosa ran her hand across one as they passed. She could barely make out the number 1902 on one.

"Get down!" Basil said, and he threw his bike to the side and pulled Rosa behind a gravestone. They fell onto the grass, and Basil looked around the stone like someone would shoot them if they peeked their heads out.

"Whatchu do that for?" Rosa demanded, dusting herself off.

"Quiet, *perra!*" he whispered at her.

"Don't call me *perra!*" she snapped at him. To Rosa, it felt just like they were married. She liked it. He was just trying to impress her by being a macho.

He leaned his back against the gravestone. Then he looked at her. "You pretty," he said. He smiled a little. He brought his hand up to touch her arm.

"Go 'way, Basil," she said, pushing off his arm.

"Why you be like that?" he asked her, keeping his hand close on her arm.

She stopped fighting and let him touch her a little. It felt nice. His face got soft, kinda curious. Rosa knew what he was curious about. Before he could think too much about that, she said, "You gon' take me in or not?"

He looked like he wasn't sure anymore, but he wasn't going to back down. "You sure you want to?" he asked her again.

Rosa nodded. But she was scared, too.

"Just stay close to me," he whispered, and he turned onto his belly and crept around the gravestone.

Rosa followed him through the scrubby grass behind a bunch of white stone pillows until they were right up behind the old grey building. She could see the stained glass windows along the side of the Church. A little light was coming through them. She wondered if they looked prettier from the inside.

Meanwhile, Basil was checking something out by a white door near the back. Suddenly a loud bell from somewhere high above them rang out. The sound made Basil panic, and he jumped, looking all around. "Let's go!" he whispered, and vanished through the door.

From over the hill, Rosa saw some shapes. They all moved towards the Church, coming from every direction. Each one had a different kind of walk. Some kept their heads way up and spoke to the sky. Others skated with their feet and never took their eyes off the ground. Then there were some who could have been normal if you didn't know.

All these people were the faithful, the addicts come to worship.

Basil grabbed her hard by the arm and yanked her in through the door.

She didn't have a chance to complain about being treated rough. She was too scared to make any noise at all. They were *in the Church*. Rosa wasn't supposed to be there. She wasn't even supposed to be *outside*. They crept up this old flight of wooden stairs, and she knew Basil was sweating it every time a step creaked. Finally they got to the top and, creeping on their hands and knees, went out through another door until they were on some kind of balcony with a high rail. She couldn't have seen over without standing up, but she could hear all sorts of shuffling and muttering from down below, only the words didn't make any sense. It sounded like seventy people having seventy different conversations. But it was quiet, too, like nobody answered anybody else, like everyone in that place thought they were all alone.

They kept creeping 'til they got to the middle of a big dent in the floor that was a different color from the other wood, like something big had once been sitting there. Rosa saw some old wires splayed around, the sliced pieces of rubber-insulated wires sticking up from the floor like two crazy hands. Basil curved his finger at her and pointed her to a little hole in the dent just big enough for the two of them to peek through. They had to keep their faces real close to one another to see. Ordinarily she'd like that, but this time she was too scared.

Down below she could see a very long room stretching out with rows and rows of benches all facing some raised platform. There were a couple of high tables, and on each table many bags and bottles. In front stood two people dressed in black robes with hoods over their heads, waiting while two lines formed, made up of all the chatterers who had been walking towards the Church.

"What they doing?" Rosa whispered to Basil.

"That the faithful lining up to get the Body and the Blood," Basil answered.

"What that?"

"What they need."

"How you know what they need?"

"It our *job* to know," Basil said, trying to sound wise.

Now each person in line was stepping up and showing them their arm or opening their mouth, and the robe-people were applying tourniquets or giving them whatever it was they asked for.

"We got to learn about seventy different kinds of drugs," Basil told her, "and they got to be the *right* ones or the faithful can die or lose control."

Rosa didn't know what to say. She just watched it for a while. It made her feel taller inside, seeing something that she knew her Mamma and Daddy never saw.

Basil squawked, and out of the corner of her eye Rosa saw him being pulled away. She was too terrified to move until she heard the other deep, dry voice.

"This is abomination," it said. Right after came a hand hitting somebody's face. That's when Rosa turned around real quick and scooted away, looking up at the Padre, Basil's father.

He looked down at her.

"Infidel," he said, like he was spitting a bad taste out of his mouth.

Rosa didn't know what "infidel" meant, but when she saw Basil with his face all twisted up, she could tell by that look that he was going to get it and he didn't want her to see. So she ran out the room, down the stairs and away from the building through the cemetery.

She didn't figure on one thing when she got out of there: How she was going to get back home before the school game let out? She couldn't steal Basil's bike. She couldn't pay for a ride. So anyone could guess what happened when it took her three hours to walk it.

"*Where you been?*" Mamma screamed when she saw her coming down the street. Rosa didn't say anything. "I have the *whole neighborhood* looking for you!"

Rosa rolled her eyes. That was the wrong thing to do. Mamma grabbed her. "Ow, bitch!" Rosa said, and that got Rosa slapped. "What *wrong* with you?"

"What's wrong with *me*?" Mamma demanded, gripping her daughter's arm and shaking it back and forth. She was doing like she always did when she was mad. She was about to tell Rosa she couldn't hang out with her friends in the cul-de-sac tonight. Rosa didn't want to hear it, so she pushed away. She ran past her mother and fled into the house. They were in the middle of another blackout, so the lights were all out. In the dark, she found a box of Sugar Noke-O's with some little bits still in it and stole them off to her room. She didn't want to see her mother. But it's hard to lock a curtain, and when her Daddy came home, both her parents just walked in.

The power was still out, so Rosa couldn't pretend she was studying on her AVE. "You could *knock*," she said to them.

"Rosa," Daddy said.

She waited for a minute, but he didn't say anything else. She looked over, ready to shout out "What?" and saw her Mamma with tears in her eyes.

"Mamma! *Naz!*" she cursed. "*Okay.* I snuck out. I'm really *sorry.* I'll never do it again." But neither of them said anything, and Rosa wondered just how much trouble she was in.

"Rosa," Daddy finally said again. "Something happened. Something bad."

She blinked. She didn't really understand what "bad" meant.

Mamma crossed herself. "Our President will take care of us," she said quietly.

"Rosa," Daddy said, almost like he was whispering through a mouthful of crackers.

"What, Daddy?"

"Mamma's—"

"I lost my job," Mamma blurted out, covering up her Daddy's words.

Rosa sat quietly and didn't answer. She didn't want them to know how confused she was. As long as she made her parents do all the talking, she had some kind of power.

Her father went on. "I want you to gather up everything that is important to you in a small bag. We're going to try to get passage on a bus heading to DC tomorrow afternoon."

"Tomorrow! *DC?*" she exclaimed. "That's a million K away! We ain' never gonna make it all the way up there! What about my friends?"

"We have cousins in DC," Rosa's mother said in a voice pushed forward by strain. "If we can get up there, they may be able to help us...find another job."

"But ain' there crazy white people out between Atlanta and DC? What about the crazy white people?"

Rosa's Daddy looked at the floor. Then he looked back up at her and said, "Get packed and get some sleep. Don't forget to make sure the lights don't come on when the blackout ends."

For a while Rosa lay in her bed and listened to her parents whisper, whisper. They were fighting, and Rosa really wanted to know why.

At one point her father's voice got kind of loud. "We don't have enough *number* for vouchers..."

"Shhh! I know somebody..." said Rosa's Mama, and her voice went really quiet.

"We'll have to withdraw the rest of this week's water to make..." her father went on, his own voice dropping. After that, Rosa couldn't make out any more, but she knew that things were bad, especially if her parents were fighting.

When the blackout finally ended, and Rosa's parents were snoring, she was on her AVE watching commercials. *"Yo! Join the Young Guns, slice!"*

That was one of her favorites—about the Young Guns, the soldiers for the Corporation. She always liked the way it started, flying over the City Proper. You could see the tall buildings sparkling in the sunlight, surrounded by all those little blocks of white nothing, and then you were past it and all you could see were the empty lots on the other side that kept people like her out. Rosa loved the way the Proper looked.

"Yo, join the Young Guns. Defend CUSA against the Axis of Evil. Y'daddy did it, y'granddaddy did it, now it's yo' turn, cuz."

Then she got to see the Young Guns in action, running across a grassy field, firing sprayers at enemy combatants, smiling, looking slick. There was this one soldier with hazel eyes she saw every time in that commercial. You could see him up close, good teeth. When Rosa was a little girl she used to fantasize about being married to him. There were female soldiers in the commercial, too. They looked tough, slick, confident.

"*We all in this together.*" Fade to black.

"*Oooo...I love it.*" Now the AVE showed a bunch of stuff on a golden shelf that Rosa would never get to own: better shoes, better clothes, better AVE. Rosa pulled out of the sensation-envelope and lay back on her bed, only able to hear the AVE now.

She didn't want to leave Atlanta. Maybe she could run off tonight and join the Young Guns. Would they take her? She imagined herself in that uniform, coming home, telling her Mamma and Daddy that it was going to be all right, that she'd take care of them now.

Rosa heard a what sounded like a rock bouncing off her window. She looked over but didn't see anybody through the bars, just a roach balancing on the window sill. She double-checked to see if her parents were sleeping, then swung the bars aside and slipped out into the dark.

Basil was out there. She could see the red tip of his cigarette, and he held it out to her as she came close.

"Whatchu doin?" he asked her as she took the cig.

"*Nada,*" she said. She kept quiet for a minute, inhaling the smoke. Then she asked him, "You get hurt?"

"Nah," he said. "I get in trouble all the time.

"We movin'," she said. She felt like crying all the sudden.

"Movin'." He seemed surprised. He looked down at his feet and watched her through the side of his eyes. "Why?"

"Mamma lose her job."

He whistled. "What you gon' do?"

"We don't know," she said.

"You ain't got no place to go?" he repeated.

"Gaw, you quick," she said.

"Don't be cold," he said back. Rosa just stared at him. Then she held his cigarette out to him.

"Where you gon' go?" he finally asked, taking the butt back.

"DC," she said.

"DC?" he repeated, like he couldn't believe it. "Why you go there?"

"We got cousins."

Basil didn't say anything, but he was being quiet in a different way. He looked pretty agitated. "Why'n you come to Church?"

"To Church?" Rosa said after him. It was hard not to laugh. "My father, he never go there."

"We take people in," he said. "It part of our mission."

"My Daddy even knew you was here, he prob'ly throw me out."

"You be better off," Basil said.

"What *that* s'posed to mean?"

Basil shrugged. He seemed to be struggling with something he wanted to say. "I know some shit," he finally said.

"What?" Rosa demanded.

Basil looked like he didn't want to answer. "All I know is that it ain't safe not to have a job anymore."

"Whatchu mean?"

Basil looked up at Rosa. "You come live with me," he said. "Forget your parents. You come marry me."

"What?" Rosa cried. "*Marry* you?"

Basil tried not to look embarrassed at the way she responded. He turned a little angry. "You can laugh if you want," he said. "But it ain't safe not to have no job. You stay with your parents, you see. One day someone come—"

Something began pounding in Rosa's ears. She couldn't listen. "Our President take care of us!" she screamed, to block out his voice. She had forgotten it was the middle of the night and she was outside. "*Vaya*, punk! I never want to see you ugly ass face again."

She turned and ran back to her window, slithered in, and fell to the floor. Her heart was beating so fast.

She lay there in the darkness, thinking. He didn't need to scare her like that. *Pendejo*. Marry her! He just wanted to see her naked. Rosa couldn't believe she'd ever liked him.

One bag didn't hold much of Rosa's stuff. She had to leave some of her clothes, her souvenir CUSA pen, and her "Torture me" doll. "Help me..." the little person struggled and screamed when she picked it up. "*Oh, God, won't somebody help me?*" Rosa smiled at it as she took it upstairs. It went on screaming hysterically until she put it on the floor in front of the door at the top of the staircase where her little neighbor Enrique would find it.

They left before dawn. The nearest convoy depot was in Vinings, not too far from them down in the I-285. They had to get up at five in the morning and hitch a thirty-minute ride out there with a cart-driver who knew Rosa's Daddy.

The driver let them off just at the top of the ramp, and they walked down into the old 285 loop. This was the old expressway that used to run cars around the outside of the city a hundred years ago. Now even city-carts couldn't get down there because it was off the grid, and there wasn't nearly enough room anyway. Only bicycles, rickshaws, and people could move along the little passageways between all the stalls and tents, and they did that slowly.

Rosa had been down there when she and her friend Maya met some boys one time, but her parents never knew. She remembered how wherever you went it smelled rotten and sweet. It was always crowded, full of people with a leg missing or bumps on their faces, and at night you saw the escorts and little mamas selling themselves. You got pushed or run into at least once for every half-hour you spent walking around. Exterminators never went down there, and the mosquitoes and flies could be so thick on the 285 that sometimes it was like walking through a fishnet. There was always shouting off in the distance, and lots and lots of firecracker explosions.

They walked for nearly six hours with a small crowd of people who, like them, were trying to get to another hub of CUSA. Rosa's eye was drawn to a tall woman with a tennis-racket case. Several little Korean kids were walking with them in the caravan. Once a passing hooker knelt down and told them how cute they were.

Rosa's feet hurt after a while. The ground was just old concrete, torn up. In some places it had big gaping holes, fenced off with chicken-wire so people wouldn't accidentally fall fifty feet down. The stalls formed a messed-up maze that they had to walk through as best they could. Poor Mamma had to leave one of her suitcases behind because it got too heavy for her. She tried not to cry, but it had a lot of family memories in it. She gave it to a woman who ran a junk stall. Mamma told her to keep the valuables but asked her if she would send the little things to her. The woman nodded, but there was no way to do that, and Mamma knew it.

"Look," said a hungry looking man in a thirty-year old suit who had been walking just to Rosa's left. He called himself Mr. Sucher. He had a big nose, a bony chin, and black, wiry hair that had a few streaks of grey. He had been an accountant, but he lost his license when the rules for examinations changed and he hadn't gotten the update, and he had gotten busted for practicing illegally. Now he was in the caravan with them, hoping to make a new start in DC.

As they passed under an old sign that said "Dunwoody Exit 1 mile," he pointed at it. He had tried to make casual conversation with Rosa a couple of times, but she had just nodded politely, not really answering. It seemed he really wanted to talk, though, and now he was talking about something Rosa was really interested in.

Mr. Sucher moved his finger to point at the sun glinting off shattered windows like a hundred dead eyes staring out. Two old skyscrapers rose up forty stories over the river of rocks that used to be Georgia 400. "That's the King and the Queen," he said. The two buildings were facing away from the neighborhood of Dunwoody behind them, like they knew what kind of hell it was. He smacked his neck, killing another mosquito. "They used to be really nice buildings." Mr. Sucher looked at her for a second. "My family was from Dunwoody, years ago."

"Mamma always told me Dunwoody was the first place to fall apart after the Correction," Rosa said to him.

"That's true," said Mr. Sucher, nodding. "It used to be really beautiful, like an enormous garden, with restaurants, shops, apartments. If you went up there now, you'd see empty buildings and smashed glass all the way to the horizon—a concrete wasteland. Smack in the middle of it is Perimeter Mall. That was the old Governor's Mansion, I think."

Rosa cut in. "Once my friend Tauna's older brother went down into Perimeter Mall as part of his gang initiation, and he made it back alive. He said now it was like a life-sized jigsaw that you could get lost in and never come out. He said that even if you didn't get killed by some warlord on the streets up above it, you might starve to death inside."

Mr. Sucher nodded again. Rosa tried not to look as the ruins of the mall sailed by them on the high bank to their left.

There was some kind of disturbance a few stalls away. Lots of people were streaming towards the noise and confusion. Rosa could hear shouts, mostly of men, but of women too. A few Uniforms were running towards the buzz, their guns out. The escorts quickly steered the convoy away from the excitement, their faces tense but not stressed. Soon the noise disappeared into the other sounds of the 285.

They moved past Perimeter into Chamblee Dunwoody. Everywhere people were selling worthless junk. The smell of the noodles started to be irresistible. Most of the people spoke nothing but Spank, the mix of Spanish and Black English that changed so fast that if you stopped speaking it for more than about a year you couldn't understand it. One real old woman came right up to Mamma and tried to sell her some fried potatoes. Mamma spoke some Spank, but it was the Spank of about twenty years ago, and they couldn't understand each other, so Rosa had to translate for the woman and then tell her no. The woman laughed a smoker's laugh and tried to hand Mamma a potato anyway, but Mamma wouldn't take it.

At about four in the afternoon they saw the GM Assembly Plantation off to the right. Mr. Sucher, who was walking on Rosa's left, spoke up again. "That means we're almost at our departure point. We'll get our vouchers evaluated somewhere very near here, and then board transportation out of CUSA Atlanta."

The GM Plantation was a huge residential compound for people with a lot of number who weren't in the City Proper. One part of it was a huge black square building with huge, dirty-white English letters visible, some of which had fallen off over time. It was supposed to be fabulous inside. If the commercials were true, there were fountains in there and an amusement park and pretty shops, as well as hundreds of nice homes just like the Proper.

"This whole complex goes on for more than a kilometer," said Mr. Sucher. He acted like it was his job to tell Rosa as much about the world as he could. "The part of the Plantation we want is still a ways on to the east, under those train-tracks and past a hill." As the group of travelers went over a rise, four or five big exit ramps shot up into the sky from 285, moving off in different ways like a concrete aloe plant. "And there's Stone Mountain," he said. The huge rock looked like a hazy half-moon on the horizon; the abandoned mansions stuck to its slopes were like garbage clinging to the sides.

The way onto the ramps was blocked by Uniforms. Nobody who lived on 285 was allowed to go anywhere near those ramps. They flowed around the blockades like ants working their way around a rock. Every once in a while you could see a tiny motorbike with the City Police lights flashing on its back making its way up and down one of them. Only two things ran on I-85: City police and Bus Transports leaving the city.

They finally got a chance to rest. They had been picking up people all along the way, and now they were a group of about twenty. When they got to a huge break in the 285 stalls, guarded by police, their guide took them off the road along a little path that led to a building with a hole in the side.

Everyone went through the hole, then moved along a tunnel towards the southern half of the Plantation. They couldn't see what the Plantation looked like because the tunnel was completely covered up. Shareholders didn't like little people to see the way they lived except on the AVE. When they got through to the end, they were in a small section of the Plantation that was the only place people like them could go. Some offices were there, like for the cheap lawyers who represented ordinary CUSA dwellers, and loan-sharks stood in front of their shops, talking to one another out of the sides of their mouths and watching, half-bored, half-ready to come over if anyone looked at them. Mamma and Daddy made sure they stayed far away from the sharks. Daddy told her they always made it sound like they were doing a favor to people in their situation, but he'd seen too many of his friends get into worse trouble. He didn't even want to be tempted, he said.

A man in a dress-skirt, with his legs close-shaved and scarred with bug bites, came to their group. Even though he was dressed well, he had a mean look, and he didn't sound like he cared if they heard him or not.

"My name is Vic," he said. "I'm going to check your vouchers and then take you to the Bus. Have your voucher out by the time I get there. If I don't see it, you don't go, and I'll give your space to somebody else. There's a whole group over by that wall that's waiting to grab a spot. I won't check you twice.

"You can't take those animals," Vic said quickly to some people holding cages with chickens in them. "You can try to sell them to those lawyers." He pointed curtly to the sharks.

Everyone moved fast to do what he said. They lined up, and Vic moved along towards them, the transplants looking like five-year-olds with their little pieces of paper sticking out of their hands in front of them. Vic checked the vouchers really quick, like he'd seen a million of them. One woman at the front of the line had a ticket Vic didn't like. Vic just shook his head and moved on. The lady didn't even argue. She moved quietly out of the line and disappeared.

While Vic was checking vouchers, all of a sudden this little child came bursting through the line right where they were. Mamma jerked up her hand really quick, and it was a good thing, because without even stopping, the little child grabbed the voucher of the next person to her right and slipped into the crowd.

Vic saw the whole thing with his clever little eyes, and he called out "Stop!" and made a gesture. Then two Uniforms came out of nowhere and ran after the kid. But that kid was gone. The next thing you knew, the police were staring at a crowd of people who were looking back at them. The kid was nowhere to be seen.

The kid's victim was Mr. Sucher. He stood there now, stunned, empty handed. He didn't move out of the line. He didn't say anything until Vic got to him. Vic didn't even pause at the man's empty hand. He just moved on to Mamma.

"But I had a *voucher*," said Mr. Sucher. Sweat, or a tear, dropped down the end of his big nose.

"You should have held on to it," said Vic. He hardly looked up.

"But everyone *saw!*"

"You have to have a voucher to go," said Vic. He looked down at Mamma's voucher. He hadn't moved away from her yet, and Mamma was getting nervous.

"You can't do that!" said Mr. Sucher. He sounded like he was trying to mean it, but he didn't have a prayer. "I paid everything I have for my voucher." He was pleading, but no one would look at him except the

Uniforms. They watched him carefully, with their hands on their sticks, until Mr. Sucher moved very slowly away out of line. In a minute he was gone just like the kid.

Vic was still staring at Mamma's voucher. Then he looked at her. He looked deep into her eyes with his own little beady ones. It was the scaredest Rosa had ever seen her Mamma.

Really quietly, Vic spoke to her "How'd you get this voucher?".

"My cousin Lotta Luka in Washington, DC—she arranged it." Mamma was speaking fast, like she had done something wrong, even though Rosa knew she hadn't. "We picked it up in Vinings from the Cater Depot."

"The Cater Depot?" Vic said.

"Yes," Mamma said, nodding.

Vic's eyes flitted over the voucher. "This has a black stripe in the wrong place." He looked at her like she was supposed to know what to do about it.

But Mamma didn't know what to do about it. Daddy wanted to say something, but he was afraid.

"You arranged this through dot net?" Vic asked.

"Yes!" Rosa's Mamma said, nodding hard. "T733585dot-serial seven dot net."

Vic nodded. "The dot net connection is really old. A lot of forgeries come from the dot net."

"This one is real," Mamma said in a faint little voice, like she was begging for it to be true.

Vic kept looking her in the eye.

113

"It's real," he finally said, "But that's only because I say it's real. I'd know if it was a forgery. This is just an old template. I wouldn't buy anything off of dot net anymore." Then he moved past them with his eyes like little slits.

Mamma looked like someone had just given her back her life. She was shaking. Daddy rubbed her back and pulled away a little moisture from the corner of his eye. "You see? The President is taking care of us," Mama whispered to Rosa. "The President always takes care of us…"

They got on an old-time bus, one of those noisy, gas-smelling vehicles that you only ever saw on roads heading out of CUSA. It had some newer parts sticking out around the outsides, and it wasn't that big. It had old blue painted stripes, and the tires were all worn at the letters. Rosa was scared about that until she got on the bus and saw the smelly pile of tires inside at the back.

Fifteen people followed her on, besides the driver. The first was a tall, skinny man named Firoz. He had circles under his eyes, which were very red. He stumbled when he walked, like he didn't know the ground was there. He was alone and didn't have any bags except for one tiny one hanging from his shoulder. He got on, sat in the back corner, and looked out the window.

A noisy family of eight, the Kwangs, came on together. First was an elderly couple who had to hold on to each other every now and then to keep from falling. After them came a big woman who swayed very heavily onto her right foot when she walked. Every time she swayed the soft parts of her body would rock over to that side like water sloshing in a bathtub. A dark man, her husband, came after her, tall and strong like an oak tree. He had to be strong, because half the time his wife was leaning on him.

A younger woman came next, kind of like a miniature version of Mrs. Kwang—maybe a sister, only not as fat. From the front you could see she had one eye missing, with a black scar where the socket ought to be. If you saw her from the side with her good eye, she still looked kind of pretty. She was leading three little kids in a line down the aisle, holding the oldest's hand. The three kids followed after her in a train, the very littlest trailing along at the end, holding the paw of this nasty-looking stuffed bear. Its ear and part of its face had been chewed off, and it had a funny smell. Everyone, adults, kids and the stinky bear, sat together over two rows. Except for the old couple, they made a lot of noise. They had more stuff with them than Rosa's family did, probably because there were more people to carry it.

Next came the woman with the tennis-racket case. She was about the same age as Rosa's Mamma, with a bandana wrapped around her forehead. The tennis-racket case was the only thing she had. She put it on the rack above her head and sat down, but she kept looking up at it every few minutes, like she wanted to make sure it stayed put. When she noticed Rosa looking at her she smiled. Rosa didn't smile back.

The last three people to get on the bus were a Chinese couple traveling with a young woman who must have been their daughter. Everyone was shocked at how pretty she was. Even Firoz sat up when these folks came in. You usually never saw anyone that good-looking who wasn't part of the Corporation. By her face, she could have been a commercial-girl.

Those three kept near the front of the bus, and when they sat down there wasn't any more room. The whole bus was full of luggage and tires and spare parts and some food rations that were beginning to spoil. There was a little path to the bathroom at the back, but when Rosa went back there she saw that it was just a seat over a potty hole that went straight to the street. You could feel a breeze when you went, and it was even worse when the bus was moving.

When the driver got on she turned to slip into her seat. She didn't speak to them at all, didn't check their vouchers, didn't look to see if everyone was there. She just pulled the door closed and started up the long, slow ramp that took them from 285 to 85 going north. It went way high, higher than Rosa had ever been in the sky before, and for a minute, looking back out the window, she could see all the way to the City Proper, the whole skyline, just like when you flew over it in commercials.

I-285 looked like a cast-off piece of bread with thousands of ants crawling around on it. Rosa could see it wind away into the distance to the east, full of stalls and barriers, swarming until it curved out of sight. Just past the curve was Stone Mountain again, with all the solar panels reflecting the afternoon sun, winking and blinding. Scattered south across the skyline was a sea of tiny golden prayer arches growing smaller and smaller as they spread out towards the horizon. Then the bus came down and the view was cut off.

They drove for a while pretty quiet. The bus hummed and shook like an overfilled washing machine, but it seemed it was going to hold together all right. Nobody used this road anymore except veeps and Uniforms, so there weren't any other vehicles in sight, just them cruising up the middle of ten lanes all by themselves. You could see the train-tracks off to the side with trains rushing past them to the north.

Everybody was talking just to the people they knew, everybody except for Firoz, who didn't talk to anybody, and the lady with the tennis-racket case who looked like she was listening to something. Rosa didn't know what it could be; she couldn't hear anything except the bus. Whatever the woman heard, she seemed to be enjoying it a lot. She just grinned and tapped her fingers on the seat next to her.

They drove like that for about half an hour. Rosa looked out the window at the vast stretches of outer Atlanta. It looked pretty much like what she knew.

Neighborhood after neighborhood after neighborhood, people walking, people sitting on curbs, strip malls turned into houses, houses turned into supermarkets. Some parts looked nice; other places looked pretty bad. There were blocks dressed up to look proud, surrounded on all sides by cemeteries full of old and dead buildings.

The bus driver pulled out onto a ramp leading to a collection of cottages that had snuck up on them. She pulled off to the side of the road. Then she stood up and turned around. She was kind of short. She had straight black hair pulled back into a bun. It just barely peeked out under her blue cap. Her face was pock-marked and tan, and it was perfectly round. She was pretty old, but she looked solid, firm, like if you ran into her she wasn't going to be the one to fall. "We're coming into Georgiatown," she said. She spoke with a little accent Rosa didn't recognize. "Anybody wants to buy anything, exchange anything, or talk to anyone, you have to do it now. We can't stop anywhere on the route. Also" —she looked them all in the eye, one by one —"anyone who wants to get off, now's the time, okay?" She was quiet for a second, just looking at them. Then she said, "I'm not going to lie to you. It's a very dangerous trip. You know that. You want to get off, do it here. I wouldn't recommend changing your mind in the Unincorporated States." She stopped again. She looked down at the floor of the bus. Then she looked up and said, "We don't give refunds." She turned around, eased back into her seat, and pulled the bus back on the ramp towards Georgiatown.

The Georgiatown buildings appeared outside the bus' left window. Georgiatown had started as a mall a hundred years ago. Then during the Correction people started living there, building on top of it. Finally it got so crowded it became its own little Proper. Now it looked like a wedding cake: a group of tall, skinny buildings rising out of one huge base. It was exclusive, like the Plantation, but people like Rosa could still visit if they had enough number.

Rosa thought they would finally see some Shareholders and walk around with them, that they would get to pretend they were big, powerful people with lots of number, even if it was just for a second. But Mamma told her that the Corporation people all shopped in different parts of Georgiatown, and nobody wanted them to mix in.

Where Rosa's family got to go was pretty lousy. A lot of lawyers' kiosks and cheap clothing stalls. But when Rosa looked past the dirt she could tell that it had once been a really pretty place. There had been a big glass window in front of every shop, and some still had beautiful pictures and designs on the door. Some even had the old signs hanging above so you could tell what they used to sell there. Rosa spent ten minutes just staring at one that used to be a bridal shop. The sign for it was in English. All around it was a picture of a tall, white woman in a pretty gown that draped all over her feet. Rosa asked her Mamma why they used a white woman in the picture. Mamma said that was a picture of the woman who owned the store. Mamma seemed really nervous now, and she didn't want to answer most of Rosa's questions. She just kept looking around like she wanted to buy something but couldn't decide what to get. Her face got sadder and sadder the whole time.

Rosa didn't think they were going to buy anything, but Mamma and Daddy used most of their number for cigarettes. Mamma said their number wasn't any good on the road. So they bought cigarettes, because they could be traded in an emergency.

Still, they didn't end up with a lot of cigarettes.

The bus driver told everyone her name was Chassis. She didn't say much after that. Rosa wanted to go over to ask her questions, but she stayed by her Daddy instead. He was looking at Firoz like he hadn't seen him before.

"What's the matter, Daddy?"

"Nothing," he said. He just glared at Firoz. Meanwhile, Firoz wasn't looking back. He was still gazing out the window, looking exactly like he did when he first sat down.

Rosa was nervous about the way Mamma and Daddy were acting, and she wanted to get away from them for a while. She tried to get up and move to the front of the bus, but Mamma put her arm around her and kept her close. After about twenty minutes, the bus slowed down. Rosa thought Chassis was going to pull over, but she just stopped under a covered booth. She leaned out the window and started chatting with this woman in the gate. Real friendly. Chassis had her head out the window for maybe fifteen minutes. Rosa never heard a word, but she heard Chassis laughing. Chassis' laugh sounded like two bricks scraping together, a laugh that could put you on edge or make you feel real safe, depending on whose side you were on.

The woman in the booth came out and walked around the back of the bus. She walked slow, Rosa guessed, because she was looking at things. Rosa wondered if she was going to look up the potty hole.

Finally, she got to the door and Chassis let her on. She was wearing a black and gold body suit with gold stripes down the side. She was heavy like Chassis, but a whole lot younger. Her hair was cropped short under a tight cap with a brim that shaded her eyes. Mamma and Daddy got nervous again, but this woman didn't look like she would cause them any trouble. She didn't look like she even saw any of them. She just started talking in this dead voice.

"You are about to leave the Corporation of the United States of America. This bus is headed for the MidAtlantic Protectorate. You are expected to remain on this bus until it reaches its route."

She sounded like she'd said this stuff five million times already, maybe even five million times today. She sounded like she didn't care if they lived or died.

"CUSA makes no claim of your safety. Anyone traveling over the Unincorporated States by land does so at their own risk. Once you cross the border behind me, your connection to CUSA exists entirely in your voucher. If your voucher is lost or damaged, you will not be allowed back into CUSA. This is for your own safety."

She looked around at them like she was waiting for somebody to argue. Nobody said anything.

"As citizens and protectees of CUSA, you will be allowed back into CUSA territory upon presentation and surrender of your voucher. You must surrender your voucher to re-enter CUSA."

She stopped again. It was like the pauses were part of the speech or something.

"CUSA is not liable for anything lost or damaged in the Unincorporated States. Any disputes arising in or with the Unincorporated States must be taken up with the Office of Foreign Affairs in Baltimore. This includes all loss of property and/or life. Are there any questions?"

"When do we eat?" asked the woman with the tennis-racket case. Everybody on the bus chuckled. Even Chassis.

The border lady nodded like she thought the joke was okay, but she didn't smile. "Have a good day," she said. Then she stepped off.

Chassis pulled the bus through the booth, and they started heading for an underpass. They went underneath a big road that Rosa could see had a bunch of fences and barbed wire on it. "That's the outer loop," said Daddy. "Are you ready?" He looked down at her and ran his fingers through Rosa's hair. That irritated Rosa, and she shook him off.

They went through three gates that were tucked under the tunnel. Once they got through, Rosa tried to look back, but she couldn't see behind them because the bus didn't have a rear window and Mamma wouldn't let her open theirs.

On the outer side of the loop everything was really green. Rosa was surprised. Nobody lived out here. Nobody. No Churches, no buildings, no houses. Just the road and a bunch of trees and weeds. At first, when they went under bridges, you could sometimes see old towers or something, but after a while it just looked dark and green.

They rode for a while with everybody keeping their seats. Rain started tapping on the windows. The tap became a torrent, the rain pounding against the roof of the bus, the hard wind rocking the bus sometimes like a boat. Rosa sat in the crook of Mamma's arm and watched the scenery through the white curtains of water. She thought about lots of things, then about nothing. She wished she had an AVE to log on to. She wanted a cigarette bad enough that she didn't care if Mamma and Daddy finally found out she had started smoking, but she knew they were saving them as number.

The Kwang children had started getting up, making lots of noise. Mamma Kwang and Aunt One-Eye tried to keep them in their seats, but Mr. Kwang didn't do much or say much about it. He just sat there like his oak-tree self and kept quiet, letting his women do all the work. After a while Mamma and One-Eye got tired of slapping the older one on top of the head, tired of yanking the younger one by the arm, and they fell back in their seats and let them run.

Nobody seemed to mind. The kids were noisy, but they weren't bad, mostly just coming up to different people and staring at them.

The Chinese family were too polite to look unhappy when the kids came over. The really pretty young girl played with the middle child and made him giggle. Then when he started squealing she tried to send him away, but he wouldn't leave.

The tennis-racket-case lady watched everything with a big smile. Rosa wanted to know what she was so happy about. Rosa wondered if she was an addict. She acted like she was proud, like the kids were hers, the way she caught the eye of grandpa Kwang. He smiled too and nodded quickly, showing his yellow, broken teeth, but he didn't look her in the eye.

The oldest kid and the youngest came to the back of the bus. First they went down to Firoz and checked him out. He didn't seem to notice them. He hadn't moved since he sat down. He was still staring out the window like those trees outside were really something interesting. The kids tried to get his attention by playing near him, then by poking him with their fingers and running away fast. He didn't move, not even to scratch.

Finally, they got bored and came up to Rosa. Mamma and Daddy smiled at them, but they were looking at her.

"I'm Leethee," said the littlest one.

Rosa nodded.

"Where you from?" the oldest one asked.

"Buckhead," Rosa said. The tattered bear the littlest one was carrying smelled even worse up close. It reeked like sweaty socks and spoiled chicken soup.

"Where you from?" Rosa asked him.

"Fairburn," he said.

Rosa knew about Fairburn. It was rough down there. Lots of old strip-malls falling apart, with people living in them.

"Come play with us?" asked Leethee for the both of them. Rosa didn't want to be around the stuffed bear, but Mamma patted her away, so she went. They took her up to introduce her to the Grandma and Grandpa, then the Mamma and Daddy, then the one-eyed lady they called Aunt Kin.

The pretty Chinese girl at the front of the bus was still trying to get the middle child to go away, but he wouldn't go. The other two finally pulled Rosa up to where he was, and she and Leethee and the older one all bounced on the seats, laughing and making lots of noise.

125

They settled on the row in front of the Chinese girl's parents and stared at them for a while. Rosa never would have been allowed to stare if she hadn't been sitting with the Kwang kids, who were too young to know better. Rosa got a good look at them.

They didn't look like much now, but she was getting the idea they used to be pretty number, just from the way they sat. They looked uncomfortable, but they tried to pretend they weren't, as if the spongy seats were some kind of couch they were reclining on and this was a royal bus. Most Chinese, maybe all of them, lived in the City Proper, usually high up. Rosa didn't know what could have happened to these people to make them leave their home. Their clothes were old and faded, but they would have been expensive if they'd been new. She guessed they'd been in them for some time.

The man kept his eyes far away, but the woman would look back and smile really sweet, then look down. She did this three times. Rosa knew she was making the Chinese people uncomfortable, but she just couldn't resist getting a good stare at someone, especially someone interesting. Finally, the Chinese woman tried to make friends.

"What are your names?"

The Kwang kids wouldn't answer. Rosa waited for a second, and then she said, "Rosa."

"What does your father do, Rosa?" she asked.

Rosa didn't want to tell her that her Daddy had been out of work so long. "He works for the neighborhood," she said, just to come up with something.

"What does your mother do?"

"She was a code checker," Rosa said. "But she lost her job and now we're going up to DC to find a new one."

The woman nodded. "That's what happened to me, too," she said.

"Really?" Rosa asked. The older Chinese woman nodded again. "What did you do?" Rosa wanted to know.

"I worked for Noke," she said. Leethee had started stroking the hair of the Chinese daughter because it was so smooth and black. The daughter tried to sit there like she didn't feel it, and the parents were making like it didn't bother them, but Rosa knew it did.

"Noke? Wow! Us too! That's who Mamma worked for. Did you live in the City Proper?"

"We did," she said.

"That must have been great," Rosa said. "We just lived in Sandy Springs. Do you have a brand?" Rosa knew her mother would go crazy if she found out she'd asked someone about their tattoo, but her mother wasn't here, and she really wanted to see one.

The woman nodded again.

"Can I see it?" Rosa begged. The Kwangs stood up on the seats, interested.

The woman reached up to her shoulder and pulled a flap away. Underneath was a pattern of blue bars painted on her skin. It looked like an air-conditioner vent. She elbowed her husband. "Show them yours," she told him.

He did what she told him. His tattoo looked a lot like hers. You could see the hair growing all over it. "Don't you have to shave that, mister?" asked the oldest Kwang.

The man glowered and looked away. The woman answered for him. "We don't use them anymore." The man turned on her suddenly like he wanted to argue, but she shut him up just by looking at him.

"Why not?"

"I don't work for Noke now," she said.

"Did you get fired?" Rosa asked.

"Yes."

"That's what happened to my Mamma," Rosa said, trying to sound sympathetic. "You couldn't find a new job in CUSA?" She figured it had to be easier for them than for her family.

The woman looked down at her feet. "Things don't work that way in the City Proper," she said.

Rosa didn't understand that. She wanted to ask more, but she got a feeling that her Mamma would really pull her away now. The Kwang kids had already gone down the aisle, and Rosa wanted to follow them. "See you," she said. The Chinese woman nodded back.

By the time she got to the middle of the bus, the three Kwang kids were all gathered around the tennis-racket-case lady. She was showing them something.

Rosa crept over and peeked across the seat. She couldn't believe the tennis racket the woman had taken out of the case: It was made of orange wood, shaped like a kidney bean, with a scrape down near where her hand touched the strings. Rosa couldn't look away. She'd never seen anything like it.

"What kind of tennis racket is that?" asked the middle child, who had never seen one.

"It's a guitar," she said. "A hundred years ago, people used to play them when they sang special commercials called 'songs.' Want to hear one?"

"Can I play?" the oldest asked.

Instead of answering, the lady started singing some wordless melody. She held the guitar still the whole time and didn't play it. "Do you all like that?" she asked. They nodded. "How about you join me?" she asked.

Then she added some words. *"I'd like to teach the world to sing..."* Her voice came out so beautiful. She let them sing after her. *"...in perfect harmony..."* she went on. The woman smiled as she sang. *"I'd like to buy the world a Coke..."*

"Rosa!" her Mamma called.

"I have to go," Rosa told them. She left the woman and the Kwang kids singing behind her and went back to her Mamma and Daddy. She noticed that Firoz had fallen asleep against the window. The rain seemed to pour into his head as it fell in sheets against the glass.

"What are you doing?" Mamma asked her.

"Nothing," Rosa said. She sat down next to her Mamma and leaned on her arm. Mamma wrapped it around her.

It was getting dark outside.

Rosa didn't think she was tired, but she woke up later in complete darkness, feeling the bus bouncing under her. She didn't know how long she had been sleeping, but everyone was quiet. Even the little kids in front had gone down. Only the bus driver was awake. Rosa could see her looking all around as she drove, even though she was just looking into the blackness.

Rosa got up and went towards her. The bus driver's comfy chair was set just a little below the floor, and she moved all around in it as she drove, like she was dancing on her bottom. When the driver heard Rosa coming she looked up out of her little cockpit. Rosa wasn't sure if she was mad at her for coming up, but the driver didn't say anything. She just turned around and kept dancing.

There were a lot of interesting things in Chassis' cockpit. All in front of her were dials and switches, some that were working, others dark. Some of the big switches were obviously missing, and some metal pieces were pointing out where plastic used to be on top. Along her left side were a bunch of hundred-year-old photographs taped to the wall. The images were really small and they didn't move, so Rosa couldn't make them out. She wanted to get closer, but she thought it would be rude.

Finally Rosa noticed the little box by Chassis' left hand that sounded like it had bees inside. But then instead of buzzing, it squawked.

"What's that?" Rosa pointed at it.

Chassis looked at Rosa's finger. "The radio," she said. "Old-time AVE."

"Oh," Rosa said.

"You've been asleep five hours," Chassis said. "You should go back to sleep."

"When are we going to be there?" Rosa asked.

"By noon tomorrow. Maybe sooner. It depends."

"On what?" Rosa asked.

"Lots of things," she said. "I know the roads really well, but things change out here. Depends on the route."

Rosa nodded like she understood. She tried to look smart because she had decided she liked Chassis and wanted to impress her.

"You log on to school?" the driver asked her.

"Yeah," Rosa said.

"What game?"

"*Ultimate Acquisition VII.*"

"They still play that one? That's a classic. You like it?"

"It's okay." Rosa said, shrugging. "I wouldn'a chose it, but that's the one they assigned for my neighborhood." Before the driver could ask her another question, Rosa said, "Where you from?"

"I'm from everywhere," Chassis said.

"No you ain't," Rosa said, waving her head around.

"Yeh I is," she said in Spank.

That surprised her. Rosa answered her in Spank. "How you learn to talk like that?"

"Spank been 'round a lot longer than you!"

"You don't look like you speak Spank!"

"That 'cause Mamma 'Bangladeshi!" she said. "But I been 'round."

"You Bangladeshi?" Rosa asked.

"Mmm hmm."

"From there?"

"When I was little."

"How little?"

"Littler than you!" and she smiled. "We gone right before Bangladesh get taken over by Pakistan."

"You remember?"

"Nothin' to remember," she said, shaking her head. "I been lots of other places since then."

"Where you go?"

"Everywhere!"

"Where?"

"You name it."

"Washington."

"Uh huh." she said.

"Houston."

"Mmm hmm."

"LA."

"Yep."

"How you go so many places?" Rosa asked her.

"'Cause I done so many things."

"Like what?"

She didn't answer. She was slowing down. She was looking at something in her headlights. She cussed in some language Rosa didn't know.

"There's a bridge out," she said in Spanish. "It's collapsed."

"How you get around it?" Rosa asked her.

"Wait," she said. She reached down and grabbed a little box off of the squawking thing. It was attached with a funny piece of coiled rubber. She talked into it, quiet, so Rosa couldn't really hear.

The box squawked back at her, and Rosa caught a little of it. Whoever was squawking told Chassis they didn't know about the collapse.

"It must be a recent one," she said. "They go out all the time, now. They're finally beginning to fall apart."

"How you get around it?" Rosa asked her again.

"We go up this ramp and down the other one," said Chassis. She was looking around more intently now, like she was trying to see through the dark. She moved the big wheel at her chest to the right, and the bus pulled over and started turning around. She took them back the way they'd come a little ways and then wheeled the bus onto the ramp going up.

"What you used to do?" Rosa asked to get back to the conversation.

"Everything."

"Like what?"

"When I was just a little older than you, I got my first job. I used to monitor websites for illegal activity. You know what websites are?"

Rosa nodded her head, even though she didn't.

"Then I made deliveries in the boondocks."

"The what?"

"I delivered things for people like those that live in the shacks on the I-285."

"Oh," Rosa said. "Like what?"

She smiled. "And I was a swimming instructor. You swim?"

Rosa shook her head.

She went on. "I drove my first bus when I was twenty-three. Took it all the way to Chicago. That was before—" Her voice died. She was looking ahead at the road. There wasn't any ramp back down. Just trees. She cussed again.

"What is it?"

"There's no return access ramp," she said. "Now I have to figure out where...wait a minute." She talked into her radio again and waited. The radio squawked back at her, and she nodded. Then she smiled. "Okay," she said. "I know where we are. That's fine. That will even save us some time."

"What?" Rosa asked.

"I know a good route we can take," she said, and she started moving the bus to the right again, down the road into the darkness.

"Is it all like this?" Rosa asked. It looked even darker through the windows than it did along the highway, if that was possible.

"Like what?"

"Woods. Woods."

"No," Chassis said, cocking her head. "There's some cities out here."

"*Cities?*" Rosa said. "In the US?"

"Sure," Chassis said, moving her hands up and down the steering wheel. "Richmond is still pretty big. Charlotte. Wheeling. They even have electricity."

"No way!"

Chassis laughed hard. "What they teach you in that game you play now?"

Rosa shrugged. "We learn about the President, how great he is, how he gonna take care of us..."

"Yeah, yeah, yeah," Chassis said, like she'd heard it all before. Rosa raised her eyebrows. She was surprised that Chassis wasn't more respectful. "What else?"

"We learn about what we need to do to get a job, who we need to talk to, how we get around, how we stay safe..."

"Don't you learn any history?"

"Sure," Rosa said. "We learn about the Dow and the Great Correction and how the President saved us."

Chassis chewed her lip. "Huh," she said. "So they don't teach you any history."

"What you mean?" Rosa demanded.

"You know why the white people left?"

Rosa was quiet for a minute. Then she admitted, "No."

Chassis waited like she wanted her to ask. Rosa wanted to know, but she didn't want to sound any dumber than she felt. So she kept quiet. Finally, Chassis said, "You know what the Correction was?"

Rosa shrugged. She thought she did.

Then Chassis started rattling off facts like she was an AVE and Rosa was buying. "In what they used to call the Twenty-First Century, about a hundred years ago, people were living on borrowed time. Everybody knew something was going to come down on them, but nobody knew when. Nobody knew how.

"Well, one week, a bunch of people defaulted on their home loans. A huge bunch of people. Back in those days people didn't have tattoos, and the credit companies weren't part of the government, so you could get into a lot more trouble with your number and nobody would mess with you. Well, when all of a sudden everybody couldn't pay, there was a bank-collapse."

Rosa didn't understand every word Chassis was saying, but she was really interested in the story anyway, since nobody had ever bothered to tell her this stuff before.

"Well, things got better for a while, but then they went bad again. Up and down, a bunch of falls, each one worse than the last. They take all of them together and call them the Correction. That would have been bad enough.

"But out west, the Colorado River had dried up because of the heat, and everyone left Las Vegas, pushing into the East Coast and West Coast. Right about then the ocean levels were getting high enough that when a bad bunch of storms hit the East Coast, all the major cities out there got flooded. New York, Baltimore, DC. The levels never did come down again, and everybody was just stuck.

"The people with all the number got out, you know? They fled to higher ground. That was happening anyway, though. After Iran took Mexico in, a lot of Mexican Catholics fled north, into the big dry cities where their families were.

"So when the government became a Corporation and changed USA into CUSA, it was mostly darker people living there.

"Then they built the levies around DC, and the walls around the Southern Protectorate, the Northern Protectorate, the Texas Protectorate...you know them all, right?"

Rosa nodded. Yes, she knew all the Protectorates. She was glad she knew *something*, anyway.

"Well, Richmond and those other cities got left out. Charlotte almost made it, but they had that *coup* and the President didn't want to waste his number protecting it anymore. So now it's one of those Unincorporated States.

"They got electric power," Chassis said, getting back to that subject. "Though you can't rely on it out there like you can in CUSA. There are lots of blackouts and things, especially when someone tries to take over as Governor, but it's not as bad as out in the country where they make do with candles."

"Do the Young Guns protect them too?" Rosa asked.

"*The Young Guns?* No way!" Chassis said really loud. "CUSA's not going to use its troops and its number protecting a million little backwards White States, even if they are all gathered in one big place. No, they're just out there, like the little towns in the woods."

Before Chassis could go any further, Rosa heard a noise from the back of the bus. Chassis looked into her mirror. Rosa couldn't believe the noise, because she recognized the voice. It was her father. He was screaming at Firoz.

Firoz was still sitting in the back of the bus, but Rosa couldn't see him because her father was in the way, hanging over the seat. She quickly ran back there to see what was going on.

"Nobody said you could do that here!" he was yelling, his accusing finger pointing down.

Firoz didn't answer him. He just looked out with big, sad eyes. Rosa looked down at his arm and saw the needle hanging from it.

Rosa's father turned towards the front of the bus and began screaming at Chassis. "Nobody told me there was a drug-worshipper on board!"

Now everybody was awake. The little Kwang children and the beautiful young Chinese girl were all looking back at Rosa's father like they couldn't figure out how he had gotten on the bus. Everybody else was trying to ignore him.

"Daddy," Rosa said. "Forget it." She pulled his arm.

"Go sit down, Rosa," Daddy said.

"Daddy—"

"Sit down!" he shouted, and he shoved her away so hard that Rosa stumbled and had to catch herself on the hard rubber floor. The lines on the mat cut into her hands.

Rosa's father didn't even notice. He had turned back to scream at the drug addict. "If you don't get that needle out of your arm right now, I'll squeeze you by the throat until you choke!"

Rosa couldn't see Firoz's response, but before her father could do anything, Chassis had stopped the bus. She stopped it so suddenly it jerked everybody forward. Rosa fell over again onto her knees.

"What's your problem, mister?" Chassis shouted, rising to her feet from the front.

"Nobody told me there was a drug-worshipper on board!" Rosa's father answered her.

"So what?" the driver said. "He paid his money like you did; he gets to ride on the bus!"

"Not with me!" Rosa's father insisted.

"You want off?" Chassis replied, threateningly.

"I want *him* off!" Rosa's father said, the spit in his throat making his voice gravelly.

Rosa's Mamma was up by now, and she had pulled Rosa to her feet and out of the aisle. "Eduardo!" she said.

"Nobody gets off this bus unless I throw them out," Chassis said, coming towards Rosa's father.

"No, Katarina," he said, holding out his hand, stopping Rosa's mother from coming any closer.

"You need to tell me what your problem is, mister," said the driver. She shoved past Rosa's Mamma and was right in her Daddy's face. He should have been scared, but he was crazy, now, like Rosa saw him only when he was talking about drugs. His black eyes were wide open like big, bottomless pools.

"No prosperity without sobriety," Rosa's father quoted in English. "Genius is 10% inspiration and 90% perspiration!"

"There is no fear like a cockroach eye!" Firoz answered loudly. It was the first time he had spoken. Rosa could see the addict's face now. He was looking all around like he saw things moving down the walls that frightened him.

"Look, mister, I'll give you one warning," Chassis said. "And then I'm going to throw you out, with or without your wife and daughter." She was tense, like she was getting ready to move on him.

But Rosa's father hadn't heard. "Your fear is not as my fear!" Rosa's father shouted, pointing at Firoz. "And your bread is not as my bread. Therefore the body is not the body!"

Something exploded, and the bus rocked once to the right and stayed there.

Chassis braced herself against a seat, and then she cursed in Spanish so everyone could tell what she was saying. There was another explosion, and the bus rocked again. Now it was leaning towards the front. By the time Chassis got to the front of the bus, there were four more explosions, and the bus rocked and leaned a different way each time.

Then Rosa heard glass shattering, and Chassis got back to the front really fast. The pretty Chinese girl started screaming. Rosa noticed through her terror that the Kwang kids didn't make a sound. They had already gotten down behind the seats. Even Leethee was completely quiet and still. Obviously those kids had been through something like this before.

The bus door shattered into a thousand pieces and folded in. Chassis watched a large man coming up the stairs with a shotgun in his hands. As he got to the top a little old lady stepped up behind him.

The man was like a huge toddler—his face puffy and pink. His hair was cut down to a pimply scalp and looked like the bristle on a pig's back. Among the bands of the sleeveless T-shirt he was wearing, you could see bumps of various sizes all over the bottom of his neck and shoulders. He spoke to all of them in a voice like the gunshot that had demolished the bus door. "Y'all are trespassing!" He was speaking English, of course. Rosa knew a little English because all the prayers were in English, but his accent was so strange she almost couldn't make it out. "We welcome you to the great sovereign nation of Steaksbury Under God." He held his gun across his chest.

The old woman creaked out from behind him, "Y'all speak English?" She was tiny compared to the man, but she didn't look fragile. You couldn't get a pin inside the folds of her prim old-fashioned suit. Her steely blue eyes were sweeping from side to side, and everything they touched was knocked away immediately. The little grey bun on the back of her head was so tight it could have been glued to her.

"I understand you," said Chassis, stepping up to the man and looking at his face. She didn't seem much afraid. She actually looked like she was trying not to laugh. That made him mad, and he glared down at her like he was ready to step on her.

"Any of these other folks?" the old woman asked, nodding with her head at all the passengers.

Chassis shrugged.

"Tell them they've entered our jurisdiction unlawfully by God's good graces, but if they do as they're asked, no one will harm them."

Chassis turned back towards them and spoke to them in bored Spanish. "This is obviously a tribute ambush. I'm sorry. It happens from time to time. Just do what I tell you. Don't listen to them. Listen to me."

The woman waited for a second. "You tell them yet?" she asked Chassis.

"What do you want?" Chassis asked.

"We ask what's fair in the name of the Skelton Treaty," she said. "Ten percent of all valuables on the bus."

"The Skelton Treaty was repealed," Chassis told her. "Virgilina breached—"

"That's *Virgilina!*" the old woman snapped, showing her teeth. Her eyes were like cold iron on Chassis' face. Rosa couldn't believe how Chassis didn't flinch from her glare. "We're a sovereign nation unto God, separate from Virgilina. You have a compact with *us*."

Chassis shrugged. She turned towards them and said in Spanish, "They want ten percent of everything you own. That's one tenth of your cigarettes, some of your food. Just use your common sense and give them something valuable. Don't hold anything back or they'll just get angry."

Quickly the passengers started fishing through their stuff, finding things they could get rid of. When Rosa looked out the window she saw people pointing big guns right at their heads.

"Don't just give them any old thing," Chassis said in Spanish. "It's got to be something that will satisfy them."

"You," the little old woman said to Chassis. "Sit in the chair." She had a small silver pistol in her hand, and she was pointing it, waving it towards the driver's seat.

Chassis nodded and moved past the big man, then eased herself down into her chair. "Go on," the woman said in English, and the oversized, greasy baby man started walking down the aisle with an empty burlap sack. He looked over everything people handed him. Sometimes he nodded and took it. Sometimes he shook his head and roared in their faces until they gave him something else. He looked like he was concentrating very hard on his job. The lady with the tennis-racket case had to open it and show him what was inside. The man looked at the guitar like he couldn't tell if it was valuable or not. Then he gestured at the strings. She took the strings off of it like she was undressing somebody. After she gave them to the big man she turned away so he couldn't see her face.

The man got to Rosa. She gave him a little gold chain that wasn't worth anything to anyone but her. The man looked at it real close, then stuffed it in his shirt pocket. He reeked like musk mixed with feces. The smell was so strong it made her want to throw up.

When the man moved on to the back of the bus, he found Firoz just staring at the ceiling. The drug worshipper probably didn't even know what was going on. "Come on, spig!" the man shouted at him. He slapped Firoz on the face with his huge hand. "Up!" But Firoz didn't look at him. His face just went where the man's hand took it.

"He's a drug worshipper," Chassis told the woman at the front of the bus. "He doesn't have anything but his drugs."

"No food?" demanded the woman.

"Probably not," Chassis said.

The big man went all over Firoz's body, feeling for anything he could take, but all he found were needles and empty plastic bags. He just threw those to the side and glared down at Firoz.

"He ain't got nothing," the man said back to the woman.

"I told you," Chassis said.

"Then he's got to die," the woman said, shrugging.

"No!" Chassis said, standing up.

"Yes, he *dies!*" the woman shouted at her. "He ain't got no tribute. He's in violation of the treaty. Penalty for going against a treaty agreed upon under God is death!"

"He stays on the bus," Chassis said to her. "He's in my care. You got plenty. Now you get off this bus."

The woman clicked her gun and pointed it at Chassis' head. "You talk to me like that, you ugly old spigger, I'll put a hole in you like—"

"See this?" Chassis gestured towards her radio. "That's my radio. It's on and it's connected to my home base in Atlanta. They've been listening to everything that happened here. They know where we are, because you told them. You harm anyone on this bus, and the Young Guns will come out with sprayers and kill all your sons."

The woman stared thin-eyed at Chassis for a second. She looked at Chassis' feet.

Then she nodded. "Okay," she said, satisfied. "Come on, Porter. Get on up here."

He shambled up to the front of the bus, bumping each seat with his legs and his burlap sack. Just as he got to the front, he noticed the pretty Chinese girl and her parents. He was so surprised that he stopped still. The old woman and Chassis both watched him as he carefully put his bag on the ground. He reached out his hand, amazed, and ran it down the Chinese girl's black, soft, silky hair. She started to tremble. Her mother was talking to her in some language Rosa didn't know.

"Look, Mimi," the big man said softly, his voice gentle. "A China doll! Real pretty."

"Come on, Porter," the old woman said, sighing.

The Chinese mother was watching the big man stroking her daughter's silk. Rosa never saw anybody so still in her life. She kept her hands from trembling by holding them in little balls in front of her mouth.

"I want this one, Mimi," Porter half said, half asked, looking back at the old lady.

Chassis didn't say anything this time, but the old woman did. "That ain't under the agreement, Porter. Come on."

"I want her," Porter insisted. "I want her for me!"

"No!" the old woman shouted. "It ain't part of God's agreement with Skelton. We keep our word. One tenth. Now git on!"

"I want her for the night, then!" Porter said. He grabbed a hank of the girl's long hair in a huge fist. The girl screamed. The mother and father cried out and clutched at her.

"No!" the old woman shouted. She moved up the stairs and came right up to Porter. She slapped him hard across the cheek and stared at him with her steely blue eyes. The blow stunned him, and he let the girl drop to her seat, moving his hand to feel his face. "Now we keep our agreements or God takes vengeance," snapped the old lady. "You don't get to take a woman out of marriage."

"But for the night," Porter protested.

"*No!* Not for the night! You follow God's Law or we throw you out!"

Porter stared at the old lady. Rosa couldn't see his face, and she wondered if he was going to hurt the old lady. But then he sniffled a little bit, turned, and looked around the bus. His eyes fell on Rosa.

The look in them changed from being frustrated to something Rosa don't want to say. She suddenly knew the smell of his breath, could feel his stubble pricking her throat.

"Rosa," muttered her Mamma, like she was thinking the same thing.

All of a sudden, the old lady turned, and her gun went off with a jerk.

The tennis-racket woman lurched as if shocked, then slumped over. Rosa could see the guitar strings fall to the rubber floor from her hand. She had been trying to take them back out of the burlap sack while the old lady and the big man were arguing.

The old lady came, picked up the strings from the floor, then put them back in the sack. She looked up at Chassis. "We stick to our agreement," she said. "One tenth." Chassis just nodded and didn't say anything. "Go, Porter," the old lady said to the man. "Or I'll shoot a hole in you for the same reason." Porter sagged a little. He moved to the front of the bus and down the stairs.

"You'll have our protection all the way to Clear Point," the old lady said to Chassis on the way out. "No one will harm you here. Throw six of your tires out, and my boys will put them on for you."

Chassis nodded again, and she and Rosa's Mamma and Mr. Kwang started throwing tires out the front door. They felt the bus shake some more. Rosa sat and listened to how quiet it was and how loud the pounding of her heart was. Rosa's Daddy didn't say anything. Not about Firoz, not about anything. He just looked straight ahead and sat really quiet.

Then Chassis started up the bus again and drove them away.

Rosa's father didn't open his mouth after the incident. He didn't say a word to Rosa's Mamma or to Rosa. Mamma was pretending he was okay, but she was tugging obsessively on her own sleeve. Rosa could tell she was pretty shaken up.

"Why isn't Daddy saying anything?" Rosa asked.

"I don't know, sweetie."

"Is it 'cause of Firoz?"

"I don't know, Rosa."

"Why—" She was afraid to ask, because he was sitting right there, but he didn't look like he could even hear what she was saying. "Why do we hate drug people so much?" she whispered into Mamma's ear.

Mamma looked like she didn't think Daddy was listening, either. She shrugged, and she looked really tired. "I wasn't *chuseno* before I married your father," she said. "His grandparents were true believers. They came from really bad neighborhoods." Mamma shifted like she was uncomfortable. "Drugs weren't legal when your great-grandmamma was a child the way they are now. Back then, people that sold drugs ran those neighborhoods. But a bunch of residents got together and kicked the drug-people out. That's what started it, the *chusenos*. They all got religion and swore to keep the drugs away."

"You mean like Jesu religion?"

"Yeah," Mamma said, nodding. "It was some Jesu and some Islam. Your Daddy was raised that way, and it's just in him forever. They put it in him really hard."

"Is he gonna be okay?"

Mamma nodded. "Yes, honey."

Rosa didn't ask any more questions. She didn't think Mamma wanted to answer any more anyway.

"Daddy," Rosa said, quietly, patting him on the arm. But he looked like he didn't feel or hear.

After a while, Rosa got up and walked towards Chassis at the front. On the way she saw the families. They were hunkered together. The Kwangs were talking with each other too quiet to hear with the wind whistling through the busted door. The old couple were asleep on each others' shoulders. The kids were playing already. If what had just happened didn't faze them, Rosa hated to think what they had been through already.

The Chinese family looked really bad. The three of them were all clutching at each other really tight like they didn't want to even look up, like Porter and the old lady were still standing there. The daughter sat like a statue, and the mother kept close to her, holding her hand, crying a lot.

Rosa didn't look at the body of the guitar lady as she passed. Even out of the corner of her eye she could still see the blood pooling on the floor under the seat. The smell made her stomach turn over. Rosa rushed past and tried not to think about it.

Chassis was calm and quiet at the front of the bus. The wind coming through the shattered door was cold, and it was making the little pieces of glass hanging from the rubber wiggle and flap a lot.

"Are we gonna be okay?"

"Yes," Chassis said. Rosa didn't think the driver meant it. She just didn't want anyone to worry.

"I'm not scared," Rosa said to her.

Chassis looked up at her for a split second before returning her gaze to the road. "Yes, you are," she said. "But you won't feel it 'til later."

Rosa didn't believe her.

"Are *you* scared?" Rosa asked her.

"You'd be crazy not to be scared," Chassis said. It wasn't a real answer. Rosa wasn't sure whether she meant she was scared or she was crazy.

"Our President will take care of us," Rosa said, over her shoulder.

Chassis looked back at her again. "You believe that?"

It surprised her when Chassis asked her that. Nobody had ever asked her that before. "That's what Mamma always says," Rosa told her.

"What does it mean?" Chassis asked Rosa.

Suddenly Rosa felt mad, being asked that question. Chassis *knew* what it meant! Rosa recited what she'd learned, trying to keep from messing up. "Mamma said the market rises and falls. She says it's designed to come round again if you trust in the President. The President takes care of us. You just—"

Rosa had to stop because Chassis was snorting, looking away.

"Why you laughing?" Rosa demanded.

But Chassis didn't answer. She just shook her head and smiled the rest of her laugh away.

After a few minutes, she started looking in her side mirror. Then she kept looking in it.

"What's wrong?" Rosa asked.

At first Chassis didn't want to say. But after Rosa asked her a few more times, she finally admitted that someone was following them.

"It may be for our protection," she said. "But I don't like being followed." She started to speed up the bus.

She kept looking in her mirror, and it looked like she didn't feel safe enough because she sped up again. And again.

Then they passed a sign that Rosa could see read "Clear Point." "That's where our protection ends," Chassis said. As she said it, a pair of headlights came up in the side mirror like a pair of cat's eyes opening. Then another pair appeared behind it.

"They're behind us," she said. "And I think we'd better speed all the way up." She stepped on the gas hard, and the bus jerked forward.

"How fast will it go?" Rosa asked.

"I didn't want to go too fast on this road," she answered. "But if it's that or the alternative—"

"What alternative?" Rosa asked.

"You ask too many qu—" With a sickening lurch the bus leaned down, and this time everyone on the bus screamed. The bottom of the bus scraped against the road and lit up the windshield with blue sparks. Chassis pushed really hard on the brake pedal and pulled hard on the lever by her right leg. Rosa grabbed a metal bar behind Chassis' chair and hung on while her legs whipped out from under her. The bus screamed like it was about to flip over onto its side, but somehow Chassis hung on to the wheel and spun them right and left, and they stayed upright until the bus skidded to a stop.

For the first time, Chassis actually looked mad. This time she reached under her seat, and Rosa saw the huge gun she didn't get a chance to pull the first time heavy in her hand. She said something into the radio and muttered at Rosa to get back to her seat.

Chassis turned back to all of them and spoke out. "Folks, this isn't good, but it's still not the end. Everyone needs to keep quiet and let me handle it."

While Chassis was talking they heard heavy footsteps on the stairs, and Porter came up with his big shotgun in his arms. But there was no old lady behind him this time. Just a bony white man with a lot of scraggly beard and a long, sharp nose.

Chassis had her gun pointed at Porter's head, right at the temple. He looked surprised, but he didn't back down or put up his hands. "You better not," he said. "You can't get back on the road without us."

"What have you done to my bus?" she asked him.

Porter grinned. His mouth was a big black hole. The man behind him said "I guess we didn't put those front tires on quite right. Your front right axle came right off. We can fix it back up if you want."

"Then do it," Chassis said, each word crisp like the scrape of a knife against a whetting stone.

Porter still didn't seem to care about the gun at his head. "I want something," he said to her.

"You got everything you wanted in your agreement," Chassis told him.

His cheeks puffed out. "My *Mamma* got everything!" he yelled at her, pouting like a child. "I didn't get *nothing* that I wanted!"

Chassis didn't react to Porter's tantrum. "You can't have anything else," she said, not backing off.

"You better put that gun down," said the man behind Porter. "Phil is standing just outside with a rifle pointed at your head."

Chassis' shoulders tensed, and then sagged, and she sat down. "You know," she said to Porter, "that the people where I come from can hear what you're saying on the radio. If you do anything—"

"I ain't gonna harm you," Porter said. "I just want what I said I want. I want the China girl for the night."

"You can't have her," Chassis said. "She's not part—"

"*I want her!*" Porter interrupted, spit spraying from his mouth. He moved his big belly towards Chassis. "I want her, or you ain't going anywhere! You give me that China girl..." Then he paused, and his eyes found Rosa again.

Rosa tried to shrink away, but she was afraid to move. "Or I'll take that pretty little spic there." He gestured at her. Even though her Mamma was all the way at the back of the bus, Rosa knew she had stopped breathing.

Chassis looked at Porter, and Rosa saw her eyes get as little as slits. Meanwhile the mother and father of the Chinese girl were watching Chassis like they were afraid she'd vanish if they looked away.

Chassis finally nodded her head towards the Chinese girl. "Half-hour," she told Porter.

"No, the night—" Porter said, even while the Chinese father and mother were crying out at her.

"No, one half-hour!" Chassis snapped, bringing her face into his. "You take that, or you see what happens when the Young Guns get here."

"You can't," said the Chinese woman to Chassis, shaking her head. "You can't you can't..."

"Be quiet," Chassis said to the woman. She pointed her finger. "Give him the girl." To Porter she said, "Me and one other person are going with you to make sure you don't go any farther than those trees. And when you're done, you're letting us out of here."

Porter had been thinking while Chassis was talking. Finally, he looked like he was satisfied. Rosa saw her Mamma's and Daddy's faces. They seemed like they were going to be sick, but they didn't want to say anything, not them or anybody else on the bus.

"Mr. Kwang," Chassis said, nodding at him to come away from his large family.

Porter came over to the girl and started stroking her hair with his filthy, hairy, enormous hand. His voice was low and tender. "Pretty pretty," he whispered. It was like he wanted her to answer him.

"You can't! You can't! You can't!" pleaded the Chinese mother. Her hands were together, and you could see she was ready to get down on her knees.

But Porter had already picked the girl up in his arms, carrying her like she was his bride, and was moving towards the front of the bus. The beautiful girl was shaking, floating in front of him, light as a feather. It was such a strange scene that no one was watching anything else.

Porter made a sound like someone was sucking the air out of his lungs, and he fell on his knees, dropping the girl clumsily. He made a huge thump when he came down on the tilted bus floor. He was squirming, trying to get to the hole in his back where the Chinese girl's father had stuck him, but his arms were too big and he couldn't even touch the knife handle. The girl's father was looking down at Porter where he had stuck him, and when Porter wriggled all the way to the floor, Chassis and the man on the steps could finally see what he had done. Chassis' face got all scrunched up. "Do you know what—" she started to say as the bony-nose man practically fell down the bus stairs in his hurry to get off.

Rosa knew what was about to happen next because she was watching the Kwangs. When they got down, she got down. Then everything in the world got shattered in the space of a few seconds.

After the crashing of the glass finally stopped, Rosa didn't hear any cars driving away. That's why she was scared to move. Her and everybody else. She thought they were just waiting, standing around the bus with their guns pointed at the windows, ready to shoot off the first head they saw peeking out.

So nobody made a sound. Rosa guessed it was for an hour. She didn't know. There wasn't any way to tell.

Later, she began to hear animals moving around, and she figured they wouldn't if there were any people out there, but she still didn't get up. Her ears were ringing, and she was positive that she belonged on that bus floor.

Chassis was the first one to move, rasping out, "Okay. They're gone. Everybody, let me see you."

Rosa was up fast. At first, it was hard to tell who was dead and who was alive, because some people wanted to stay on the floor forever. But finally, everybody who was getting up did.

Three people didn't. First one was little Leethee. When old Mrs. Kwang saw that her baby was gone, a wail came out of her mouth, a horrible, practiced sound. The little girl had taken a bullet right through the side of her head. The mama tried to hug her, but the child's body flopped around in her mother's arms. Her eyes were rolled up towards the left and her mouth was open a little, drooling. The smelly face-eaten bear fell onto the rubber mat and slid towards the front. Nobody

157

touched it. None of the family was trying to keep the mom from crying, or to help her either.

The Chinese man was dead, too—the father of the girl that Porter wanted. He must have been standing there in shock when the guns were firing. He looked like such a mess Rosa couldn't have said who he was if she hadn't known. The Chinese woman and her daughter were rocking over him ritualistically, the blood leaving huge stains on their beautiful clothes.

The third person who didn't get up was Rosa's Daddy.

He was crouched down, like he had a cramp. He was breathing really hard and grinning a little. Rosa was so scared when she saw him that she was afraid to run back to him. She just stood there while Mamma checked him out. She followed Chassis down the aisle and they slowly made their way back. The driver knelt down on one knee with care.

"Mr. Chaves," Chassis said. Her voice was tired and ragged. "Mr. Chaves. Are you okay?"

"My side hurts," Rosa's Daddy said.

"Which side?"

"Left side." Then he grunted and bent over more.

"Don't move," Chassis said. "Don't move at all. Okay?"

Daddy looked like he was nodding, with his head bent down low towards the floor.

Rosa followed Chassis up to the front of the bus. The driver was moving slowly and carefully towards her seat.

She stopped, and her head came over her shoulder. She didn't look at Rosa all the way, but she said, "Don't follow me. Get back there with your Daddy."

"What can I do?" Rosa asked.

"Keep your head," Chassis grunted. Then she moved forwards. Rosa went back to where her Mamma was kneeling.

"Daddy, does it hurt?" Rosa asked him. He didn't answer. "Does it hurt, Daddy?" She was afraid he was already dead. Mamma tried to calm her down.

"No, baby," Daddy finally answered. It was like he was speaking up to her from the bottom of a well.

Then Aunt Kin Kwang came up to Rosa's Mamma. "Our President will take care of us," she said.

Mamma looked up. Rosa could tell she really appreciated the comment, especially since the Kwangs had already lost their little girl. The one-eyed woman held Mamma's hand until Chassis came back.

It took longer than Rosa thought it would, but Chassis finally moved down the aisle with a box with a red letter "t" on the side. She laid it down by Rosa's Daddy, then asked him some questions, really softly.

She must have asked if he was able to move, because he finally lay on his back in the aisle. That's when Rosa saw how much blood there was. He was holding his side, and his hand was soaked. Rosa started to make a high-pitched squeal. She was embarrassed and scared at the same time.

She cried all the time Chassis was wrapping him up. Chassis worked so slowly, Rosa thought he would bleed to death before she was done. But after she finished, he did look more comfortable. His eyes were closed, and he was breathing—little shallow breaths, but regular.

The Chinese mother stood up. "What do we do now?" she asked like she was demanding an explanation.

Chassis sighed and sat down heavily in her seat. She grunted as she hit the chair, then her body sagged in relief.

"Ms. Chassis," the Chinese woman said, again. "What do we do now?"

Chassis didn't look at the Chinese woman. Rosa didn't know if she was mad at her for her husband having caused all of this, or what. But she kept looking out the shattered front window. "This bus will never drive again tonight," Chassis finally muttered. "Maybe—" She faded out for a second.

"Should we stay here?" asked the old man Kwang. He and his wrinkly old wife looked like they hadn't moved at all since they left port, even during the gunfire.

"Yes," Chassis rasped. "I've called into Washington. We're a little closer to them than Atlanta. They may send help."

"May?" her mother said.

Chassis didn't answer her. She just kept looking out the front window.

Nobody spoke for a little while. It was like they were waiting for Chassis to go on. But she didn't. Finally, the whispers started. Rosa wanted to talk to Chassis some more, so she got up and started walking forward.

Mamma grabbed her by the arm, yanking Rosa back. Rosa pulled free, escaped her Mama's clutching, and ignored the calls. When she got to the front of the bus, she said, "Chassis."

Chassis was sagging down in her seat like she was exhausted. She didn't look up, and she didn't answer.

Rosa didn't want to look too closely. She never saw a wound, but that didn't mean there wasn't any. She didn't know if she should tell everyone or not. Mr. Kwang noticed her standing there, looking stupid. "What's wrong?" he asked, like he knew but didn't want to guess.

"She's dead," Rosa told him. "Chassis's dead."

Then all the whispers stopped again.

"We have to determine what to do," Rosa's Mamma said. She looked worried, but she sounded real firm. Rosa knew that tone of voice. Mamma was going to *decide* something.

"We have to leave the bus," the Chinese woman said.

"No, we need to stay on the bus!" one-eyed Kwang said. "That's how they're going to find us!"

"I don't think they're coming," Rosa said. But nobody listened to her. They kept talking like she wasn't even there.

"What are we going to do with my husband?" asked the Chinese woman. "I can't leave him. If those people come back—"

"She's right," nodded Mrs. Kwang. "They might come back."

"But where do we go?" asked old man Kwang. "We don't know where we are."

"Chassis would have—"

"*Quiet,* Rosa."

"I don't think CUSA's coming for us," old man Kwang said. "They aren't going to risk anything for us."

"That's what *I* said!" Rosa exclaimed.

"They have to," said the Chinese woman. "According to the laws of the Corporation, all vouchers are strictly binding. As long as we have our vouchers—"

"Those vouchers are just pieces of paper," One-Eye said. "You think the Corporation worries about pieces of paper?"

"The Corporation keeps a record of all transactions," the Chinese woman said. "It's all they care about. Lost vouchers have to be accounted for."

"So they write us off as dead!" Mr. Kwang shouted.

"No, I was an accountant for the—" the Chinese woman argued.

"Are we going to get off this bus?" Rosa demanded.

Rosa decided the only reason people listened to her this time was because they were already asking themselves the same question. Mamma glared at her.

"Her father is hurt," Mamma explained to everybody apologetically. Like that needed explaining. Mamma went on. "If we stay on this bus, we have a little protection, and a location where we can be found. If we get off, we just have to hope we can—"

"Why don't we just get off the bus a little..." Rosa started to say. Mamma took her hard by the shoulder and tried to pull her in.

Old grandpa Kwang pulled out a cigarette. "What are you doing?" exclaimed the old lady when she saw him light up. "Don't waste those!"

"We won't need them now," he retorts. "We're all going to—"

"Why don't we just go somewhere a little ways away from the bus," said Mr. Kwang, "so we're off of it, but where we can still keep an eye on it?"

"That's what *I* said!" Rosa yelled, exasperated.

Mamma pulled her aside. "Rosa," she whispered at her, word by word, harsh. "Your father is sick and we're trying to figure out what to do!"

"But I'm—"

"That's enough, Rosa!"

Rosa shut up.

Rosa started hating them all. They all thought they knew *so much*, the grownups. But they were in the same mess as her. Chassis had been the only one with any brains.

Rosa had to go where they went. They all got off the bus and moved a little ways into the woods. Someone took Chassis' gun and gave it to the one-eyed woman to carry. They left the dead bodies on the bus where the animals wouldn't get to them. Mamma Kwang didn't want to leave Leethee, but she finally came off, crying, holding tight to the little maimed bear instead.

It was much colder out in the woods than on the bus. At least the bugs weren't too bad. Everyone hunkered down in a big circle and just sat still, not knowing what else to do. The moonlight was blocked by the branches of the trees, so they couldn't make out anything more than the shapes of each others' bodies.

Rosa's Mamma and Mr. Kwang carried her Daddy to a flat spot and laid him down. They had wrapped him up in a blanket, but he was still moaning a little, complaining of the cold. Rosa tried to talk to him, but Mamma said to leave him alone. Angry, Rosa moved as far away from her Mamma as she could.

That put Rosa next to Firoz. She had forgotten all about him. Through all the shooting, he had just been in the back of the bus, not moving. Rosa didn't even think he had gotten down when the guns went off. He had just sat there like it was part of the ride. The only reason he got off the bus with everyone else was because Old Lady Kwang spent the time to try and explain to him what was going on. Rosa didn't know if he had even understood. But he had gotten up and followed.

So now they were all sitting around, and she was next to Firoz, and he was the only one Rosa didn't hate right now. Because he was quiet, probably because of the stuff he had taken earlier, keeping him calm. Even though this whole situation they were in was kind of his fault, because he had tried to take drugs on the bus and her Daddy had yelled at him.

"Why do drug-worshippers take drugs anyway?" Rosa whispered.

He didn't say anything back. Rosa waited a long time, but he kept quiet. She felt tears stinging her eyes. She wanted to talk to somebody, but even Firoz didn't respond.

"The drugs require it," he mumbled after a while. Rosa looked at him. At first she couldn't even believe he had said anything.

"What do you mean?" Rosa asked him.

"We do what the drugs tell us," he said.

"Why?" Rosa asked.

"They're trying to teach us a lesson."

"What lesson?"

"Not to do drugs," he said.

Rosa stared at him. He didn't look down at her. "I don't get it," she said.

"It's hard," he answered, nodding. Like that was an answer.

"Rosa," her Mamma was whispering. She was looking for her. Rosa was glad it was dark. She didn't want to be close to her Mamma.

You could hear things moving around in the darkness. Rosa was scared to death. She had never been that near to wild animals before except for squirrels and rats, never even seen any other kind except in commercials. Now everywhere she heard scratching and sniffing. She heard chattering next to her ear, and way off in the distance she heard a dog howling. At least, she hoped it was a dog. Rosa felt herself starting to lose it. She wanted to scream. Then she thought about Chassis and what she said about being scared, and she got calm again.

Somebody spoke out into the dark. "Does anybody want to pray?"

Her father was groaning louder now, and her Mamma bent over him. Rosa wanted to be there, too, but she didn't want to be near her Mamma. She wanted to be with her Daddy alone. Where *she* could take care of him.

"I said, does anybody want to pray?" It was old man Kwang.

"I have a Century Report," said One-Eye. "It's in my bag. But it's too dark to read."

"I know it," said the Chinese woman. She got to her feet. Rosa could almost see her looking sad in the dark. "I know a lot of it by heart. I'll pray for us."

She raised her head and started speaking in English. "Dean Witter, Seven, Twenty-three through Forty-seven." She paused and took in her breath. The next time her voice came out, it was clear and strong. Rosa didn't even recognize it.

"The last quarter of the 1970s were a difficult time for us," she said. "Interest rates had skyrocketed, the price of fuel tripled, and violent crime was on the rise. The outlook was bleak. Few could have forecasted any kind of reprise. But the Corporation elected Our President, and he saw to it that smaller companies were able to grow. He took money out of the hands of big government and gave it back to the common people. And the companies grew and thrived. And there were more rich people to spend money. And it was good.

"But Our President looked and saw that all was not well, because the people were not happy. They sent out annual reports, telling the people that all was well, but people were still not happy. And they asked if the people were better off now than they had been four years ago, and the people said yes, but they were still not happy.

"'How can we brighten your portfolio?' asked Our President.

"'Help the smaller people to become rich,'" answered the people. And Our President nodded. It would be so."

Rosa remembered this story from when she used to watch the devotional commercials. It was one of her favorites. She could tell a lot of people liked it. She could hear a few of them coming in at places to say the words after the Chinese woman. Her Mamma probably knew it too, but she was keeping quiet.

"And Our President evaluated his surroundings, and the Corporation thought outside the box, and this thought gave rise to the Internet. And the President told our Corporation, 'Nurture the Internet and make it grow.' And the Corporation did so.

"And the people saw the Internet and saw what fruits it bore, and they invested. And the Internet grew. And Sun begot JAVA and JAVA begot Amazon.com. And even the smallest among the people grew rich. And it was very good." The Chinese woman bowed her head. Then everybody knew what to say:

"In the name of the Corporation, the President, and the whole Portfolio."

It used to make Rosa feel better to say that, too, when she was little. But something about that night made it seem kind of stupid. Here they were out in the middle of nowhere, the Corporation had already said they wouldn't help them if they got stuck, and now they were praying to them. Rosa just felt like the whole thing was fucked up.

It got even quieter after that, Rosa guessed, because the animals heard them and stopped moving. Her Daddy was moaning, though, even louder. Then one of the Kwang children started to whimper. She wondered if they were finally getting scared.

"We have to keep him quiet," said Mr. Kwang about Rosa's father.

"What do you want me to do?" demanded Rosa's Mamma. She sounded angry.

"I don't know," said Mr. Kwang. "But if they come back—"

People were starting to get antsy. Rosa noticed that the prayer hadn't made them feel that much better. The panic spread from one person to another. Now the Chinese girl was crying, and her mother was holding her and telling her to shush.

"*You* aren't being very quiet," said Old Lady Kwang to Mr. Kwang.

"Shut up, stupid bitch!" said Mr. Kwang, turning to point at her.

"Don't tell *me*..." the old woman began.

Mr. Kwang didn't let her finish. "I said shut up. You're only here because you're married to my father."

"Your mother was a *hooker!*" she rasped at him. "The best in the neighborhood. Didn't he ever tell you..."

"Quiet!" Rosa's Mamma told them, before Mr. Kwang could push his father out of the way. "Rosa, where are you?"

"I want to pray," said Firoz, standing up. "Will anyone pray with me?"

Nobody was listening to him. Rosa was mad for him. They didn't listen to *her* either. But Firoz didn't care. He was fiddling around in his pouch.

"We're going to die here," the old woman said, "and I don't want to be quiet any longer. You all haven't done anything to get us out of here."

"That's all you ever do!" Mr. Kwang shouted. "You complain. You moan and complain."

Mrs. Kwang said to her husband, "Stop it. This isn't—"

"Rosa!" her Mamma shouted. "Where are you?"

They were making more and more noise. But Rosa was sitting still. She was watching Firoz. He had taken out a little cigarette and was lighting it. He breathed in. The smoke curled around him and drifted away. She caught the scent. It was sweet and strange.

Firoz moved through all the fighting people straight towards Rosa's Daddy. Nobody was paying Daddy much attention at the moment, but now she could see that her Daddy was shivering really hard.

Rosa followed Firoz to her Daddy's side. Daddy's eyes were closed, but his head was bouncing around from side to side.

"Hold him steady," Firoz said to her. So Rosa took her Daddy's head in her hands and stroked his hair. He stopped moving enough for Firoz to stick the cigarette in Daddy's mouth. Daddy took a puff.

"Rosa!" her Mamma shouted. "What are you doing?" Then she gasped, unable to believe what she was seeing. "You!" She pointed a finger at the addict. She had seen Firoz giving Daddy the cigarette.

"Mamma, wait!" Rosa cried. She could see that Daddy wasn't shivering anymore.

"What are you *doing?*" Rosa's Mamma screeched. "Haven't you got any decency?"

"I'm praying," Firoz answered.

"Get away from my husband!" she frothed. "Get that drug worshipper away before I *kill* him!"

"No, Mamma, he's trying to help!"

Mamma slapped Rosa so hard that she lost her balance and hit the ground. For a second, she lost her sense of direction. She could still hear her Mamma shouting at Firoz.

When Rosa was able to look around, she saw Mamma kneeling over Daddy. "Eduard," she said to his face.

"Pestilence!" Mr. Kwang said to Firoz, coming over to him. "Parasite? Why don't you leave us be?"

"You're the reason we're in this mess," said the Chinese woman, pointing a finger at the drug worshipper accusingly.

Rosa wanted to stop them. But they were rising to their feet one after the other, starting to take out their fear and anger on Firoz. One of them picked up a rock. It seemed to bounce off the drug worshipper before he knew it had hit him. He looked around suddenly, bemused, as if he had an insight. The next rock let him know what that insight was.

Stumbling to his feet, looking around curiously at all the people shouting at him, moving towards him, then scuttling away like frightened dogs, he acted like he didn't know what to do. Finally, he turned and stumbled away.

The people chased him out of the dim enclosure, yelled at him until he had disappeared into the night, and stared after him, making sure he would not return. Terrified by their fury, Rosa got up and shuffled off away from all the sound. Her face hurt, and she didn't understand why she felt so ashamed when she hadn't done anything wrong. She really didn't want to be around these people anymore. They were all falling apart. She wished Chassis could have been here to shut them up.

First she started walking away from the noise. And then she started running. Because it felt so good to move away from all that stupid yelling. She pushed through the trees and let them close behind her, to protect her from her Mamma and all those other stupid *chicopes*. But she could still hear them.

She could hear her Mamma shouting "Rosa! Rosa!" way off in the distance. Rosa was glad her Mamma was worried. She wasn't about to answer her. She hoped her Mamma was scared shitless. She wanted her to be sorry she'd ever yelled at her daughter, much less slapped her. So she ran farther. She ran until her heartbeat was louder than the shouting.

Once she couldn't hear them anymore it occurred to her how dumb she was being. She considered that it was pointless to be running through the woods in the middle of the night when she didn't know where she was going. So she stopped running.

Rosa had thought that if she just turned around, she could walk back the way she came and she'd bump into everybody, no problem. But it didn't work out that way. For a while, she didn't hear anything. Then she made out their voices, way off in the distance. She thought someone was calling her name. But she couldn't tell which direction the sounds were coming from. It was really hilly out there in the woods, and the hills were steep, and the noise was echoing off them. She slid down some places and then couldn't climb back up. And even when she did make it up somewhere, she only heard the sounds coming from some other direction.

She kept trying to follow the sounds, but the more she wandered, the fainter they got. Rosa wanted to call out, but she was too scared. She didn't know who else was out here.

So she kept quiet and tried to listen, but the sounds got farther and farther away, and she thought she was heading in the wrong direction. She didn't know where she was going anymore. Then she fell two or three times and totally lost her bearings.

She wasn't sure if she was crying. If she was, it wasn't on purpose. She didn't remember feeling bad enough to want to die, or to stop walking, even though she was getting tired. She did remember hearing Chassis' voice in her head, telling her it was okay to be scared, and to just keep going. Keep going, the voice said. Don't worry about what anybody thinks.

So she kept going. And she didn't stop until she reached a clearing where the moon shone full on her. At that point someone grabbed her by the shoulder and she screamed very loud.

She cursed in Spank, and she flailed and hit at him. The man didn't fight back; he just kind of stood there like a tree, taking her blows, with his hand on her shoulder.

When Rosa realized it was the addict, she stopped hitting him.

"Firoz!" she said, out of breath. "Were you looking for me?"

"Hey," said Firoz, like they were friends who had run into each other. He was amazed as he looked at her. Amazed at what, she couldn't say.

"Hey," she gasped. His black shape looked funny through the darkness. "You know where the others are, or what?"

"Are you an angel?" he asked her. Rosa considered that, lit up by moonlight, she must look kind of ghostly.

"I don't think so," she said.

But Firoz didn't seem to hear. "I was hoping to find a Church out here," he said. "I'm out."

"What?" she demanded. "So you don't know where everybody is, either?"

"I know where everybody is," said Firoz. "But I'm out."

"Where is everybody?" Rosa asked.

"Everybody is in the future."

"In the future," Rosa repeated, looking around. She had no idea what he was talking about.

Firoz nodded. "You want to go to the future?"

"Sure, Firoz," Rosa said. She turned away and started walking off. Something about seeing him had made her less scared, but she wasn't exactly happy to know that he was by himself.

"The future is this way," Firoz said, and he started loping in another direction.

Rosa watched him for a second. Maybe he did know the way back. Maybe he was trying to tell her but didn't have his words all straight. Grumbling, Rosa took off after him. She figured following after him was just as good as wandering by herself, at least until she could find the voices again.

He seemed to know where he was going. He started moving faster up the hills than down them. Rosa tried to keep up with him as best she could, but it was hard. She was starving, her legs were sore where they were cut in a couple of places, and she just wanted to find a warm place to lie down and go to sleep. She wished she had Basil to talk to, or somebody, or anybody.

"Hey, Firoz! Where are you headed?" she called.

He didn't answer. He didn't say anything to her at all. For a while, he was moving pretty fast in one direction. Then he started walking a more and more jagged path. Then he was making big half-circles around places where he could have gone straight. Then

175

he stopped to look up into the trees a couple of times. When he started looping around the tree trunks, Rosa knew they were both in real trouble.

"Firoz, what are you going around those trees for?"

She knew, though. He was messed up and didn't even understand what he was doing.

She thought about ditching him then. She thought about leaving the last grownup behind her once and for all and taking her life into her own hands. But there was no way that made sense. Firoz might be crazy, but at least he was big. If they got caught by some other nasty people they might think he was protecting her.

She called out to him again. *"Firoz!"*

This time he stopped. He turned towards her like she had said his name for the first time. Then he sat down. He watched her as she came up to him. He was breathing heavy. "What do we do now?" he asked her, like she was the one who had been making the decisions.

"What?"

He kept his eyes on her as she got real close to him, looking up at her like he was a child.

"Firoz, get up," Rosa said. "We have to get out of here."

He started rummaging through his pockets. He looked through each one slowly and calmly. Then he looked again, less calmly. By the fourth time, he was beginning to panic.

He looked up at Rosa again. "Can you offer me absolution?" he asked.

"No, Firoz!" she told him. "We're in the woods, you freak."

He started looking much more frantically in his pockets.

"Angel," he said to her. "Can't you tell me?"

"Firoz, we have to—"

"Tell me..." he moaned. He started to rock back and forth.

"Tell you what?" Rosa asked.

The addict didn't like that. He looked up at her like he was four and she'd told him he couldn't have a dog anymore. He opened his mouth and began to bawl. She wanted to run away from him, but he kept staring at her with big horrified eyes, and she couldn't move.

Firoz fell quiet for a while and looked at the ground. Then his legs gave way and he half-fell, half-sat. After a second, Rosa tried to talk to him. "Are you okay?" she asked. She tried to pull him up. She lifted his arm, but he brushed her away.

Firoz groaned and started to shiver. He wrapped his arms around himself and shook. Never taking her eyes off him, Rosa backed away and sat down so she could lean against a tree.

Rosa decided they probably weren't going to make it.

"Where are we?"

His voice croaked out of the darkness like an old frog. Rosa was so startled she nearly shit her pants.

"Firoz!"

"Who are you?"

"I'm *Rosa*. Firoz, you *followed* me out here."

He didn't answer. She heard him grunt.

"Little boy."

"I'm a *girl!*" she shouted before she could stop herself. Her voice echoed through the hills, and the animals went a little quiet.

"I only need the Body and Blood."

"I don't have any," she said.

"That's a lie," he said. "I know you have some in that bag of yours."

"You crazy," she said. She had no idea what else to tell him.

"Why do they take the Body and Blood?" he asked her, softly.

She was getting scared. It was like he was accusing her of something. Quietly, she said, "You said they take them because the drugs teach them a lesson."

Firoz's eyes opened wide. "That's right!" he said.

She hesitated because she didn't know what else he was going to say or do. When he didn't say anything, Rosa asked what she had been dying to ask him since he had told her that.

"What's the lesson?"

He answered her immediately, like he'd been waiting since the beginning. "The drugs make everything backwards. You see from the outside looking in."

He was silent again. "That's weird," she finally said, shrugging.

"Yes," he agreed. "And it's really weird because you find out in CUSA that when everything is backwards it makes sense." She didn't understand what that meant, but he kept talking before she could ask him another question. "The economy doesn't support us. We live to support the economy," he said. "Backwards. We find something that conflicts with what we already believe, and so we decide that the new something must be wrong. Backwards."

He stopped. He swallowed hard, and she heard his Adam's apple thump the bottom of his throat.

"A million people die so that I can live. Backwards."

"What are you talking about?" Rosa asked him.

He said it again. Louder. "A million people die so I can live. Why, angel?"

He was scaring her again. She didn't notice her own tears, dripping down her cheeks. "Look, Firoz," she said. "Stop, okay? We going to be okay, right?"

But he was just like all the other adults, just in his own drug way. He just kept on saying what he'd always said, only louder and louder. "Why, angel? Tell me why?"

"Why are you calling me that?" she demanded. She was getting tired of hearing him. Tired of looking at him, smelling his pukey smell.

"A million people die so I can live!"

"Shut *up*, Firoz!" He wasn't paying her any attention at all. He didn't look at her. He didn't cock his head like he had heard her. Just said the same thing again and again, like he wanted to shout it, but was afraid.

"Tell me why!"

"Who died, Firoz?" Rosa yelled, trying to be louder than him. She wanted him to say something else, anything else.

"A million people die so I can live! I see it now, only now I can't pray! Tell me why, angel!"

She didn't want to listen to him, or listen to her mother, or see her Daddy lying on the ground. She didn't want to come out here on a bus and get nearly raped by some big hairy freak. She didn't want to be in the middle of the woods with a drug addict who was coming down off of who knows what. She just wanted to *leave*. She just wanted to go home.

"It's okay, Firoz," she said to him. "Just shut up!" But he had begun to shake and writhe on the ground.

His hands were on his ears. "Tell me why!"

"Shut up, Firoz!"

"Tell me why, angel!!"

"I'll tell you, Firoz! Okay?"

"Tell me why!!!"

"I'll *tell* you, Firoz, you *chicope pinga!* I'll *tell* you! I'll *tell!* I'll *tell*, okay? *I'll tell!*" She was starting to cry hysterically. She wasn't making any sense herself, now. She didn't know what she was going to tell Firoz. Her voice was going ragged, and it scared her how old she sounded all of a sudden. She didn't care who could hear her anymore, or what was going to happen. Porter and all his ugly friends could go ahead and stick their guns in her chest and blow her away, because it didn't matter now. She didn't have anything left to save.

"You will?"

It took her a minute to hear Firoz. She was too busy wiping her eyes, coughing snot. The addict was lying on the ground in a pool of his own spit, looking up at her. His eyes were bloodshot, and one of them was half closed. But he looked like he was amazed by her.

"Don't worry." The voice came from behind her. She whirled around to face the person who owned it. Her hands were clenched in tiny rock-hard fists, and she would have tried to kill the man if she hadn't thought he looked like her Daddy.

He had the same dark eyes and the same kind face. Rosa even said "Daddy" to him. But then she collapsed, either right then, or sometime after.

I love you...

I've learned that, in the old days, before they refined the drugs, addicts in recovery would often have the sensation of bugs crawling on them. Now, ironically, the bugs crawling on me are real. I have been clean enough long enough to see that I am in a decent bed in a small room with a window overlooking a woods. The room has been kept scrupulously clean, but bugs still get in my blanket and my eyes from time to time.

When I took to the Body and Blood I followed two gods. I took the hallucinogens to see, and the syringe to feed me. Now that the hallucinations have gone, all that remains to me is the emptiness of the syringe, the cruel hunger. And the never ending pain in my arms and legs.

When I think over my life, it seems like a mural on the wall behind my head. If I turn my head, I can see myself, two-dimensional, moving through the scenes.

A man who looks something like me, thin, grey, and tall, is holding a gun about six inches from my face. I am a child. There I am looking up the barrel, wondering if this is the end of my life, understanding what beginnings and endings mean.

Further to the right, in the same direction that the gun is pointed, I take up my duties, feeling too young for them, because my father was dead and there was no going back for him.

There I am taking the sacrament for the very first time. Over here I can watch myself escape miraculously from the dulled eyes of the Corporation. Here I am, dwelling in the Churches, waiting in the lines for the Body and the Blood. There I am, learning how to become a Fryer from one of the Brothers who carry their sacrament with them. Free from the need to attend services three times daily, I am able to ride a bus. The bus explodes.

I emerge from the mural to fall onto my head on a hot, flat mattress.

The grey Pastor comes in the afternoon. Sometimes he talks in English, and when I'm too tired to translate, I just let the sound of his voice wash over me because it's very pleasant, like music. It is of the Pastor that I finally ask my first coherent question.

"Where am I now?"

He smiles. "Clear Point," he says.

I don't really know where that is. "What suburb?" But as soon as I ask it, I doubt myself. His accent is so strange. At first I can't place it, but before he answers I remember.

"No suburb, *señor*."

A commercial. I've heard the accent in some comedy commercial where a hick from the outside gets lost in the heart of CUSA. This man has that strange tinged accent, the accent of an English speaker.

I'm not in CUSA.

I manage to consume dinner, even with my headache, but my body forgets I am clean and I throw it up. I shake so badly I can't even see. I jerk around in a sweat-soaked bed like I'm controlled by an epileptic puppeteer.

I have so many dim memories, but it's impossible to distinguish them from delusions which seem equally real. Whenever I close my eyes I feel myself go through the endless process of preparing myself to receive, only I never do and I snap out of it again, still drained.

The Pastor calls me "*señor*" out of reverence, not for my former status but for all living creatures. The woman, with beautiful grey eyes and soft peach skin is always looking at me silently. She doesn't speak Spanish.

"You want more water?" she asks in English.

"No. Thank you." My English must sound as strange to her as anything she has ever heard.

The more coherent I get, the less she seems to talk. Every time I try to be polite to her, she gets silent. I think she has been very kind to me.

There is a child, a little boy, who is watching me from the corner. He sits there so long, I decide I am hallucinating again. He is too blond to be real. His eyes are long-lashed, and they open and close slowly. His red lips are almost the color of blood from a pin-pricked finger.

I try to speak to him, because that's what I do with my delusions. "I can't pray," I offer. "Do you have—" But my mouth is not used to obeying my commands. It goes off on its own, and I am not even conscious of what I am saying.

A man's voice speaks from the other room, and the boy gets up quickly and flies out the door. Then I know, as I fall back onto the mattress, that the child was real.

I get out of bed for a few minutes in the morning. My legs are so rubbery that I fall to my knees. Luckily, no one is around to see. I get back in bed quickly, my thighs trembling, the pitiful muscles twitching. I am determined to get back my strength soon because I'm sick of going in the bedpan.

That afternoon, I try to walk again. My self-control has deteriorated during my time away. It is hard to decide my direction. I jig towards the window. The boards are as smooth as stones under water.

From this room I can see the sun shining on birch trees. Nothing else is visible from the window. My legs do a dance that somehow gets me back to the bed.

Just after dark, the woman comes in carrying my dinner and a small lamp, an oil burner or something. She sees that the curtains have been disturbed. She looks at me out of the side of her eyes, then lays the plate of greens and sweet potatoes on my side table next to the lamp.

I don't remember eating, but the tray is empty as she is still sitting there. Seeing that I am done, she quickly takes the tray away.

The Pastor is sitting at my bedside and wants to talk. I don't tell him that I'm still not sleeping. Instead I lie to him that I am feeling tolerable but am always starving. He smiles and nods and says he will see to it that I am served larger portions. That only makes me want to retch again.

"Why am I in here?" I ask him.

"You required sanctuary," he replies. "Jesus doesn't turn his desperate children away."

"Jesus?" I wonder how far I am from a hub. "How did I get here?"

"We found you screaming in the woods."

I have no memory of that. I sit up higher in the bed and look around, but I regret it almost instantly. Every flash of dust which sparkles as it passes through the light from my window is like an explosion in my eyes. My forehead begins pounding as if someone were trying to let me know they are trapped inside. My arms and legs fill up with glass shards. "How much longer do I have to stay here?" I manage, falling back down. I wince at the sudden blooming pain. "How much do I owe you?"

He blushes. Instead of replying, he begins to talk about his parish.

The Pastor took the oath as a young man in a conscientious effort to repair the state of the world around him. Although he grew up here in the Unincorporated States, he shares little of the suspicion that overtakes his congregants since the war. He believes that his mission is to bring light to the darkness that has overtaken the land of Virginia. By doing Jesus' work, he is spreading the message of charity and good will.

"That's why you took me away from my drugs?" I ask.

He nods.

"The people of this town, they're fine with me being here?" I demand, incredulous.

The Pastor looks away from me. "It's best to tell them as little as possible until you are well."

"And then what?" I say.

"What do you want?" he asks me, his eyes returning to mine.

"I want to get back to the Body and the Blood."

"That's impossible," says the Pastor. "I don't have it to give you."

"Then let me go," I demand. "Turn me loose."

"We're hundreds of miles from the nearest city," he reasons with me. "Following a road will take you into towns much more dangerous than ours. Stray from the roads and you could wander forever in the woods."

"Isn't there any fucking way *out* of here?" I say, raising my voice, looking around.

"My friend," the Pastor says, keeping his voice quiet. "I won't allow you to return to your demons. No...you must stay with us."

After the woman brings me my breakfast and I try to enjoy it in front of her, I roll over and pretend to go to sleep. She walks so carefully it's hard to hear her, but after a while I make as if I'm rolling over with my eyes closed, and I peek. She isn't there.

I pull myself out of bed and take a second to get used to the way the floor buckles under my feet. When the sea is calm, I start carefully walking towards the bureau, the glass shards in my legs cutting me bloodless. Arriving at the chest, I find some clothes are inside that look like they might fit me—a lot of clothes. Did she make them for me? I put the shirt on and find it fits.

I experience a wave of nausea as her face passes through my mind. Why would she take care of me? Is she some kind of idiot who doesn't know how to do anything else? Suddenly contemptuous of her, I dismiss her image from my mind.

They have left my old shoes under the bed which aren't comfortable but are familiar, and when I slip them on, they tell my feet to start searching again. I walk out the door of my room, quiet.

The space around the other side of the door opens into a large rectangular room, a chapel with hand-carved benches going back to the door and forward to a simple raised pulpit. It looks exactly like the kind of Churches that have always served me, and my scalp sparkles with joy. I can already taste the Blood again. What I recognize as a Christian cross hangs on the wall over a carpet that once was red but now is so faded that it is practically white. The windows are open to let the musty smell escape, and when the breeze blows in you can smell flowers from the outside.

The Body and Blood are always somewhere behind the cross. I tiptoe up along the pews, looking left and right. There are books tucked into the pockets behind the benches. They are so worn and ripped that their pages would have to be held together in the hand like a bouquet of flowers.

Behind the cross is an empty sack.

Nothing.

What kind of a Church is this?

Getting more reckless, I dive noisily down behind the cross display. My eyes scan the dusty, worn cardboard placard holding it in place. The whole setup is disgusting, dilapidated, and tired. Even the dust looks bored. Some small animal's droppings are barely hidden in the shadow.

Under the placard in the corner I find a small decanter of wine so I open it and pour the whole thing down my throat. Even this small stim is enough to bring me back to myself.

I creep up and swing off the pulpit to the door along the left side, heedless of what might be behind it. My heart is thumping in my ears. There *must* be more. There must be. They're just hiding it from me.

I come to a little room where the Pastor keeps his bed and study. On the surface of a desk lies an old bible, open to something called James, the place mark lilting casually over the pages, like a whore sitting on a divan with her hand draped over her thigh. I have the urge to close the book, but there is a pair of spectacles sitting upon it as well, protecting her. I can't disturb them.

The rest of the room is plain. The little twin bed is made up neatly with a cotton blanket, a white sheet and a small pillow. Empty bookshelves sit by the bed, and a small extinguished lantern sits on a table in front of the curtained window.

Muttering to myself in a loud voice, convinced there's nothing in this place worth taking, that these barbarians don't have a gram, I lope off out the front door and into the open air. A man is there, standing by a woodpile. Rangy and unshaven, he looks up at me with blood-rimmed eyes and says nothing, does not move to shout or to urge me to stop. After a second of us staring at each other, I determine that he is not going to raise any alarm and I take off for the woods.

The country is hilly, peaceful, and flowery like a commercial. The terrain in front of the Church is rugged, and the ground slopes very steeply until it crests. I reach the top of it, breathless, forgetting for a moment my search for some absolution.

Beyond is a long strip of pasture running across my eyesight like a roller-coaster, its grass untouched by any mower, insects buzzing over the stalks of the snapdragons. Huge silver power-line towers follow the contour of the land, but the wires are long gone, and only the rusted towers remain. Beyond them sits a tiny blue country house. I am being minutely scrutinized by the windows of the house. I turn, slow and deliberate, back to the woods. Trying not to look back, I resist the urge to run.

I almost stumble across an old road at the top of a long uphill before I finally feel safe again. The pavement is cracked like all the roads out here, frozen in bursting like the top of a volcano. You have to walk a maze to take a straight path. After about ten minutes I see buildings to my left and right, but no one is living in them. As the road continues, the buildings taper off for a while, but soon an old downtown arises from behind the trees along the path, and people are moving along it.

What were once houses converted to businesses two hundred years ago are now businesses converted back to houses. No one is living in the buildings as they were meant to be lived in. People have made homes on top of them, or along the side of them like tumors or

191

fleas on a dog. There are no cars parked in the parking spaces that jut diagonally from the storefronts; they were pulled apart for scrap long ago. A chain of steering wheels descends from a rooftop to the street, used as a ladder by a girl in overalls that is coming down. As I wander a little ways down an avenue, the girl catches sight of me and stares with her mouth hanging open.

All talking has stopped. I'm in the middle of an intersection, sharing the road with a few horses and some bicycles, and everyone has come out from behind their boarded-up windows to gape. I feel like an AVE. People seem to be expecting something to come out of the top of my head. I could speak to them. My English is very good. Was I unwise to come out here? No one comes forward.

There on a stoop is a little blond-headed boy, the one I thought was a hallucination. He stares, too, at the dark lumbering giant.

These people are dressed in the meanest rags, their clothes either handmade and awkward, or hundred-year-old remnants of a city's throw-offs, faded, dirty, and comical. If I was seeing them in a commercial, I would laugh, but seeing it real in front of me, there's nothing particularly funny about their poverty. Even the dog lying on the front porch looks poor with its matted fur and bald patches.

I continue along slowly up the street, the people turning just as slowly to watch me pass. I round a corner to find myself in a central square. A large stone courthouse dominates the scene, squatting like a Sphinx, its eyes looking past me at nothing.

A man with a large hat, tall boots and a rifle in his arms comes out of a door in the front of the courtyard and limps down the stone steps. He stops and stands across from me in the street. Considering that he is armed and I am not, it is somewhat ridiculous the way he stares warily at me from such a distance, as if I had a forked tongue that was about to snap him up into my mouth. The man gestures, and five other men come out from the same door. They rush at me, and before I know it I am under a pile of them, not struggling but being hit nonetheless.

"What you going to do with him, Sheriff?" calls someone from off to the side.

"Pick him up!"

Still gasping with the pain in my stomach and ribs, I find myself launched to my feet, my hands securely fastened behind me. I try and spot the boy, but he has vanished. A rifle-butt presses into my back. In order to avoid it, I am compelled forward.

The Sheriff is behind me. I hear his uneven gait through the heels of his boots on the asphalt. The other men have scattered, all but one deputy, who holds his gun at my back. He never touches me with his hands, not the whole way down the street. Always it is with the barrel of his rifle. Does he think I'm radioactive? Perhaps he is afraid he will catch my disease. Except he has no notion of what that disease really is.

The people watch me in silence as I lope down the cracked road, doing my best to keep to my feet with my hands secured behind me in steel rings. Some of these people are missing teeth, others have small growths on their faces. Only the children are free from defect, except that they are dirty and very curious. The mangy dog has been following us. The Sheriff scares it off with a swift kick.

Soon the buildings end, and we continue onward down the road. The trees begin to form a canopy over me like I'm on my way to a wedding. Abandoned houses peer through the overgrown holes made possible only by the cracked driveways that used to serve them. Are these men planning to shoot me out of sight of the town?

After a minute I see a flicker of light through the trees, and we head towards that. My feet roll over gravel, and the sounds of the crickets are obscured by the crunching of the little stones. The light comes closer, torches and candles dancing in a dozen windows of the huge Church that looms suddenly overhead. It looks from the top of a high hill and dominates the scene below. The building itself is several stories high and extends palatially in wings to the left and right.

We are moving through some low hedges. I can see shapes in the shadows. Perhaps they are statues, or perhaps they are men standing watch. The light through the windows by the two front doors obscures my vision of them as I am escorted in. Off to the left I see a side door, where two men are handing out small potatoes and wedges of cheese to four townspeople with wheelbarrows.

Just a whiff of the tobacco hovering in the air makes my skin writhe unbearably. The smoke is fresh, coming from behind a closed door.

Opened, that door reveals a foyer now converted to a parlor, medieval but ageless, like everything out here: a long-misused carpet, faded paisley-covered chairs, and a sofa that has been recovered so that it looks new, but the way it sags on its tired wooden legs anyone would know better. Lush, faded curtains hang over the picture window overlooking the woods. A hand-rolled cigarette, fit into a holder, smolders in an orange clay pot by a comfortable chair where a man is sitting.

On the table in front of him is a small scale-model grey airplane, the kind that used to be flown in great numbers a hundred years ago. It is only partially assembled, still waiting to be brought together, little plastic parts making imaginary alphabets on the surface of the table. Where did he get this toy? The model itself could be a hundred years old. In the corner of the desk sits a small pot of glue, and beside it is a tiny paintbrush.

The part of the model that is complete has been done carefully. All unused parts lay organized in neat stacks, arranged by size and function. No seams mark the joined spots for the wings of the plane or any other joint.

Next to the man is a short grey-haired woman in a tattered dress and half-worn sandals. She stands with her hands clenched before her stomach, her knees frozen in a half-curtsey. She has turned her face only a tiny way around, obviously wishing I had not interrupted.

The seated man now looks up at me with interest. No longer seeing the woman in front of him, he dismisses her with a curt wave. She completes the curtsey and whispers "I love you, Elder Oughta." With a barely acknowledged nod, he looks away as she scurries out.

The man turns to look at me as though I were a circus animal brought in for his inspection. He leans back in his chair.

"Well," he remarks. His voice has a scratchiness which suggests something jagged inside that has been forcing its way out over time. The skin of his face is full of old bends and creases that give him a permanent gaping expression. His eyes are sharp as they take me in.

He has scrupulously clean fingernails, which sets him apart from almost everybody else I've seen out here. He's admiring the ones on his left hand, fingers bent in a little wave towards himself. His right hand is lowered. His eyes flit up to us both, the ash-blond lashes coming to strike the brim of his woven white straw hat, which is as clean as his hands. He stares at me for a second, then his right hand comes up and I can see what has been weighing it down.

A heart-shaped stone, black as obsidian, polished as smooth as a mirror, which he clutches as though it is his actual heart, removed from his body. He admires it, turning it this way and that, and absently brings it up to his rough face as he asks me, "What hell did you climb out of?"

I have no answer. Still caressing the stone, the man frowns and gestures at Sheriff Lyman. The butt of the rifle is inserted between my shoulder blades, and shoves me swiftly towards the ground.

"Speakee English?" he says loudly.

"Yes," I answer from the floor.

"Then get up," says Elder Oughta, "and tell me where you're from."

I get to my feet cautiously, sure that I will soon be pushed down again. "I'm from CUSA."

"That I'd have guessed," says the man mildly. "Are you an escapee?"

"You might say that."

"I might?" Elder Oughta laughs, looking at the Sheriff and the deputy. "I might? Well! What else might I say?" The laugh dies away, but the smile continues. "What are you escaping from?"

"From CUSA," I growl. "I didn't mean to come here."

"Good!" cries the man. "That's good—that you didn't mean to come here. You haven't been given permission to be here." He glares and frowns. "You know how I know?"

"No."

"Because *I'm* the man who decides who stays in Clear Point. Me. Not that Pastor. Is that who took you in?"

I glower, but the man seems to assume he has guessed correctly. "Damn," he says. "Damn him. Another refugee in his stinking church. Why can't I punish him?"

"You don't dare, Elder Oughta, " replies the Pastor from the door.

Elder Oughta looks up, surprised at the interruption. He smiles again, a tolerant, patient smile. "Pastor. You're becoming truly rude."

The Pastor steps into the room. "Jesus teaches me to be bold, to take in the hungry and the naked."

The Elder has nothing to say to that. He gestures with his stone. "I want the Citizen out of here."

The Sheriff's deputy grabs me from behind. He tries too hard. When I do not resist, we both fall back a step.

"Let him go!" the Pastor insists. "Move past your hatred."

"Hatred?" laughs Elder Oughta. "I have no hatred for him. You do not hate the dog when it shits on your doorstep. You expect that of him. This man is such a dog. He's come to spread his vile CUSA darkness on my stoop. His grandparents kicked my grandparents out of my city, and now he's come for my scraps. You do not hate the jackal for hovering over your last meal. You just shoot it." Carefully, the Elder puts his stone down on his desk where it rests with a sharp thud. Opening a drawer at his belly, he reaches in. A revolver emerges in his hand.

The Elder points the revolver at my face.

"No," says the Pastor. "Wait!"

"Wait?" cries Elder Oughta. "Why wait? Don't you understand? He's come for the rest of our freedom!"

"He has been under the influence of terrible demons," the Pastor says. "Now he is redeemed. He can't go back to CUSA. I have to take care of him."

"You want to keep him?" demands the Elder. "Like a pet?"

"Like a human being," replies the Pastor.

"You have no idea what you're doing," snarls the Elder. "He's not human. It's only a matter of time before he corrupts our world."

The Pastor is undaunted. "I want to make a place for him at the Church."

"I won't allow it."

"You can't stop me!" exclaims the Pastor, rising up to his full height. "Jesus protects me."

Elder Oughta regards the Pastor with a bored expression. "He won't protect you forever."

The Pastor is not cowed. "Then kill me," he says, extending his chest outward like the breast of a pheasant. "Kill me first."

Elder glares at me for a long time as if waiting for me to speak . I have nothing to say to him, which is probably for the best. "All right," he says, grinning wearily and lowering the revolver. "Maybe Jesus has something to teach us all. He can stay, then. If you keep a leash on him."

The Pastor bows his head, greatly relieved. "God bless you, Elder Oughta."

"Save it," the Elder says, waving the Sheriff to get us out of there as he returns to his model airplane. "It's going to be very bad for him here, and maybe for you, too. But that's not my concern."

The next morning, after I have eaten, the Pastor pays me a visit.

"So," he says, "Seeing as how you are well enough to go roaming around the countryside endangering your life—" He musters a small smile as if to show me he means no harm. "Perhaps you could do some work around here?"

I dress myself while the Pastor watches me, lost in thought. When I am fully clothed, he leads me outside.

Next to the Church is an old strip of a building. Above the door, the words "Fellowship Hall" are still visible as faded spots where the letters used to be. I've watched the woman who has been taking care of me going in and out of that building.

The Pastor takes me out to meet Whitaker. He is the rangy man who saw me walk away yesterday. We three stand outside the Fellowship Hall. Whitaker is wearing black overalls with white paint stains on the knees. He looks at me with his hard blue eyes and bristly face.

"Whitaker," the Pastor says. "This is Firoz."

Whitaker says nothing, only chews on the inside of his cheek.

"He's going to be joining our family, and I thought he might be able to help you with some work, since you...since things have been slower around here."

Whitaker's face collapses towards the dirt into a scowl, but he does not reply. The Pastor clears his throat and smiles a little. "Elder Oughta has given his permission for Firoz to stay with us. While he's here, Firoz will do anything you need help with." Again, Whitaker does not answer but gazes at the ground without moving. Shrugging and nodding at the same time, the Pastor turns and leaves us.

As soon as the Pastor has gone Whitaker also turns away and heads towards the Fellowship Hall. He does not tell me to wait, and he does not tell me to follow. He disappears through the first door, and it closes behind him with a click.

I stand in the oven heat for about five minutes, waiting for him. Finally, I decide he is not coming back. With nothing to do, I casually approach the Hall and look in the window. There isn't much light inside, but I can make out a few pieces of furniture.

I try the door, made of flimsy particle-board, which wobbles on the hinges as it flies open. Passing through, I close it quietly and stand at the doorway. The Hall is sparsely decorated with only two pictures faded to near blankness behind broken glass frames. They both depict, in slightly different versions, a solemn bearded white man holding open his palms to the sky.

In the corner I see an old piano. I used to have one in my office in Atlanta, but no one there ever knew what it was. I walk over to it and run my hands over the top of it. Even water-damaged, the wood is smooth, with dingy black paint peeling everywhere. I pull up the key-cover. The keys are all there, but the plastic strips are gone from some of them. I lay my finger on the wooden middle C, and a frightful rattling comes from the belly of the instrument.

Whitaker bursts through the door, his face an expression of incredulity. He storms right up to me and shouts in my face, *"What are you doing?"*

"I was waiting—"

"Waiting? Waiting for what? The *fucking bus* to take you home? Not here! Doesn't come through *my* house!" He stares at my nose now, his bottom lip working back and forth.

Finally I say, "The Pastor wants me to help you."

"Then go fix the roof!" he snaps, waving his arm like it's asleep.

"I don't know how," I protest. I feel sheepish, ashamed of my ignorance.

"Then I don't need you."

"I—"

He continues to stare at my nose. He waits.

"What should I do in the meantime?" I ask him.

Instead of answering me, he turns away and is swallowed by the door from which he came. It does not close all the way, but it blocks my view of him. After wiping my face of the silence that he leaves behind, I turn to go. My eyebrow twitches, and I have to try very hard not to remove the particle-board door from its frame as I pull it to.

This place is a prison. They have nothing for me here, nothing except bugs, and more bugs, and prayers. None of that can relieve the pain in my hands and shoulders. I can't think about anything except where I might get my next shot of redemption and relief. I can't leave the Church for fear of Sheriff Lyman. I can't stay in my room all day. So I wander around the Church property, achy, humiliated, watching Whitaker from a distance as he tries to keep himself busy ignoring me.

By the time I dine with the Pastor that evening I am ravenous. As I wolf down all the food he can provide me, the Pastor fondly observes me as if I am a feeding animal, which I most likely resemble. He asks me what Whitaker has given me to do, and I shrug, not wanting to create more trouble. The Pastor sighs and drinks.

"Firoz," he says.

"Yes?"

"What is your relationship to Jesus?"

While I am taking bite after bite out of a huge chunk of bread, I describe the commercial I saw about Jesus many years ago that CUSA aired to sell their instant breakfast drinks. The Pastor gazes at me with his chin in the heels of his hands, fascinated. When I stop to take a breath, he tells me, as if I had asked, how the story he knows about Jesus differs from the commercial. I have no real interest, but it breaks the silence.

"Did you worship the Lord before you turned to the Drug Church?" he asks.

"CUSA broadcasts inspirational marketing on Sundays. You can get the messages any time at any AVE."

"AVE?"

"Audio-Visual Envelope. Shows you pictures, smells you smells, offers you anything you might want to buy. Some people call it God."

He nods, a fork full of lentils just in front of his mouth. "Did you ever listen to the messages?"

"Occasionally, when I was a child."

"Do you think you were searching for Jesus as an adult when you took to the Drug Church?" he asks.

He is prying for details about my past. "That would be an interesting way to describe it," I say. He will have to be satisfied with that.

The Pastor looks thoughtful. He says, "There never was a time when I could say that those who lived in the cities and those who lived outside of the cities saw eye to eye." He takes a drink. "We were all one people once, so I'm told. *Red and yellow, black and white* went the song, but like the Tower of Babel, we built too high and we were separated.

"Now they speak Spanish in the cities, Chinese, a hundred other languages. And English has become the old Latin, used for business transactions and religious ceremonies, if one can now separate the two. Meanwhile, we English speakers in the Unincorporated States cannot speak to one another even so far as the next valley." The Pastor's expression turns angry. I would think he was accusing me, but he is far too self-effacing for that. "We bicker and fight like monkeys in the jungle over the size of our territories while the Corporation flies back and forth above us, keeping its huge cities connected to one another with invisible tight wires.

"Where has God gone? Do they broadcast him from the AVE screens that dot your cities? Is he hidden in the numbers that make up your bible? Or perhaps he really has gone into the syringes that inject the forearms of the drug addicts. He certainly has not come to dwell with us in Azazel." The Pastor has forgotten me. His eyes are far away, looking through the patched ceiling above us into the clear starry sky.

Of course, I do not know the answer. I take another spoonful of beans and think about which town nearest here might be able to help me pray.

I have finally learned my keeper's name: Glory, the woman with the skin like the scent of a peach. Every day she cleans the Church from top to bottom, doing to its insides what Whitaker does to its outsides. Now that I am well, she will not look at me. When we cross paths, her eyes fall quickly. She will not answer me when I say "Good morning." This makes me angry somehow.

She is promised to Whitaker. She keeps her room in the Church, but will soon be joining him in the Fellowship hall. The Pastor says they are to be married in the fall. This also makes me angry.

I am shuffling aimlessly around when Whitaker comes out his front door. "Hey...*Hey!*" he shouts, stabbing at me with a finger.

I stop, wondering what I've done. He comes over to me and stands about an arm's length away.

"Where in the hell are you going?"

"I don't know."

"You my God damned assistant!" He stares at me.

I shift from one foot to the other without answering.

"Go to the shed and get me seven cord of two-by-fours," he orders, pointing with his face to the third building, behind the hall and the Church.

Shrugging, I nod and start walking towards the shed. Whitaker follows about five paces behind my right shoulder.

"They call you a *spigger?*" he demands to my back. I can feel the spit fly as he says the word. I shake my head. No one has ever called me that. "You know what my granddaddy would call you?" Again I shake my head. "Spic," he says, as if he's clearing his mouth. When I do not respond, he gets in front of me, blocking my way. "Then again, he might have called you a coon," he says, rubbing my head. "Which are you, anyway?"

I have no idea what he's talking about. I walk around him. As I get to the shed he shoves past me, snarling, and vanishes into the gloom.

I find the two-by-fours lying against the wall in bundles and begin carrying them from the shed to the side of the Church. I stumble over my awkward feet, my legs with their broken glass shards. My useless arms drop the cord which clatters like someone shouting at me from everywhere. I don't see Whitaker again for the rest of the day.

When I'm done I'm completely out of breath, so I go back to my room and lie on my bed.

I can't sleep. After three hours of twisting and turning I am brought still by the sound of whispering. I sit up, alarmed, and look around through the empty dark of my room. No one is there.

But the sound comes again. I glance over at the window. There is a little shape, a roundness by the sill on the outside. I get up and creak across the floor to look down.

It's a boy. Though it's hard to see in the dark, I recognize the blond-headed boy I saw in the town. He's gesturing at me, making a motion like he wants me to come out.

Pulling on a pair of trousers and a shirt, I move quietly out my door and through the Church, trying not to rouse the Pastor. The boy is waiting for me on the stoop when I open the front door.

He looks up at me and waves his arm in a "follow me" gesture.

"Why?" I ask.

He continues to wave his arm. Then he turns and disappears into the night.

I follow as quickly as I can, keeping sight of the shape of his head in the gloom. Once I lose sight of him. I call out in a loud whisper and he reappears, checking to see if I am still following. I make sure to move faster now, to keep him in my field of vision.

He is taking me somewhere in the woods. I don't think to ask for a rest. There's no chance to talk to him anyway. We move out of sight of the Church property. He fades in and out, but I can still hear his footsteps crunching just before me.

Then I have lost him again, and his footsteps seem to vanish from my hearing. I stop. "Hey!" I call out as loudly as I dare.

A large form rises up in front of me, the shape of a tree trunk. From it comes a sound like the gibbering of a loon. Other sounds echo it behind me, and as I turn I am surrounded by five more shapes.

I wonder if I am dreaming, or perhaps if I have finally received my drug benison and am hallucinating.

"Spook!" mutters a gravel voice. "We're gonna *string ya up.*"

Something in my head tells me this is not a hallucination. And the hands on my shoulders are very heavy. Somewhere from deep within me comes the instinct to escape, even before I fully think through the danger I am in. I bellow.

The figure in the sack in front of me recoils from the sound, as if genuinely afraid I will turn into some kind of demon. Before he or the others can recover themselves, I take off in whatever direction seems open.

Only my feet can be trusted now. They find the curve of the land in the dark, and I ride upon each crest like I am surfing from channel to channel.

Behind me the gibbering of the loons comes calling. These men in the sacks—surely they know the land better than me. Are they leading me into a more deadly trap? I couldn't possibly know. There are only my feet to trust.

And then I am clear of the woods, and the town in darkness comes rushing upon me. I dare not scream in the empty, muddy streets, but the men have gathered behind me like a pack of wolves and are calling to one another.

At a loss for ideas, I turn abruptly at one of the buildings, hoping the darkness will cover my escape. But I hear the men shout, and I know they have seen. In the gloom I stumble across something hard, and I fall face first into wet gravel and iron. A cat, hidden by the night, snarls at the noise and scuttles off.

Though my face stings, I look to see what I've tripped on. It's a handle. Pulling on it, I open a door to a stairway that leads downwards. Quickly I descend and pull the door to, hiding breathless upon the steps beneath the closed panel.

I can hear the men surge by me, grunting, swearing. They do not yet think to look beneath the door, but they are calling out loudly. Surely they will double back and find me. And then what? "String me up." My neck tightens with some ancestral memory. I back away and collide in the dark with a small pile of jars and cans, which clatter mercilessly to the floor all around me.

Footsteps come up to the door. My heart beats louder and louder. My cover is ripped from me as the door is yanked wide.

There stands an older woman in her nightgown, shocked, staring at my frightened face. She looks at me for one endless second, then throws the board back down at me. I hear a clicking sound.

Has she locked me in? Tentatively, I test the board. It no longer gives. Trapped. Afraid to test the darkness of the cellar for another exit, my mind races with the final possibilities.

More footsteps coming up to the panel. A rough hand seizes it and pulls.

It shakes, but the lock on the outside of it does not give way. "Mrs. Bell's cellar is locked!" calls the man from the other side.

"Then come help us check these!" says another voice, far away.

The terrible sounds fade into the distance. I wait a long time, but the noise does not return. I lie on the cold black steps as if they are my only friends and wait in the dark for something I can't predict to happen.

When I realize I have been nodding, I start up, forgetting where I am. My heart beats vindictively against my chest, insisting that I am not in my grave.

I try the panel again and it opens. Terrified, I peek out, searching for any movement, the least sign of it, but there is none. The darkness outside the cellar is as complete and silent as the darkness I have left behind.

Taking care to make no noise, I emerge from the cellar, sure that at any moment someone will slice my head open with a machete. The attack never comes. No one is here.

I close the door to the cellar as quietly as I can, and slink away. I cringe at every noise and rustle as I creep through the shadows by the buildings in town, as if I am escaping some haunted, deserted prison. The more complete darkness of the woods finally embraces me. Grateful, I make my way quickly back to the Church.

Finding my way to my room, I grab the pillow from the bed. I pull it and myself underneath the frame and press the dirty pillow into my face. At first I dry heave into the misty pillow.

I'm not going to cry. I'm *not* going to. But I do. And then the sobs come without my permission.

I do not sleep. Finding myself under the bed in the moments before dawn, I know for sure that what happened was no flashback.

Eventually I decide I don't want to be found under the bed, and I pull myself out. I climb under the blanket, but it doesn't feel nearly substantial enough. I close my eyes, but every time I start to drowse I jerk awake again. I keep my lids squeezed shut as if they could keep out the danger. I lie there, curled up double, pretending to rest.

When I finally open my eyes again, the light is considerably brighter. Looking over, I find a new suit of clothes waiting for me on my chair. They are somewhat old-fashioned. When I venture out to look at them, I find the Pastor standing at the door. "Glory tailored them for you," he says. "She's a wonder. I'm sure they'll fit."

They do, and perfectly too. The Pastor beams when he sees me in them.

The Pastor tells me that it is Sunday, and that people will be coming. He asks me to help him set up for the service that he offers each week.

I ignore the shaking of my legs and try to help. Moving into the sanctuary, the Pastor and I pull out two plates, a worn velvet cloth that fits over the pulpit, and the Pastor's bible. He asks me to be sure the pews are clean and that there is a hymnal of some kind in each row.

The first two to arrive in the sanctuary after us are Glory and Whitaker. This is the first time I have seen them together. They do not speak to one another, she walking with her eyes down, he stiffly with his head up. They take their seats off to the side in the second row.

Other people come in and make their way to the pews, walking by the Pastor, who is at the door to greet them. They are dressed in their Sunday finery, which means exhausted, moth-eaten neckties, dresses with the ribbons missing, a tattered straw hat on the head of a woman with strands of her iron-colored hair showing through the holes.

I sit by myself in the front row. No one comes to sit next to me. I hear and feel the Church fill up until the mumbling is substantially loud. Then I can smell the congregants sweltering in the thick, close air.

When I was a small child my mother took me to Martin Luther Kingdom. The Ebenezer Recreation Center was still used by the small number of Christians who came to the little segment of the old sanctuary that had been cordoned off for them. People used to gawk at the worshippers. There were tall candles in a row in the Catholic section, a tired little washtub in the Baptists' section, and a light-bulb hanging by a piece of thick, dirty string from the ceiling where Jews were supposed to come, though I never saw one.

These people are praying the way those few Catholics used to. They worship with a fervor that surprises me. They close their eyes and sing strange commercials with words I don't understand, patting themselves on the thighs. The little children are respectful and quiet as the older ones bow their heads during silent meditations. It's beyond anything I ever experienced in my own worship: a unifying sense of purpose, born out of their desperation.

The full room has gotten very quiet. I turn to look at the door and see the Elder dressed in his finest, holding his beloved rock in his palm and supporting himself with a walking stick. Sheriff Lyman, who has escorted his fearless leader this far, turns and limps back towards town in the company of his deputy.

The Pastor makes his way to the front of the sanctuary. In a moment he has climbed the few stairs to the shaky podium. Now he reads from his great old bible, half of which I can see is missing. Was it always, or did he leave some behind in his office for safety? The Pastor seems hesitant to touch the pages, and I wonder if he reads from the same spot each week.

"'*Therefore, beloved, since you wait for these, be zealous to be found by him without spot or blemish, and at peace. And count the forbearance of the Lord as salvation. So also our beloved brother Paul wrote to you according to the wisdom given him, speaking of this as he does in all his letters. There are some things in them hard to understand, which the ignorant and unstable twist to their own destruction, as they do the other scriptures. You therefore, beloved, knowing this beforehand, beware lest you be carried away with the error of lawless men and lose your own stability.*'"

I think about the commercials about the worshippers in Mohammedtown all bowing at the big mosque in the abandoned airport concourse. Once they ran a long five-minute spot about how the Muslims saved the old airport from burning down. It was the longest commercial I ever saw. I used to get half of my fixes in Mohammedtown. I fantasize about getting in the line to receive. My scalp itches, and before I know it I have calculated how long it would take me to get to Richmond from here.

I realize that the little boy who came to my window last night is standing at the front of the pews. I am furious at him, but he does not look at me. He opens his mouth and begins to sing, and the beauty of what comes out hits me like a barrage of bullets to my face. He is only an arm's length from me, and the purity and the innocence of the melody are undeniable, even as I remember the trap he set for me just last night. Something inside me moves and slides like a rock-shelf deep under the earth. I am very uncomfortable, but I cannot shut out the call. Only when he has finished do I realize that for a few moments I have not been scheming for a way to get back to my habit.

The Pastor comes to stand in front of me, and he holds a plate towards me expectantly. He asks me to take it and pass it along the rows on my side of the Church.

When the people see me passing the plate, their faces crumple. Some stare; others turn away. Only the

Elder looks straight in my eyes as he passes the plate on without contributing. I manage to collect three black and tarnished coins. I've never seen real coins before. I can't tell if they are valuable or not. In the plate the Pastor has been passing around on the other side, there are a great many more. I take that as an indication that the community doesn't like me. That and the fact that they tried to "string me up" last night.

At the end of the service, the people file out in an orderly fashion. I expect to be able to watch them go, but the Pastor takes my arm. "I think it would be safest if you stayed with me," he whispers in my ear. He and I move behind the exiting townfolk. Whitaker and Glory do not follow, but remain behind to clean up the sanctuary.

The Pastor and I follow the solemn crowd out the door and along the path back down the wood-shrouded road to the town center. At our approach, the buildings loom left and right like silent witnesses to our passage. As we come to the courthouse I see Sheriff Lyman standing with several of his men. Next to them is a slumped figure with his hands behind his back.

The figure is a young man with a shock of unwashed, dirty blond hair. His face is young, but lined with defeat, and his eyes are bloodshot. As we get closer I see that he is dressed in something like a sack, and that his hands are tied behind him.

The Elder, who has led this procession, stops suddenly, and the crowd stops behind him. At this, the

Sheriff walks up to the man and stands in front of him, facing the crowd. "Here stands Jeremiah Bloodworthy, who has been tried and convicted by the wisdom of the Elders of the community for the crime of theft. On'y the sentence remains. Your honor?" Here, the Sheriff nods at Elder Oughta, who steps up and stands before the man, looking him in the eye.

"You, Jeremiah, you understand your crime?"

The accused nods his head, looking at the Elder.

"You know which commandment you have violated? Which of God's laws you have trod upon so casually?"

"Nosir," replies Jeremiah, the hopelessness rising in his face like a wave.

"Number eight," says the Elder. "Thou shalt not steal." He nods once as if confirming his own words where Jeremiah is unable. "Breaking the Ten Commandments is about as low as you can go. There is only one punishment available to you. You know what that is?"

Jeremiah nods, like the Elder has asked him to agree to a point of argument.

"You have anything to say?"

Jeremiah raises his head. "I din't mean ta steal," he says to the crowd. "Mamma," he calls, looking at one remorseful grey woman in a shawl. "I'm sorry." The woman nods, then rests her face in the shoulder of another woman who is wearing a straw hat with a daisy drooping out towards the ground. I recognize her as the person who locked me in her cellar, Mrs. Bell.

The Elder steps aside and asks, "Do the other Elders have anything to say?" Two older men who are standing in the crowd shake their heads. Elder Oughta then glances over at the Pastor.

"Stay here," the Pastor mumbles to me, and walks a few steps before Jeremiah. Where the accused man could not face the Sheriff or the Elder, he looks deep in the face of the Pastor as he approaches.

The Pastor stands directly in front of Jeremiah and puts his hands gently on the sides of the man's face. Bringing his face close to Jeremiah's ear, he begins to whisper something. After a second, Jeremiah nods. The Pastor continues to whisper, and Jeremiah's eyes begin to fill with tears. He whispers something back to the Pastor, and the Pastor replies quietly.

Now Jeremiah is openly weeping. "Please," I can hear him say. "Please help me, Pastor!"

But the Pastor has made the sign of the cross over the man, and he now backs away. "Please," Jeremiah cries again. "Help me!" The Pastor lowers his eyes from the man's face and returns to my side. Now Sheriff Lyman and the other men are also backing away from the man so that he stands alone upon the steps of the Courthouse.

A man comes to put a blindfold around Jeremiah's eyes. From across the square come three others, each one wearing a woolen mask that covers everything except their eyes, each bearing a rifle. They pause in a line about thirty feet from him.

Sheriff Lyman gestures with a grimace, and the men put their rifles to their shoulders. Jeremiah trembles, his head held high like a child listening for something. The Sheriff's hand falls, and three shots ring out.

The body of Jeremiah jerks like a spastic puppet.

Three more shots.

Blood appears on Jeremiah's midriff. He has fallen to his knees.

Three shots, like final pronouncements.

The sounds of the rifles echo off into the woods. No one moves, paying some homage to the lifeless form lying in a pool of blood on the courthouse stairs. Even the children watch him curiously as though he is a commercial on an AVE. A man steps up cautiously to check his pulse, then shakes his head. Two of the deputies move to raise Jeremiah a little and drag him off in the direction of the far edge of town. A woman with a bucket of water and a scrub brush moves in and begins to scrub the steps.

One by one, then in pairs and groups, the people of Clear Point turn away and head off to their homes. Someone touches me gently on the shoulder. It is the Pastor. He urges me to follow him, and we make our away alone back towards the Church.

I return to my room and find Glory there, making the bed. Usually she is careful to avoid our meeting. I know this is intentional from the way she rushes off when I come within two hundred feet of her. When she realizes we are in the same space, she begins making the bed twice as quickly.

"Hello," I say, feeling the need to talk to someone.

"Hello," she whispers, tucking the sheet beneath the mattress. But that is all. In the next second she is gone, having not looked at me, as usual. The air in the room is slightly sweet. It makes my stomach hurt. I haven't smelled her scent in many days.

Something small is on the floor by my foot next to the bed: A ribbon, a little purple ribbon that she's dropped. I pick it up and turn it over in my hand.

The next day, the widow Mrs. Bell appears at the Church with three of her children, the daisy in her hat looking at me like a white and yellow eye. She asks the Pastor if I might go with her to her house to help remove a branch from her roof.

As I walk into town I feel the inexplicable urge to walk several paces behind her. She carries herself upright like a statue, balancing a basket and an umbrella on her arm. She makes choices in style and color that prevent the ridiculous clothes she wears from demeaning her the way they do some of the others. She was clearly striking once with her aquiline nose and bright blue eyes, but at her stage and station of life such vanity is irrelevant to her.

"Are you from the city?" one of her kids asks me. They are running around me like flies swarming a picnic table.

"Yes."

"Richmond?" she asks.

"No, dummy!" says her older brother. "Richmond ain't CUSA."

"What's CUSA?"

"It's where the spegros live!"

"Hush your mouth!" Mrs. Bell scolds, looking calmly at the horizon as she walks with her little beat-up umbrella. Her daisy bounces along, once with every step. To me she says, "They know Richmond because that's where their father went to become a doctor. Poor Ellis...he died of the fever four years ago. He was a good soul...the Pastor liked him very much. You would have liked him. Even Elder Oughta listened to Ellis."

People are glaring balefully at us from the sidewalks as we breach the border of the old downtown. I look warily around for the Sheriff, or for anyone wearing a white sheet, but none of these nightmares are in view.

Mrs. Bell's house is among the nicer residences in town. Instead of a reclaimed store-front, she lives in a real house whose outside has not been too badly marred by time. Though it has not been repainted, the grey and white trim clearly has been restored within living memory, suggesting that Mr. Bell, when he was alive, had been not only respected, but somewhat well-to-do. At least four cats are visible strolling and lying about, making it clear they own the place now.

I can see the branch peeking over the edge of her roof, as if gawking at me like the townspeople. After I rescue it from her rooftop, Mrs. Bell comes onto her porch with a pitcher of lemonade and a small cake. I eat standing on the sidewalk in front of her boarded window. It does not occur to her to invite me in. I notice that, but I don't think she does.

"Are you getting along better now, Firoz?" she asks me while I munch.

"Mrs. Bell?"

"Are people treating you better?" She has apparently not noticed how the town stares.

"Yes," I lie.

She moves a little closer to me and speaks confidentially. "We're good people here in Clear Point. You'll see. People will get used to you."

"I'm sure." I say casually.

"Many of them are very curious," Mrs. Bell whispers to me behind her hand. "Once they get to know you, it'll be fine." Her voice comes up. "Have a good day now," she says, taking my plate.

This is the insanity I begin to see in the town: a sort of neurotic combination of fascination and dread which follows me everywhere. Even Whitaker seems content now to use me however he can. After a few days I am no longer an ink blot on a white tablecloth, but a story people can tell.

Aside from the strange request from Mrs. Bell, this promotion from bane to stranger does not lessen my solitude. Not that I can blame it all on the townspeople. I have never been in the habit of sharing my thoughts with anyone. After I received my first communion I used to talk freely to the spirits, and this was a great relief to me, but since I gave that up I have been reticent again, afraid to speak, finding silence to be much safer.

Yet, I am becoming foolish in front of the Pastor. He has seen me at my worst. I have very little to hide from him. I haven't spoken much lately, but when he asks this time, I respond.

"What's it like back there?" he wants to know.

"Back where?" I ask.

"Where you came from."

"It's cold," I say. I'm silent again for a long time. Surely the Pastor thinks I'm about to retreat once more. It's just that those two words sum it up for me so well I hate to continue. But the Pastor wants more. So I talk.

"Different kinds of cold," I go on. "The first is CUSA, where everything is ordered for you, synchronized, tailored. No mistakes are ever made there. Even the mistakes are recycled into something that looks palatable. No one would ever admit to moral decrepitude."

"But you have religion," the Pastor urges.

"CUSA is the religion. There are the prayer-booths, and you can always log on to a higher-power if you're in the mood for absolution." I take a drink. "Some of the old religions are represented feebly as amusements in games available on the AVE. Unless you're Islamic and want to live in the protected area and manufacture components and never come out. There isn't anything like what you have here. Everybody worships themselves."

The Pastor nods sadly over his glass.

"Outside the City Proper it's a little different," I continue. "There are hundreds of Drug Churches all around, sponsored by CUSA."

"Sponsored?"

"Yes, CUSA pays for the upkeep of the Drug Churches, ostensibly as a kind of charity cause. But even that's tainted, Pastor, because it gives them control and access to the drugs for their own purposes. They export them and they keep them for themselves. Drug-parties are high-level entertainment. Even though they're hallucinatory and chemical, they're a step closer to reality than all the holographs we see everyday instead of real people."

The Pastor watches me carefully.

"Let's see—" I pause, feeling a wave of vertigo. I reach for my drink and take a swig. "There are the *chuseno* Churches. Anti-drug. Those are largely neighborhood organized, a way for some of the people to convince themselves they're free of the taint of CUSA, even though everyone's as good as CUSA property from their first birthday. I suppose there are other religions, too. Plenty down on 285, probably. Nobody knows what goes on down there."

I don't think the Pastor understands anymore, but he doesn't interrupt me.

"I don't know," I say, feeling suddenly forlorn and angry. "I just lost it, I guess. If you're born to any kind of conscience in CUSA, you're born to pain and suffering." I shift, agitated. My heart has begun to beat faster as I remember. "There's no room to consider what you're doing, not an hour in your schedule to contemplate. We fill it up with work or recreation, or we lie down in our beds and are vibrated into a perfect night's stasis. Anyone who questions, or who might pass for intellectual at all, ends up in the drug church. That's where I went."

"Are you happier now?" the Pastor asks.

I want to hurl my cup at him. "Happier?" I cry. "Sure I'm happier! I've run away from everything I cared about, and I'm hiding in the middle of the fucking woods!" I scrape the chair away and rise to my feet.

He is alarmed. He sees that he's offended me, but he doesn't know why. He wants to call me back, but his courtesy restrains him. I pound off to my room.

The door is ajar. I look in, my head still throbbing. Glory is there, searching around my bed in the dim candlelight.

"What are you doing?" I demand.

She jumps up, alarmed.

"What are you looking for?"

"Nothing," she says, barely audible, and curtseys.

"Don't make that bow to me!" I yell at her. "You're not my *servant!* I didn't ask for you. What do you want?"

"I...I lost..." she tries to begin, but now she is unable to speak. Why am I so angry?

"What, *this?*" I say, abruptly pulling out the little purple ribbon from my pocket. "Did you lose *this?*" I hold it right in front of her face, forcing her to back away a little. But there is nowhere for her to go, and she backs hard into the wall.

"Y...yes," she nods. She is trembling, trying to look away.

"Well, here!" I throw it at her face. She recoils as the ribbon hits her eyes. It plummets to a spot halfway between us on the floor. I stare at her for a second, too close. Then, abruptly, I turn away. "Take it and get out! And I don't want to see you in here anymore. *Ever!* Do you *hear me?*"

Her chest is heaving as she reaches down to pick up the ribbon. I watch her run from the room. After she goes, it's quiet and pleasant again in my little corner.

I feel physically sick, like I just got out of bed for the first time. My head is singing, my eyes are crossed. I have to escape from here, no matter how hard it is out there. I have to get out!

I leave the Church without making a sound.

The shaking of my hands is the shaking of my resolve. I am thirsty for any kind of stim. The road has got to be around here somewhere. I top a hill. He has had a relapse, I think about myself. I can feel myself injecting.

It's like Sunday morning, like the best Spikey, vanilla and nutmeg slowly combing the insides of my mouth as it descends. But I look down and see there's nothing in my arm.

I cry out. *Where is my arm?* Where? The needle in my arm is flapping around. No. There's no needle. So *thirsty!* The spirits are talking to me, but I can't hear them from this angle. I miss them. They're saying something important. I haven't had my updates in so long I'll have to listen for weeks to catch up.

I'm running through the trees, peeling away the layers of night to find more stifling darkness underneath, emerging into clammy fog banks, my own hot breath on my face clouding my vision.

I am in the field, the moon high above and full, howling down at me. Across the expanse I can make out the blue country house, unlit, staring, menacing. It's waiting for the moment to leap high in the air land on top of me, devouring me with its overbite mouth.

I quickly stumble in the other direction, back into the safety of the woods. I fall to the ground as if someone has tied a rope to my ankle and pulled it tight. I look up. A tall, heavily muscled man with his back to the moonlit fog is standing above me. He taps his thigh with his palm and I scramble to my feet and dart a different way.

I stumble out of the woods and fall upon my face. There is the Church across the gully, so I try and rise but trip and topple again. Twigs and stones scrape my face, write their name in my cheek.

I lie on the ground. My heartbeat slowly regains its regularity. For a while I am certain the man will follow me from the forest to crush my head beneath his heel. But he never arrives. He is most likely a figment from my delusion.

A human shape is strolling past me through the fog, a dim shadow against the outline of the Fellowship Hall. I look up to see it. Is it him? No, this is a smaller shape, a more substantial one. I painfully pull myself up to follow at a safe distance, and it stops. I move in closer and see that the figure has its back to me. As I come closer the slight curves of Glory take shape through the dim mist.

I watch her in silence for a minute. She does not move, only looks up at the sky through the branches. Something turns inside of me, but it is not a feeling of sickness.

I think of a woman who has been kind to me. One that has been close to me, her body by my body. For some reason, I am feeling both a sense of nausea, of wanting to run away, and also a desire to leap upon her, to smell her scent again, the scent of a peach. But I can't do that. What would it mean? Aching, agonized, confused, I turn away and stumble back to my bed.

"Get back to work, goddamn it!" Whitaker snaps at me. We have acquired some new shingles from Edensburgh. I am hammering them on, rarely bending a nail. The weather is cooler than usual, but at midday on the roof it is still hot.

Whitaker tells me to pass him the box. We go on hammering. Today he almost seems satisfied. The sun is bright and comes crisp through the air. The edges of the trees are sharp like a hi-res holo. I realize we are both looking around. He notices too.

But my hands begin to tremble. I cannot stop the shaking. My hands are so blistered and raw from all the recent labor that I can't make a proper fist. Dripping slick with sweat, my hammer flies from my fingers, making a dent in the roof as it bounces off towards the ground.

Whitaker looks at the dent, then up at me, and cusses once. "Where'd you learn to use a hammer, anyway?" he yells.

"From you!"

That sets Whitaker back on his haunches. He is so surprised by my retort that his fingers fumble with his own hammer. Clambering for it, he is unable to catch it and watches it plummet off the edge. He stares at the place where he last saw it. Then he looks at me. I think he is getting ready to laugh, but instead he curses again, climbs down, and tells me with a wave to go have lunch.

Glory is at the table setting food on it as I approach, still sweaty from my labors. She endeavors to hurry up as I reach the table, but I catch her eye, quite unexpectedly. "What's for lunch?" I ask her.

She pauses, as if astonished to hear me ask her a question. Then, almost smiling, she gestures at the table silently, as if to say, *"Can't you see for yourself?"* Has she forgiven me?

I look perfunctorily at the food, and when my eyes come up I see that she has been watching me. But just as I register this, the door to the study opens with a rush, and the Pastor comes out.

"Hello," he says, and Glory skirts away like a frightened fish. Watching her go, I can still smell her musk on the air. As I sit down I am suddenly very tired of the Pastor.

"Glory will need your help," the Pastor says. "Independence Day is next week. The entire Church building must be cleaned for the Thanksgiving service."

But the next thing he says causes my gut to turn over, and makes my heart beat quickly. "Whenever Whitaker can spare you, I want you with Glory."

"Does everyone come to Thanksgiving?" I ask, trying to keep my voice steady.

The Pastor nods.

"Even the Elder?"

"Sometimes," the Pastor answers absently, finding his chair. "He will host everyone for Thanksgiving dinner in the afternoon. I believe he will allow you to join us. After the feast, I'll be leaving to take baskets to some of the older parishioners who cannot make it to the supper. I trust you'll be able to find your way back here from the Elder's house."

I nod. The Pastor nods back through his bread.

"Is something wrong?" I ask.

The Pastor's expression changes quickly, softening. "Why, no, my friend! Why do you ask?"

"I haven't seen you this sad before."

"It's the holiday," he says quickly. "There's so much to do. If it wasn't for Glory—" he breaks off, but I can see that he's continuing the thought in his head.

"How long has she been with you?"

He looks sharply at me as if I have asked something inappropriate. Then, checking himself, he shakes his head. "She was born here."

I wait for more. The Pastor seems reluctant to go on but, sighing, continues at last.

"She was born out of wedlock." The Pastor puts his hand over his mouth. "Her mother was stoned to death by the community for fornication. The father escaped to Wheeling and was never seen again."

I stare at him, mouth agape. "And Glory?"

"When the mother's sin was revealed, it was discovered that she was with child. Of course, the child was allowed to be born before the mother was punished. But because Glory was the child of a fornicator, no one was willing to take her. The task fell to me. Now she is promised to Whitaker, and she will be safe." The Pastor stops abruptly, and then a final indecipherable sigh escapes his lips.

All of a sudden he rises, and his smile is thin. "I have to go," he says. "Mrs. McCutcheon lost her two-month old baby last night and I will be staying up with her."

I nod, and busy myself with breadcrumbs. The Pastor walks past me towards the door to his office. I do not turn to watch him go, after too long a pause between the time the door opens and then closes, I feel his eyes on me. As I turn to look the door snaps shut.

Whitaker and I are finishing repairs on the back of the Church just after lunch when several men come around the corner.

"Hey, Whitaker!" one of them calls. He is a tall man with a clever expression set in the gaps between his teeth. Two strong hands hang on either side of his bulbous gut. His hair is parted with great precision on either side of a small tumor that comes out of his forehead.

"Cob," Whittaker mutters in reply.

There are four of them, four of the men from town, ranging from early twenties to late forties, two of the Sheriff's deputies in their shirtsleeves, the wolf-faced blacksmith still showing dirt and sweat on his collar even after his bath. I wonder if they are the same men who jumped me in the forest.

"Can you spare us the spook?" Cob says.

Whitaker climbs down off a ladder and rubs his beard.

"Well, 'Spook?'" he asks me, mockingly. Turning to Cob, he asks, "What you want him for?"

"We want to see how he'll *pitch*." Whitaker says nothing to this but looks at me absently. "Would you miss him?"

Whitaker shrugs, scowling.

"Then let us have him," says Cob.

Again Whitaker looks at me, as if sizing up a mule.

"All right," he says. Surely he knows the danger, knows what they might do to me. "Take him." He makes a vague gesture to the woods with his forefinger, then takes the ladder and walks away.

The men gather around me. "Come on, Spook," they say.

"Let me alone," I mutter. "I'm no good to you."

"Aw, c'mon," one of them says. He holds me by the arm and leads me away from the Church. I am pulled like a boat on a lead.

They take me towards the trees, and my heart starts beating faster as the sun comes down through the stained-glass pattern of the branches. I think I see Jesus at the top of them, but he is gazing up towards heaven, not looking down at me.

We come out on the clearing facing the blue country house. Now it begins to loom larger as we cross beneath the power lines that hang above the mounds.

When we arrive, I expect we will go in, but we wander past it to a barn out back. The first man releases my arm and opens the door. He motions for me to go inside. I hesitate, watching him. He frowns at me and gestures again.

Unable to run, not daring to disobey, I move through the doorway. Several other men are there, standing around in the dusty sunbeams. I look for the rope hanging from the rafters, but see no rope.

"How do you think he'll pitch?" laughs the man at my side. Everyone joins in with the same rude guffawing.

"Why didn't you ask Whitaker?" says one of the men in the sunbeams.

"Who wants him around?" replies the first. "What you got?"

"We can do it if he can lift," says another.

I am directed over beneath the rafters, where a large beam is coming down at me. Next thing I know, I am moving large boards with the other men across the space of the interior of the barn. We are erecting an interior wall, subdividing the space. I am a little dizzy, and try to do whatever I am asked without looking up.

What will happen *after* they have used me?

When it has grown too dim to work any longer, the first man comes over and grabs me by the scruff of the neck. "Pretty handy to have a spook," he says. The others laugh.

I am escorted out the back of the barn. Two spikes are sticking up from the ground. Everyone looks at them expectantly. My heart begins to beat fiercely.

Someone puts a u-shaped piece of metal in my hand, and I stare down at it.

No one moves. Finally, one of the men says, "Pitch! Pitch the damn horseshoe!"

Futilely, I toss it at the far spike. It strikes home, sings, and dances around the pole as it falls to earth. The men all shout.

"Lookit that!" someone says! "He *can* pitch!"

"Tell you what, Spook?" says Cob, an excited look in his eye. "We won't hang you tonight, okay? We'll hang you tomorrow!"

Everyone has a good laugh at that. I laugh loudly too, though I'd rather fall on my shaky knees and cry. Before I lose my balance, someone holds me up by shoving a cup in my hand that smells of apples.

And we throw horseshoes until it is too dark to play and I am too drunk to see.

Suddenly the barn door swings open. We can hear high-heel boots striking the floorboards in an uneven gait. Out of the darkness limps Sheriff Lyman, his wide hat brushing a swath of white in the dim firelight. "What you boys doing?" he asks, his voice echoing in my brain like it's coming from the far end of a long hallway.

Nobody answers. The men look at each other like little boys caught out after dark.

"Just playin' horseshoes, Sheriff," says one of the men quietly.

The Sheriff drags himself around, balancing on his high-heeled boots. After a while he says, "What's that one doing here?"

"Aw, shoot, Sheriff," says the deputy who has been pushing me by my neck. "We was just having a little fun with the spook. He helped us put that wall up in Donovan's barn. He can hammer real good—"

The Sheriff interrupts him. "You boys better be getting home."

"Yes sir," "Yes sir," they all say.

"What about the spook?" someone asks.

Sheriff Lyman crushes some straw under his heels. "I reckon he better find his way back to the Church quick before something happens to him."

No one escorts me out the door. Drunk as night, I can barely navigate the woods. I fall when the uneven ground betrays me. I jump at every sound, sure that someone is behind me with a rope.

As I make it home, I see a figure in the dim light, but this time I know who it is.

When she hears my footfall, she does not react out of fear. She moves around slowly, leisurely.

"Couldn't you sleep?" I venture to say from across the space. I'm talking so casually, even though I'm facing a vision.

She shakes her head. "I never sleep very well." Her voice is low. I feel a trembling in my belly, but I control myself as I move forward.

"What are you doing?"

"I don't know," she replies evasively. "Dreaming." She cranes her neck to look up through the fog to the invisible sky.

"Dreaming without sleeping."

"Kind of like you," she says.

I hesitate, searching for something to offer. "Are you afraid of me?"

"No," she answers. Then, as if reconsidering, "Sometimes."

"Don't be! I can't stand it that you're afraid of me. I'd never hurt you."

"You hurt me yesterday," she corrects me.

My heart stops in my throat. "I'm sorry," I stammer. "I—"

"It's all right," she says, turning a little away again to contemplate the far, misty woods. "You've had the Devil inside you."

I am standing right beside her. Our hands are just inches apart.

"I don't want to frighten you all the time."

She turns her body towards me then. "You don't," she says.

She is warm. So warm, I melt like a piece of candy in her mouth.

A twig cracks, and she breaks away from my kiss as if she has been yanked by unseen hands. "Ahhh..." she mutters, trembling, looking around. "I've got to go..." She doesn't finish the sentence. She is fading into the fog.

"Glory!" I call, whispering as loudly as I dare.

She stops as if reined in by a bridle.

I slowly walk to her, and she does not run away. She continues to face the Fellowship Hall, does not turn to see me as I slow and come to her back. I drop my scarred hands on her shoulders: still, so still, and I can feel the warmth coming through her blouse. I lower them carefully, afraid my heavy hands will shatter her like a fragile crystal, but she is solid when I land and does not give.

I rub my hands across the fabric of her blouse, smooth like a waterfall. My blistered fingers trace a pattern over it and follow an instinctive path. She still does not move. Do I dare? I bring them to her little breasts and feel her nipples, hard like pebbles. I rub into them with my palms, and she buckles slightly, still not looking at me.

"Glory," I whisper to her. "Glory."

"Yes," she whispers over her shoulder, arching her back.

We move hurriedly towards my room, sneaking so as not to wake the Pastor. Her desperation feels different from my desperation somehow.

She slips between my sheets in her thin clothes, which I quickly remove. I throw them on the floor almost with irritation. I long for the musky scent of her sex. When I receive her in the thick darkness with my mouth I drink her like white wine.

She allows me to taste her for awhile, sighing and grunting with pleasure. She is like a ripe persimmon, smells of sweat and feels like an apricot skin. She disengages me with two firm hands and finds a position over me, gently lying me back. She moves delicately above me until she is ready to lower herself. As I slip into

A Thousand Points of Darkness

her she coos gently. She moves up and down for a while until, at last, a solemn low moan escapes her lips. All at once I feel a release and I cry out, helpless and in such joy! Across my vision an image leaps out, of myself flying out the door, out of the Church, sailing into the sky and across the treetops in Clear Point, faster and faster to the distant mountains in the west.

Glory has rolled off of me and has come to shelter herself in my arms.

And I sleep.

Glory's curious hands rouse me from the first real rest I have had in ages. She is touching my shoulder, passing it over many times with her fingers, brushing the raised lines at first as if accidentally, then visiting them regularly. A few minutes later she has the courage to ask.

"What is that?"

"That's my brand."

"Why do you have it?"

"It specifies what part of CUSA I belong to."

"Belong?"

"Yes," I mutter sleepily. "Shareholders are products of the Corporation: It brought us into existence, and so it owns us."

She says nothing for a moment. When she speaks, it is in a tone a shade lower. "Do you have a wife?"

" I did. In CUSA."

"What was her name?"

"Maria."

239

"That's a nice name."

"She isn't a nice person."

"Do you think of her?"

"No."

Again she is quiet. Then, "Did you have any children?"

"Yes."

"What happened to them?"

"I don't know," I answer honestly.

"Where are they?"

I come back with a question. "Do you love Whittaker?"

She doesn't answer at first.

"I have to be married to someone," she finally says.

"Why?"

"Who will take care of me?" she demands.

I hesitate. "The Pastor."

She replies flatly, "He will never marry."

I am shaken out of my sleep too soon by Whitaker's merciless scabby hand. For a moment I panic. But Glory isn't here. She has removed all traces of her time with me. If it wasn't for her scent still lingering, I would think our night together was some kind of delusion. I wonder if Whitaker can smell it.

"Get out," he barks. "Pastor wants me to refloor this space."

The Pastor, preoccupied with the papers on his desk, quickly explains. "I'm sorry to have to move you," he says. "We have to repair the floor in there before the service. You'll have to sleep in the Fellowship Hall."

I wander over and see that a bed has been made for me in a drafty room on the other end of the Hall from where Whitaker sleeps. My clothes are piled on top of an old bureau. Looking at the large, worn bed, I begin to realize that, consciously or unconsciously, he has moved me away from Glory.

This does not curb my excitement. It only makes it sharper. Would she still come to me, there, in the house where her fiancé lives? Would she make love to me under his roof? All day I dream of her. My hands and legs shake so much from excitement that I feel as though I've taken an adrenaline shot. I wonder if Glory will also be thinking, if this excites her, if she will give me a secret smile when she sees me.

Safe in the darkness of my new room, I lie awake for hours, wondering if she will come. The door refuses to open. Finally, unable to maintain my expectation, I drowse. I am awakened by her silky skin against mine.

Instantly aroused, I grab her by the shoulders. "I thought you wouldn't come!" I exclaim.

"Quiet!" she orders me. I can feel her smiling and trying to contain a smile at the same time. She kisses me, and her face melds into mine. I am lost in a sensation of perfume and damp downy verdure. Our passion builds, and I know that she has missed me, missed me all day.

"We have to be careful," she says to me, regaining her breath. I kiss all around her mouth, still aroused. "No," she insists. "We have to be careful."

"I want to run away with you."

"Go to sleep," she instructs me.

"Why?" I demand.

"I can't stay here," she insists.

"You didn't worry about it before," I say, kissing the softness beneath her breasts.

"Shut up!" She pulls away from me, suddenly contemptuous. "You don't know anything."

I am afraid I have ruined something, but she doesn't leave. Each word a merciless barb, she says, "If anybody finds out, *anybody*, you'll be thrown out. And they'll do worse to me." Chastened, I lie still. Finally, out of the infinite silence, she murmurs, "Having you here feels like a lifeline, like a way out."

I don't want to answer. I don't want to break the spell.

"I wish you could take me away," she whispers, and she lies across my belly and strokes my hair.

"Where?" I say, astonished.

"Anywhere," she says. "Anywhere but here." After a while, she says, "To CUSA."

"No," I correct her.

"Why not?" she demands, caressing my shoulder. Her hands are looking for the physical scar of my brand.

"I can't go back there," I say. "I'm not the same person."

"What do you mean?" She sits up. "Who were you?"

"I was Elder Oughta," I say.

She blinks a couple of times. She is clearly astonished. "Then why would you leave?"

"I had to do something I couldn't do."

"What"

"I don't want to talk about it."

"Tell me," she insists. Unable to resist, I offer a little.

"I had to terminate people."

"What does that mean?"

"I fired them." Turning towards her now to change the subject, I ask, "Where would you want to go if you could go anywhere at all?"

"Oh," she says. "I'd like to see mountains, *real* mountains, not these hills. Feel the breeze on my face."

I let her dream for a while without saying anything. Then I ask, "Would you go to Wheeling?"

I know before the words leave my mouth that I have made a mistake. She looks at me like I am an accuser. "Glory," I say. "I didn't mean that. It just slipped out."

She pulls herself from my bed. Before I can say another word she is gone without even the breeze to remind me of her.

The next afternoon, still wincing at my stupidity, I make several runs to various homes to collect information about the Thanksgiving service. The Pastor wants to know who is coming. One or two people refuse to answer the door when I knock, but many are starting to accept me as the Pastor's charge. Mrs. Bell sends me off with a bag of fresh rolls. Other families, following her lead, and reassured by the gossip that I haven't molested any of their children, have begun to talk to me, send messages and requests to the Pastor through me.

As I make my way across the square I hear a noise off to my left. Looking, I see that the boy is there, standing by a tree. He gestures to me.

My head reels. Am I supposed to follow this child like a fool a second time? But people are watching. I walk to the boy and look down at him.

He takes me by the hand and leads me twenty feet into the forest. Several men are there, the same ones who brought me into the game of horseshoes. Cob is looking over his gut into the forest. Whitaker is there, too. Cob turns to regard me.

"There's another spigger in there," he mutters.

"What?" I ask.

"Another one of your kind." He is chewing his lip. His friends are looking anxious. You would think it was a band of rabid wolves hidden in the darkness. "We've seen him lately, some wandering fellow. But he's clever and he stays out of sight."

"Call the Sheriff," I begin. But Cob shakes his head.

"Sheriff is an idiot," he says. "He'll just shoot him." Cob looks levelly at me. "We want to know what he's after."

"Why?" I ask, dumfounded.

Whitaker speaks. "Sometimes spiggers come around with things to trade, things we can't get otherwise, not even from Elder. Sometimes the pirates from the other side of the highway make raids. Sometimes Steaksbury wants to spy on us or attack us." He grabs me by the shoulder and urges me forward. "You go out there and see if he's not so scared of you."

I wonder, what if he *is* so scared of me. But I can hardly refuse the men whose graces are keeping me alive. So I nod and move slowly into the woods.

At first I can't make out anyone. The stillness of the woods grows so profound that the buzzing of a million flies and mosquitoes begins to sound like an angry engine in my ears. I continue to inch forward through the bright green.

After about three minutes, I see through the branches the imposing figure of a man sitting at the base of a large tree, cutting slices of cheese with a small pocket knife and putting them in his mouth. But not a man I would expect to see there. He is not as dark as I am. More of a dusty brown. As I approach him I am overcome with a sense of familiarity. As strange as he is, as silent, as out of place, his appearance seems not so foreign to me. I can't explain it.

As I get nearer to him, he sees me and he nods, saluting me with a precision that a roaming vagabond would not have. *Do I know him?* As I gaze, he sinks into a more subservient posture and retreats into his lunch. The illusion is gone.

This is surely the effect of my previous life, another flashback from long ago. The closer I get to him the more I can see the pocks on his face, the calluses on his hands. He keeps looking down at his bread and cheese and does not salute me again.

I sit across from him and begin fiddling in the dirt.

"So," he says in Spanish. "We're a strange pair."

"You recognize me," I say.

"*Si*, I know you, Mr. Sattari," says the man. I tremble involuntarily at the sound of my name, not spoken since before I turned to the Body and Blood.

"Then I should be alarmed at your being out here," I say.

"No doubt," the man answers. He peers at me strangely. "Is this wilderness a vacation retreat for you CUSA types?"

"Who are you?" I demand.

The man grins. He does not answer me directly but looks at the wilderness behind me. "It's beautiful here."

I have nothing to say to that.

"This is far from the kind of thing we see in our commercials," he says.

"Ah," I say. It's coming clear now. "You're no vagabond. This is all just a disguise."

"The calluses on my hands are real, *señor*."

"Where are you from?"

"Mexico."

"A soldier?"

"Lieutenant Colonel Juan Alejandro at your service, *Siyo*."

I pause to let that sink in. Mexico has never dared send troops into CUSA before. "Where is your battalion?" I ask.

"My battalion?" he mimics, almost laughing at me. "You ask me where my battalion is? Would we march an invading force into the heart of CUSA when we know from your commercials that CUSA retains a mighty military force scattered throughout these territories?"

I nod.

"And yet," the Colonel says, gesturing around. "Despite the commercials you send, the brochures we receive, the holographic tours we take, the official word from CUSA that these US are fully protected by the authority and the vast might of your Military-Industrial Complex, General Ahmad Khorasani is old-fashioned and still believes the eyes are better than the AVE. So he sent me out here on my own, against the wishes of the Iranian Republic of Mexico."

The Lieutenant Colonel grins, spreading his arms, holding the cheese out to one side. "I fully expected to be humbled by CUSA's prowess. But what do I find?" He raises his arms up to the sky. "Nothing." He shakes his head in wonder. "No encampment, no buildings. When I saw you," he continues, "I finally had reason to fear. I thought I had walked into a trap."

I nod again.

"But there is no presence anywhere I have seen."

247

I do not reply.

"Tell me, what is this wasteland?" he demands, his arm sweeping across the green before him.

"This is what's left," I say. "These are the Unincorporated States, which we left behind us when we became a Corporation."

"Who rules them?" he asks.

"They rule themselves," I say. "And that badly, most of the time."

"Then you do not control all this?"

"No."

Even as I wonder why I am betraying my country, the answer comes to me. This is my chance, my way out. The Mexiranian Army will come, level this place, take me prisoner. Then I can negotiate to get somewhere else, somewhere they have the Body and the Blood.

The Colonel looks at me skeptically. "Why are you here? Dressed like this? Have you abandoned your country?"

I look away. "I haven't abandoned my country. I've just become a shadow." Rising to my feet, I turn my back on Lieutenant Colonel Alejandro and make my way to my waiting friends by the town.

They look at me anxiously as I emerge from the woods. "He's nobody. Just a wanderer."

"Good boy," Cob says, nodding and smiling a little, and looking very relieved. He pats me awkwardly on the back.

Whitaker grimaces and gestures with his head back to the road, as if to tell me we should be getting on now. I take the hint and accompany him.

In the twilight, Whitaker and I make our way back along the road to the Church. Whitaker says nothing for a long time, which is typical of him. But as the light begins to fade he reaches into his shirt and pulls out a small silver object. Looking at it, he regards it as if he were making a decision of some importance.

"You want some?" he asks, handing the flask out to me.

"Thank you," I say, surprised. I take a sip. The poison goes down like a steel blade through my throat. My right ear howls as if someone has slapped the side of my head.

"Tha's good, innit, Seenyour? Innit?" Whitaker asks again, his voice barely emerging through the howling in my ear.

I nod, my breath still gone.

"I got that from Moody across the holler." Whitaker takes the flask and downs a swallow. "Don't tell the Elder about it. This liquor is the one thing in these parts he doesn't own."

"Elder owns you?" I say.

"Hell, yeah!" Whitaker says. He doesn't look at me as he continues. "He owns everybody. But it's okay. At least he takes good care of us, gives us something to look forward to."

"What's that?" I ask, reaching for the flask.

"Reason ta hope," Whitaker says, but he is glowering now, looking down as if he is unwilling to say more. I have an inkling of what Whitaker hopes for, but I don't want to force him to say it. Suddenly, Whitaker turns to me. "You like it here?" he asks.

I nod, handing the flask back to Whitaker, who takes a manly swallow.

"Why'd you leave?"

"Leave?" I repeat.

"Leave where you're from?"

"None of your damn business," I tell him.

Whitaker stares at me for a minute, taking that in. Then he nods. "I like you," he says, still nodding. "I hate to admit it, but I do. You're all right."

The compliment goes to my head. Or is it the liquor? I reach for the flask. Whitaker obliges, and while I drink he spews forth something about himself that I never thought I'd hear.

"When I was a kid, I used to roam around from town to town with this company of actors."

I stop walking. "*Actors?*"

"Yeah."

I blink a couple of times.

"You *acted?*"

"Well, not me so much," Whitaker admits, shrugging. "I was just a little fella. But I was quick and quiet. So while they were doing their shows, I'd break into houses and steal stuff, then I'd bring it back to our camp. We'd leave town that same night and sell it in the next place."

I stare at him. "How'd you get in with them?"

"I don't remember," Whitaker says, wiping his mouth with his wrist. "I don't even remember my folks. I just remember being in the troupe since before I could walk. Maybe my Mamma was one of them in the troupe." He pauses and looks at the bottle. "I didn't like stealin' much. The only thing I liked wuz the way we used to sing some nights. Gathered 'round the big bonfire, singing songs. I don' even remember the names of 'em, the words. I just remember that I liked 'em. An' I miss 'em."

Whitaker takes a swig. "I finally left that when I wuz eighteen."

"Is that when you came here?" I ask him.

He nods. "I was wandering around lost in the woods, and the Sheriff found me. Brought me to the Elder. Elder figured out I liked music, an' he gave me to the Pastor. It was because he knew there was music here at the Church. Not much of it; just enough, I suppose, to get me through."

"Did the Elder give you Glory?"

Why did I ask him that? Am I insane? I tense, waiting for an explosion, an accusation. But instead, Whitaker glowers and looks at the ground.

"I don't know why Elder did that," he says. "I never coulda had anyone like that without someone steppin' in and offerin' her up." He takes a swig. "Elder convinced Pastor to give Glory to me." Whitaker's eyes drop. "She's so bright, you know. She...she talks more'n you'd think, when you're alone with her."

I know.

"I'm not nearly as smart as her. If I was, I'd find a way to talk back." He swallows.

We have arrived at the Fellowship Hall.

"When I was about ten years old," I hear myself start to say to Whitaker, "my father called me into his office. Usually there were a lot of servants around, but this time it was empty except for him." Whitaker is silent, listening. He doesn't even interrupt me with a swallow. "He closed the door," I continue, "and he pulled out a gun, a black, heavy pistol.

"He pointed it at me, right at my eyes. I remember I could see up the barrel. I remember thinking, 'How far back is the bullet? How many inches?'

"'Firoz,' he said, 'I need your help. I'm either going to kill myself tonight, or I'm going to kill you. Me or you, son."

"'You get to choose.'"

Still Whitaker says nothing. I have the sudden urge to turn upon him to be sure he is still standing there, but I'm afraid if I do, his image will vanish with the light.

"I waited for five minutes," I say. "He never pulled the gun down, he never said anything else." I swallow once. "The thing I remember most is the smell of my father at that moment. It filled the room. It actually made him available, made me feel close, close to him." I pause.

"After a while, I chose."

Finally I turn to look. Whitaker is standing there, a strange expression of satisfaction on his face. He looks over the top of his bottle at me. "Wanna know what, Seenyour?"

I reach for the flask.

Whitaker passes it and wipes his mouth again. Then he says, "There was this woman in the troupe, she kind of took care of me. She was a quarter-black, daughter of somebody's maid or something in the old time—I don't know." He has trouble coming up to meet my eyes. "There was something about the way she looked at me sometimes...made me think..."

I hand him the flask. He accepts it without raising his head. "I don't know," he says again. "Somehow you just know deep in yer soul who you are, what you are, and nothin' you did or you do is ever gonna change it—you know?

He waves at me awkwardly, shoves himself roughly through the flimsy door, and pulls it carefully closed behind him, leaving me in the cool darkness.

"Night, Whitaker." I say. I stand there for a while and let the sky spin above me.

The Thanksgiving service is well attended. Later, in the early afternoon, everyone gathers around a small, fenced-off field just outside the Elder's house and watches the young men play baseball in the bug-filled sunlight.

Until I came here, I'd never seen a real game before. You can play or watch simulated baseball in CUSA any time, but as for the real game, everything but the gnats vanished years ago.

The Sherriff stands behind home plate wearing a big vest, making the calls with his sour drawl. Cob is off to one side with a team of young men from town. An elder on the other side of the field holds court with Oughta's guards. Stripped of their uniforms, no guns in their hands, they just look like boys...spastic, happy.

Cob's team is doing well, leading by two runs. Their momentum is only broken when the mangy dog races onto the field, stopping game play. The men stand idle in the sunlight as the owner runs out to catch the animal.

When the game has resumed, one of Cob's men, the blacksmith, gets on third from a ball hit high. Everyone cheers as the carpenter's apprentice, a huge slugger, comes up to bat.

He lets the first ball go by him at the knees. "Strike," the Sheriff calls.

Cob glares at the Sheriff from the side. The second pitch is a slow ball and the carpenter nails it, sending it over the heads of the guards in the infield.

The outfielder is ready, and he watches the ball as it gets hung up in some branches by the edge of the field. Cob curses as the ball bounces through the sticks and drops easily into his glove.

Screaming over his gut, Cob urges the blacksmith on third to head for home. The hapless blacksmith has been so engrossed with the drama of the ball in the trees that he loses a couple of precious seconds before he takes off. This is a deadly miscalculation, because the arm of the outfielder is as good as the carpenter's bat. The ball is hurtled towards home plate.

The blacksmith slides into the catcher who swings the ball out of the air and into his chest.

"Out," mutters the Sherriff.

"What?" screams Cob, and he is waddling as fast as he can towards the two boys, locked in their embrace on the ground, both eyes on him. "You idiot! Everyone saw that ball was late."

"I said out," repeats the Sheriff calmly, watching Cob approach.

"I *heard* what you *said*," exclaims Cob. "What I don't know is what you're *thinking!*"

"I'm thinking maybe I should take you off to my jail," quips the Sheriff, not moving an inch as Cob's gut approaches him.

"Why you pasty faced gimp, I'd like to see you try it!"

"Don't talk like that to me, you ball-bellied sot!"

I hear a sound I haven't heard in years. The two players, still lying there watching from the ground as these two characters spit in each others' faces, a deep chuckle like a volcanic eruption. It's coming from me.

Glory has heard me and turns, her grey eyes almost disbelieving. My heart misses a beat as I catch her looking. Then she is watching the game once more as

Cob gives up in disgust and spins on his heel, accidentally stirring up a small cloud of dirt. The Sheriff noncommittally brushes off his vest and turns back to the diamond.

The rain comes up suddenly out of what was a clear sky, turning the earth to riddled mud in seconds. It pounds into the crowd as everyone flees and heads for the Elder's house. Dripping all over the tile floors, they talk about the unfinished game and the supper that is to come. They file into the room that must have once been the sanctuary of this old complex. The pews have been removed long ago, and only the shape of the place, the high ceiling, the columns by the walls, provide a clue that once people worshipped here.

All the families are present: the men who tried to hang me, whichever ones they might be; the kids; the spinsters; the young; the other elders. I see Cob holding court in one corner, the widow Mrs. Bell in her hat and her daisy, making her rounds to all the people with her kids trailing along, and even the mother of the man who was publicly shot to death. The long table where Elder Oughta has invited them to sit is full, and I wonder if there is a spot for me.

The Elder finally enters the room, dressed in his white finery. The Sheriff is at his side. The Elder carries his stone in one hand and a rough wooden stick in the other. He points the stick at individuals, who then come to him and greet him.

After Oughta has had his time, everyone is invited to sit. There are sweet potatoes and corn and butter beans, blackberry pies and slices of watermelon. In the center of the table, someone has brought a dozen scrawny chickens, probably smuggled from CUSA, which glisten on plates resting on the white cloth. The Pastor sits modestly along the side somewhere. The Elder takes his seat at the head of the table, his black stone resting by his manicured right hand. He raises that hand for silence.

He looks around at everyone as if surveying his own family. His eyes lose focus when they come to me and pass quickly over.

He rises heavily to his feet. He clears his throat, and in his husky voice he intones: "On September 11, 1776, our forefathers defeated the Nation of Islam at Antietam, the last battle of the Great War. At the end of the final victory they thanked God and sat down together at the first Thanksgiving feast. Today we celebrate their triumph."

With practiced slowness he continues. "Our nation was once ruled by wise and patient men, under fear"— and here he nods to the Pastor—"of God, and dedicated to the limitless expansion of His chosen people. We settled this land from coast to coast, from sea to shining sea. We made it beautiful.

"But over time we became careless and vain, and we forgot God and abandoned his ways. He warned us, but we heeded Him not. And so he sent the dark peoples of the earth to punish us. They drove us with their clever ways into the sea and into the mountains. They made us into barbarians, and they sealed our cities from us."

The Elder glares. "We cannot return until God wills it, until we prove ourselves worthy, brave enough and purified enough by suffering to take what is ours.

"We are but a tenth of the men our ancestors were. But we are still men, and we still possess our memory. For that let us say thanks."

He looks over at the Pastor. "Pastor Harbin? You want to make a prayer?" He nods at everyone. "Join hands," he says.

I find each of my hands being taken by the soft, gentle palms of the people next to me. They bow their heads and close their eyes, trusting like children that I will do the same. I keep my head up so I can watch, but for a second I realize I am fully connected to the community, by silence and respect, by reverence, and by peace.

The Pastor stands in his long black robe but does not look at me, the only one with my head up. He simply opens his mouth and says, *"Now as they were eating, Jesus took bread, and blessed, and broke it, and gave it to the disciples and said, 'Take, eat; this is my body.' And he took a cup, and when he had given thanks he gave it to them, saying, 'Drink of it, all of you; for this is my blood of the covenant, which is poured out for many for the forgiveness of sins. I tell you I shall not drink again*

of this fruit of the vine until that day when I drink it new
with you in my Father's kingdom.'"

Everyone nods and replies "Amen."

There is an awkward silence. Then a child grabs a
roll, and soon the room is buzzing with people reaching
for their own share of the meal.

After a while, the buzzing begins to sound more
deliberate. At first I am not sure what is happening, but
then it occurs to me that people have begun to sing.
Snatches of their commercials, what they call "songs,"
come to me through the conversation. I can't make out
any of the words, though.

Out of the noise, one name begins coalescing.
"Cob!" people begin whispering to themselves, then to
each other. "Cob." Now louder: "Cob!" people begin to
say out loud, and the tumor-headed man, mangling a
breastbone, looks up as if surprised, though everyone
seems to know he'd expected this.

"What you all want?" he demands. He acts like he's
offended that folk are distracting him from his food, but
he is obviously covering up his pleasure too.

"Sing it!" folks are starting to cry.

"Sing what?" he asks through the chicken pieces.
But he knows. He's already standing up to their
scattered applause.

"Sing it!" everyone is demanding now, in a single
voice.

"All right, all right," Cob says, holding his hand out,
and making a downward gesture to subdue them. He

takes a breath. His eyes shining, he sings in a beautiful baritone voice.

> *Old empty bed...springs hard as lead*
> *Feel like ol' Ned...wished I was dead*
> *What did I do...to be so black and blue*

They strike me as ludicrous, these words. Is this an attempt to mock me, to ridicule me? But as I look around I see that no one is paying me any attention. Even the Elder doesn't have a glance for me. He is as rapt as the rest of them in what Cob is singing.

> *Even the mouse...ran from my house*
> *They laugh at you...and scorn you too*
> *What did I do...to be so black and blue*

They aren't associating the song with me at all, at least not consciously. They must listen to Cob sing this every year. It goes deep for them, as though it were some kind of connection to their past. The meaning of the words is completely lost on them except as a song about sad times. It's the tune that seems to touch them and the situation in which it's sung. It's something they all know and can share.

When Cob finishes, the song seems too short. Only the two verses. Is there more? If so, that's all Cob and the townsfolk seem to know. After his short recital, only thirty seconds or so, everyone is clapping and smiling as they nod at him. Cob sits down, smiling, amidst the applause, and returns to his meal.

It is only then that Cob seems to remember me. He calls out to me from up the table, "They got this kind of food where you're from, Spook?"

I am in the middle of quietly deboning a breast of chicken, and the hall gets noticeably quieter. I look up, uncertain how to answer, when Mrs. Bell comes to my rescue. "Firoz," she says, "won't you tell us something about where you come from?"

The room goes completely silent. I look up, unsure of what I am supposed to say. Nobody offers to help me out. The faces are a mixture of curiosity and embarrassment.

"I don't know," I say. "It's not like here. Parts of it look similar, I guess." I wish I could just eat. "There are places in CUSA which never recovered from the Correction—"

All Mrs. Bell's children are shouting at once. "The what?" "What's the 'collection'?" They are used to me and are not afraid to ask questions. Mrs. Bell tries to quiet them. Once I start talking again, they quiet down quickly.

"The Correction. Essentially, it started when a large number of people defaulted on their house payments at the same time. The economy collapsed, and got fixed, and then collapsed again, a bunch of times, like little earthquakes. It never could recover because the environment had collapsed. In the end, the President was only able to save us by incorporating. So now we're all born into debt, and we spend our lives trying to get out of it."

People are nodding at me like they understand, like they even feel sorry for me.

"Can you tell us anything *nice* about your home?" Mrs. Bell asks quietly.

I consider. "Some of the commercials are nice. Especially the old ones. I used to memorize them. There was one my mother used to sing me, when I was a boy, to get me to sleep."

I don't have any intention of continuing. But someone cries out, "Sing it!" Then they all nod their heads and affirm the suggestion. "Sing it!"

After a few seconds, I rise to my feet and sway a little with nerves. In the silence, I can hear the rain pounding on the roof. I think back and recall the first verse. I'm not sure as I begin that I'll be able to recreate all of it, but once the first words leave my mouth, new ones scroll into my head.

> *"O beautiful for spacious skies,*
> *For amber waves of grain;*
> *For purple mountains majesties*
> *Above the fruited plain!*
> *America! America! God shed his grace on thee,*
> *And crown thy good with brotherhood*
> *From sea to shining sea."*

I pause. There is dead silence again in the room. Cob speaks from the corner, says quietly, "That's beautiful."

"Don't stop," urges Mrs. Bell, gesturing with her hand. So I go on.

> *"O beautiful for heroes proved*
> *In liberating strife,*
> *Who more than self their country loved,*
> *And mercy more than life!*
> *America! America! May God thy gold refine,*
> *Till all success be nobleness,*
> *And every gain divine."*

And as I stand here, looking around, I see that everyone is rapt, watching me. No one interrupts me, not even to cough. No one wants to break the spell. Some of the children see their parents crying and whisper to each other, amazed.

The little boy that has been dogging me since I got here rises to his feet and begins humming the tune under me. As if I am singing with my own memory, I begin the third verse with his soprano voice illuminating it.

> *"O beautiful for patriot dream*
> *That sees beyond the years*
> *Thine alabaster cities gleam,*
> *Undimmed by human tears!*

America! America! God mend thine every flaw…

The ending of the verse eludes me. I falter. "God mend thine every flaw…" I say again, without the tune. "God mend…" Now my lips are moving, but no sound comes out. The people stare at me, confused and wondering why I won't continue.

I can't. I look around and down at the dusty floor.

At last, someone applauds to cover up my discomfort. Their gesture is followed by others. Now hands are patting and thumping me on the back. "That's all right, Firoz," says Whitaker, as several people offer me more food. "That's all right."

All the while the Elder is glowering from the head of the table. He appears to take no notice of me, but I feel the enmity pouring out. He is occupied making gracious talk with his community, but I know that if he could he would take his heart-sized stone and hurl it at my head.

Mrs. Bell's children all gather around me like a swarm. "Firoz! Firoz!" they cry. The youngest grabs me by the shirt-tails. "Mamma wants you to teach us how to *read!*" she shouts.

Mrs. Bell is behind them. She is smiling nervously. She puts a hand to my lapel and draws me closer. "Ellis used to have a school here years ago," she says. "No one's done it since then. I know you that can read. I thought you and I could start something…maybe together…"

Despite herself Mrs. Bell flushes, but like the true lady she is, she maintains my gaze.

Someone has brought out a tiny stringed instrument and a tambourine. The townspeople begin to pair off for dancing. As the music begins, the Elder retires out of sight. I don't stop to wonder where he has gone. I'm looking for somebody else.

"Where is Glory?" I ask the Pastor.

"Washing dishes," the Pastor says, looking over my shoulder. "Will you excuse me, *Señor?*" He rushes off to get one of his older congregants a gift basket that he has brought.

A hard hand comes down on my shoulder. I turn around. It is the Sheriff. "Elder wants to talk to you," he says.

"About what?" I ask.

"That's the Elder's prerogative!" he snaps. He brings his face closer to mine and says, through clenched teeth, "You want to be a part of this town? You better just do what the Elder tells you."

I follow Sherriff down the long hallway and am brought to the model room where Elder Oughta once again sits behind a desk, contemplating an almost completed plastic model airship while the rain drips, drips, drips at a nearby window. He has an uncharacteristically thoughtful look on his face as he balances the black rock in his right palm, then puts it on the desk and picks up a small, thin paintbrush with the same hand.

I look around his study and see the dozens of models like the one I saw on the table that first day. Ships, planes, toy soldiers—all meticulously glued and painted.

Elder is working on it with determination, as though its completion is of vital importance. His concentration is extraordinary. There is, in his face, an expression I've never seen there before, a studiousness, as he paints the black stripe across the bevel of a plastic tailpiece. Though his hand shakes, he never strays outside the lines, makes no mistakes in his painting. His mouth hangs open a bit as he delicately, exactly maneuvers the brush so that it dots the edge. Then he fits it to the model by hugging the glued part on and patiently waits until it has dried.

When the door has been closed behind me and the Sheriff has taken a seat facing my back, Elder exhales once. Then, carefully, he puts down his glue, so as not to dislodge any loose model pieces. Looking at me at last, he speaks.

"You know what today is?"

"Thanksgiving."

"But for *me*?" he says pointing to himself with his manicured index finger.

I have no idea.

"It's my birthday," he says.

I raise my eyebrows.

He continues. "And on my birthday, I give gifts. You probably wonder why all these people don't give gifts to *me*." He nods, as if I'd asked the question myself. "No one here could ever give anything to me," he says. "These people have nothing. I have everything. So on my birthday, I give gifts." He looks at me. "What do you want?"

I blink. "I don't want anything."

The Elder nods thoughtfully. "I know what you want." He continues to nod, scratching his chin. "I know what you want."

I am dying to know what I want.

"You want to get away," he says, finally.

"I already did that," I reply.

"Why?" the Elder leans towards me.

"I don't remember," I answer.

"What did you do?" he asks, slipping back into the chair and relaxing. I do not respond. Sheriff Lyman slaps the back of my head. As I duck a second blow, the Elder holds up his hand, urging the Sheriff to restrain himself. "What were you in CUSA?"

"Nothing of any consequence," I reply.

The Elder considers, rubbing his cheek to the stone. "I don't believe that."

"I was a drug-worshipper," I said. "That's all I remember doing. Before that, I was probably a rickshaw driver or something menial."

"Why would you run away from being a rickshaw driver?" the Elder insists.

"I didn't like CUSA," I answered.

"You were safe there," he reasons.

"No," I answer.

"A rickshaw driver in danger?" the Elder laughs. "Come on, darkie! You can do better than that!"

"No one's safe in CUSA," I say, trying to keep the emotion out of my answers.

"Why not?"

"Because you're only a product," I say. "The Corporation can do whatever they want with you, so long as it keeps them solvent."

"Does everybody know this?" the Elder asks, very interested.

"No," I reply.

But this is a lie. "Yes," I say.

But this is a lie also. I am confused. "No," I finally manage. "Nobody really sees the truth."

"Then how did *you* know it?" says Oughta, .

"I...I had a revelation."

The Elder's eyes open wide, and he leans back, clicking his fingertips together. "No wonder the Pastor likes you," he says. "All right... *señor*." He has never used my title until now. It comes with difficulty to his lips.

"Yes."

"I owe you a present. I don't know what I'm going to do for you, yet, but rest assured, you'll receive something. I'll get back to you."

"I don't want anything from you," I say.

"Yes, you do," the Elder says, leveling his eyes at me angrily. "That's why you came here. You ran from your domain to my domain without asking for sanctuary. You've inserted your black self into my community and have given nothing back: no respect, no subservience, nothing. You want a present from me, but you don't have the decency to ask." The Elder waves his hand, and the Sheriff comes up behind me. "So you're going to get it without asking," the Elder concludes. I am quickly ushered from the room.

When I return to the feast, the warmth of the celebration has dimmed a little bit. I look for Glory or the Pastor, but I cannot find either of them in the crowd. Finally I head back to the kitchen.

Glory and two other young women are washing dishes by candlelight.

"Glory," I mutter hoarsely.

She looks up sharply.

"Go!" she whispers. "Don't come talk to me here." The other two women keep their eyes down and pretend not to hear us. I stand there silent, brooding. Finally, one of them makes an excuse, and the other follows her from the kitchen.

"Will I see you later?" I plead to Glory.

"No," she answers sharply. "Not tonight."

"But Glory—"

"I said *no!*"

I shuffle my feet. "I miss talking to you." She doesn't answer. She is scraping dishes vengefully. "I miss talking with you. I love to hear you talk." I put my fingers to her mouth. She brushes them away impatiently. "I...I want to hear you talk."

"Go away."

"When I see you, it's never for long enough. You're there, you're gone—" I sound like a whining dog. "Why are you avoiding me, Glory? Don't you—"

"Stop!" Glory cries. She grimaces, mortified that her voice has emerged so loudly.

"Let's take a walk tonight. I want to show you a special place, in the woods."

"No!" she cries, straining the whisper with her intensity. "I can't go with you. Don't you understand? If Whitaker finds out, if the Pastor—"

"They won't," I interrupt. "Listen. I have a plan."

"Get out!" she says, and her eyes are begging me. She is frantic.

"I need you! I'll do anything to have you."

"You can't."

I pound on the table with my fist so hard it shakes. "I've *got* to!"

Glory's eyes sparkle with astonishment as she stares at me. "Are you insane?" she asks.

"Yes, I think I must be," I reply. "But when I'm with you, I feel clear-headed."

"I'm sorry," Glory says quietly. "I can't. I have to protect myself."

"I'll protect you!"

Her eyes flash, like I've just spoken ill of the dead. "How?" she demands contemptuously.

"I'll take you—"

"*Señor?*" The Pastor's voice interrupts us from the doorway. We both jump. He looks down at the floor.

"Yes?" I answer.

"Mrs. Bell asked to see you before she leaves."

Turning slowly, under the watchful eyes of the Pastor, the words I have not yet said to Glory burning on my lips, I shuffle out of the kitchen with my head down. Glory does not watch me leave.

I wait for Glory in the drafty darkness of my bed, with the thunder protesting outside.

Despite her attitude, *I know* she will come to see me. She is drawn to something in me that she needs. Finally, after an hour of silent waiting with nothing but the endless storm for company, I see her tiptoe into the room and remove her gown.

We lie there, neither looking at each other nor speaking. I know she is getting ready to tell me that we have made a mistake, that this is the last time. "I wanted to talk to my demons again," I tell her, to shock her maybe, to keep her there.

"What?" she asks, sitting up and looking at me. Thunder peals, and it echoes across the hills of the woods, fainter this time.

"I haven't wanted the Body and the Blood in weeks. Since we've been together, it's been better."

She is staring at me.

"Now I want them or you."

"I have to go," she says, beginning to roll over.

"Stay," I say, grabbing her by the hip. "Just a little while, just a minute."

"I can't," she protests, but she doesn't resist, and she lies back down on her back, still tense.

"Glory," I mutter, kissing her on the side of her mouth.

She doesn't answer. Her lips don't respond to my kisses. She is stiff like a corpse. Maybe she thinks I'm only practicing her name, and maybe I am. I'm drowsy, but I don't want her to go just yet.

"Glory," I say again. "Glory."

"Be quiet!" she scolds me.

"Glory, we have to leave."

"What are you talking about?"

"We have to go," I say, still half drowsy. "There's going to be a change coming."

"A change," she repeats. There is a break in her voice. "What are you talking about?"

"I can't tell you," I say. "I don't want to scare you. But things will change soon—change in a big way. We don't want to be here when they do."

"I have to get back." She tries to rise again.

"No, Glory," I say, holding her by the wrist. She struggles a little, unwilling to make too much noise. "No, Glory, listen," I say. "We have to go, you and me."

"*Go?*" she demands in a whisper. "Where would we go?"

"You said you wanted to leave."

"That was a dream," she mutters. "I have to get *back*," she says, almost pleading, pulling her wrist.

"No, Glory, *wait!*" I exclaim, a little too loudly. "We have to run from here! This whole town...Clear Point is going to be overrun with strangers." The thunder again, restless, importuning.

"What are you talking about?"

"There are going to be soldiers. There was a Colonel from MexIran out there, pretending to be a wanderer. He came to find out if your lands are protected by CUSA. There will be others, a force larger than anything you've ever—"

"*Señor!*" she pleads. She seems unable to listen to me. "Let me *go!*"

"Glory!" I shout, desperate to reach her, to make her understand, to convince her.

"Whitaker," she reminds me. "Whitaker will *hear!*"

"I don't care," I retort. "Let him know. We have to get out of here. Don't you understand? Everything you know is about to come to an end!"

"*Señor, please!*" she begs. A close lightning strike, a huge crash. Glory is beginning to cry as she tries to free her wrist without making too much noise.

"Glory!" I beg.

"God forgive you."

The Pastor's voice.

He is standing in the doorway. His grey face, soaked with rain, is lined with deep weariness and regret. "I always knew that you had the seed of sin within you," he says.

But he is not speaking to me. He says these words to Glory. She spins around and lies on her back, facing him naked, like a cornered animal. "All these years," he goes on, "I wanted more for you."

Then Glory does something I would never have expected. She laughs, not a warm laugh. Instead it is harsh, taunting and scornful." What were you doing, Pastor?" she demands. "*Spying?* Through the *window?* How long have you been watching—"

To stop her words, the Pastor rushes at her with his wet hand and grabs her by the hair. With all the force he can muster, he pulls her from the bed and drags her onto the floor. Shrieking, Glory resists with her hands.

"I took you in," the Pastor says, trying to keep his shaking voice level, like a parent dealing with an unreasonable child. "I gave you everything I had. Now look at you!" he cries, pointing a finger in the direction of her pluming pubes. "After I took you from your mother—"

"Oh, *spare* me your devotional!" she cries, rising up from the floor, pulling herself free from him with a vicious snap of her arm. She reaches for her nightshirt which is lying on the bed. "Twenty years I've lived under your roof, and I've always known what kind of *lust* you had for me. How you'd like to run your hands all over me—"

Wounded, the Pastor recoils. Snatching her nightshirt from her hands, he forces her to stand before her, naked. "You're a whore! Like your mother!"

"God rest her soul!" Glory says, cocking her arm to strike the Pastor. "How dare you speak of her! She was stoned to death because of *your* sin, while you stood and watched!"

"What in the hell—" The low mutter from the doorway is Whitaker's voice.

Whitaker stares at us, his naked upright fiancé on the floor, me unclothed on the bed. His jaw drops. He shifts his stare from one of us to the other.

The Pastor has now gotten himself under control. His voice is low and measured again, even reasonable. "Your mother was stoned for being a fornicator. A just punishment which—"

"*Just!*" Glory howls. "You watched while Jesus wept!"

The Pastor roars, his wounded head circling. "I gave you everything I had. I treated you like you were my only child!"

"Is that why you didn't *bed* me at twelve when my body was first beginning to show?" Glory's hands rise slowly, mockingly, coming up under her breasts before him. "Is *that* why? Because I am your child? *Father?*"

"No!" the Pastor protests, thrusting her shirt towards her as if in vigorous denial of her words. As if to protect himself from this accusation he covers his face with his hands, recoiling from the thoughts that seem to be racing through his mind.

Glory is merciless. "Will you stone me for the crime of my mother as punishment, the way you did to her, for not giving in to you freely?"

Now she has gone too far. The Pastor lowers his hands and, with tears in his eyes, says, "I loved your mother. You may not believe that." Clearing his throat, he stares at Glory but seems to see someone else. In a whisper he says, "You'll be stoned for your transgression against God's law, just as she was." The Pastor comes forward and roughly pulls the nightshirt down over her head, attempting to cover her up. Impatiently, Glory seizes the garment and finishes the job herself. The Pastor seizes her gingerly by the arm.

Naked, frozen on my back by fear of this incomprehensible spectacle, I am unable to move to protect her. Whitaker moves forward to seize her other arm and help the Pastor take her away. He acts automatically, though his eyes are full of questions.

They are ignoring me, leaving me behind. I am nothing to them now. After all, I was never part of their world.

I am running along a path in the utter darkness of the torrential rain. Dressed thinly as I am, I feel like I'm still naked. I remember just after I learned to pray that I was running then, through the streets, past the offices and the warehouses and the Uniforms, and I was nobody for the first time, feeling unearthed and exposed.

I appear at the gate of the Elder's house, sopping like a dog. Seizing a rock from the ground, I smash it against the wrought-iron bars of the locked gate, and a noise sings out to wake the dead. Two guards rush out of hidden alcoves. I make no move to escape as they unlock the gates. They are shaking me in the rain, demanding to know what I want here, and I try to tell them through the thrashing, but the Elder is already standing in the doorway in his pajamas and robe.

"Let him go," he says, signaling at his guards to release me. "Let him go." The guards release me. I walk over to the shelter of his porch and stand before him. Elder stares at my bedraggled form for a moment, looking very satisfied. "Come on," he says gruffly, and he turns without another word or gesture, expecting me to follow.

I remind myself I haven't slept much in the past twenty-four hours, and I try to maintain my focus. Almost in tears, all I can think about now is how I wish the Blood were coursing through my arm, dripping me into an exclamation point.

This time, no one is following us. It's just me and the Elder. I marvel how it is that he has no fear of me at all, no caution, no acknowledgment of the danger I pose to him.

We enter his study, and he moves to his seat. He does not offer me a towel, and says nothing about the pool forming at my feet.

"What can I do for you?" the Elder asks. His right hand spasms. He regards the jerking idly as if it was somebody else's hand.

"Elder," I begin.

"You've come for your present," he says.

After a second, I nod. When he does not continue, I blurt out, "Glory—" His eyes flash up at me.

"Ah, yes," he says. "The harlot."

I stare at him in confusion. He knows already.

"Of course I know," he says, reading my mind. "I know everything that happens in my town."

"It's me you want. You've got to help her!"

The Elder is quiet for a while. After he has contemplated the situation for long enough, he nods and speaks. "When I was a boy, I wanted to be like the great Roman general Octavius who I was named after." He shifts. "Once I realized that wasn't going to happen, that we lost the chance to be generals long ago, I sought to become an Elder.

"Do they still teach you about Abraham Lincoln in the CUSA?" He looks to his left out the curtained picture window into the blue-black woods beyond.

"I suppose."

He grimaces tightly. "You may recall that Lincoln defeated the Black Regiment not far from here, at Gettysburg," he says. His eyes gleam with a strange kind of desire. "That was when God loved us. We were a nation, then, just sewing ourselves together. Repairing the breach, deciding we wanted to be one people."

He makes a fist and swings it in a downward arc towards the desk. "Ah," he growls. "To have lived in those days. How I would have loved to ride with Lincoln. Or to serve under Nixon when he ousted the Jews of China. My *God*, what times!" He gestures at his bookshelf, where a couple of books lie snoozing against one another. "I never get tired of reading about them! I tell the stories to my people because I want them to *know*. It could be so *again*."

His wrinkled face falls. He turns to stare at me. His right hand dives into his pocket and emerges clenching his large black stone. He brings it up to his cheek, just below his nose, and gently caresses the side of his face with the smooth polished surface as if he were in love with the rock.

"You want me to help Glory," he says.

"Yes!"

"Help you, Firoz Sattari of the Noke Corporation."

My shock at hearing my full name takes away my capacity for speech.

He is grinning at me now, sizing me up. "You don't think much of us, do you? Don't think us white people are very smart, out here in the wilderness. You think this is the end of the world, that we're a bunch of cavemen." Elder gets up and comes over to me. With a nubby forefinger he taps me on the forehead. "But I know you," he says. "I know who you are."

He is sizing me up, looking at me as if he had never seen me before. For my part I find myself re-evaluating him as well. We stare at each other for a moment.

"What do you want from me?" I ask him.

"I'll save your precious Glory," he says to me. "That's the favor I'm going to do for you, the birthday present you so blithely turned down. And here's what you're going to do for me. Go back where you came from. Get me weapons. The good kind. None of these little rifles and shotguns. I want the sprayers. And money—"

"We don't have money," I interrupt. "Just numbers on tattoos."

"That's a lie," he says, looking down his nose at me. "There's wealth in your world backing up those numbers somewhere, and I want my share of it. Gold, silver—I don't care."

"I'm not a *siyo* anymore! If I go back they'll give me nothing. They think I'm dead!"

"You'll go back, all right," snarls the Elder. "If you want to save your precious Glory, you'll find a way. I'll give you two days!"

"How would I get there?"

I hear the irregular clump of Sheriff Lyman's boots approaching me from behind. He has seized me with an iron grip by the arm and is lowering a syringe towards it. For a moment, I almost consider struggling.

When I became an addict I grew used to the sensation of not knowing what time it was, of confusing present with past and getting turned around, looking south and thinking it was north. So the darkness is nothing new to me, and when my senses at last begin to register sights and sounds I think they very well might be illusion, or at least memory.

When I have regained enough of myself to distinguish between dream and reality, I notice the throbbing of my head. I begin to recollect that the Sheriff has thrown my unprotesting body in the back of a horse-drawn cart driven by some hired hand from nowhere, and I have been bumping along back here for hours. The wonderful return to the Body and Blood is long gone now, and the hunger and the ache means I have to find more, even as I remain trapped in this cage. The air is cold, and the drafts between the boards seem like knife stabs.

As the light begins to emerge through the slats I catch glimpses of a greying, decayed cityscape. Not CUSA, but somewhere in the US, crumbling stone and mortar, weather-beaten monuments to an excluded society. It is nothing but a large-scale model of the pitiful shacks in Clear Point. Occasionally I see people, no better off than those in the country, making their way across garbage-strewn lanes. Sometimes there are gunshots in the distance.

The cart lurches to a stop, and I hear a heated exchange of words in a language I do not recognize. Suddenly the cart is thrown open, and a large red faced man peers down at me. He regards me for a moment, sizing me up, then hurls the door shut once more. The exchange continues, again in that mysterious tongue, only more heated now. Finally, after a climax, the conversation drops precipitously, and there is eerie silence.

A click, and then my cage is in motion once more, only faster. The bumps now rattle my teeth unmercifully. The cart must be hitched behind a motorized vehicle now, most likely an old-fashioned diesel. I am inundated with fumes and smoke, and for a while I pass out again.

I come to with a familiar nausea and an enormous headache. I am lying on my side on concrete, facing a small puddle of water lapping at the base of a low wall. The cart and all sign of a driver are gone.

In the back of my mind I hear the word "canal," and as I roll onto my back to face the grey sky, my lungs collapse in protest. I hack and cough from the bottom of my gut until a small quantity of black mucus emerges reluctantly onto the concrete beside my head. My eyes dimly come into focus, and as I register Spanish words I know for certain that I have been dumped somewhere in CUSA and left to die.

The canals confirm my worst suspicion: that I am at the southernmost tip of the Mid-Atlantic Protectorate. The Elder has clearly spent a considerable amount of his money to put me safely back behind the CUSA wall, where, he assumes, I will either be able to help him or be out of his life forever.

It was a better move than even he knows. I have nothing in CUSA: no friends, no help. With my useless tattoo I am more likely to starve in the streets than escape. The only alternative open to me is a return to the Drug Church.

As if summoned by my thought, something familiar and comforting ensnares me, a shuffling sound that pries my heart open. I sit up and see the addict, wandering aimlessly, wearing old forgotten clothes, a chewed sun-hat from some executive's throwaway pile.

Her eyes are cloudy now, and there is no intent in her stride. I walk behind her. The voice in my mind starts reciting the catechism: Follow her to get what you need. Just a chance to retreat again, be free from the uncertainty, just for a night, blissful in ignorance of all.

Then the woman turns to look at me, and she nods. The gesture turns her into Glory.

"*We all in this together...Oooo...I love it.*" The AVE blares from the lamp-post.

I've grown so used to the joys of occasional silence that I've completely forgotten the incessant blathering of the AVE, the terminals spaced uniformly about the streets. My ears cannot shut out the noise that I once filtered as silence. The pedestrians, mostly reactor-cleaners waiting for the train, are answering to the smell exuded by an ad for little cups of coffee at ten dollars each, which will be hot and waiting for them when they reach their work stations.

The bell chimes, calling the addicts to worship. It's amazing, but I don't even argue. I shuffle towards the Drug Church in a kind of eager acceptance. The decision has been made for me. All thoughts of Glory are nearly forgotten.

Glory! Is that her in the line in front of me? Looking back dolefully? Beckoning me on...

Is that a protest? Or is it a flashback? I am already standing in one of two straight lines in the middle of a large cathedral. The Padre is intoning some kind of blessing, his voice echoing off the distant ceiling. It's a commercial I must have heard a thousand times. I doubt I'll ever register it again. The person in front of me is talking to himself or to me. "The thing of it is it's so common, it's so common, it's so common," he says. "It's so common to, it's so common..." He doesn't know what he's saying, but I understand.

Glory...

Yes, I love Glory. And I cannot be with her anymore. The dream ends here. I was silly to try. Now I can go back to my delusions. I am standing before one of the acolytes. She is holding the syringe in her hand. I roll up my sleeve and reveal row upon row of puncture marks.

A hand grabs me by the arm, and I begin to submit to the syringe, but instead I am yanked upwards and stare into an astounded face.

I reel in shock. It is an angel, her childish mahogany features ringed by curly black hair. The eyes stare down at me in horror and disbelief.

"Firoz?" says the angel.

I must be dreaming. I thought she was a hallucination, thought for sure my absolution could not be real. How can this be? I haven't taken the Body and Blood yet, so I must be flashing back.

But the reality of the angel will not be denied. She was there in the woods as I cried in shame for what I had to do. She offered me salvation. I took her blessing, and now I have failed her. Ashamed, I can barely stand to look back up at her. "I know I've let you down," I stammer.

"What are you *doing* here?" the angel demands.

"There's nothing left," I murmur, wretched. "They brought me here."

"Come on!" Still gripping my wrist tightly, she pulls me out of the line as the next shambling mound files up behind me for absolution. I have to follow. It's as if I were as weak as a child, and the child as strong as indignation.

She sits me down in a pew at the back of the Church, warily looking back at the line of worshippers, who wait patiently for her return.

"Don't you know who I am?" she asks me.

"An angel," I say.

"No, I'm *Rosa*," the child continues. I stare at her, uncomprehending. The name means nothing to me. "You *saved* me!" she says, as if this will help me understand. "We were lost in the woods together, and you made such a racket that Pastor came and found

285

us! Don't you remember? Virgilina and Steaksbury and..."

She knows the Pastor. Confused, I stare into her eyes. I can tell that they have been long dulled with grief, but they are bright now, in confusion, in rage.

"If it wasn't for him, I'd be dead," the angel says. "He found me a way back here, got someone to give me a lift to the DC entry. He said you'd be okay. Why are you here?"

"I don't know!" I protest with a pleading look. "I lived with the Pastor for a long time, but the Elder threw me out, and there's no place for me."

The angel looks down, the sadness pulling her gaze to the floor. "I understand that. When the Pastor found us, he tried to get me back to my family, to the bus, but someone had already come and picked them up. So he got me here himself. I wasn't sure if I could find my parents again, didn't even know where they were. But I found my cousins, the Lukas." Large tears begin falling down her nose. "They wouldn't speak to me at first," she said. "They were afraid. I didn't understand why. But I found out. One of them finally told me. As soon as my parents got here they were rounded up and taken away." Rosa looks up at me. "Basil tried to warn me, Firoz. He told me people who lose their job get taken away." Crying overtakes my angel, and for a moment she is weak.

My angel was a girl with parents? How could evil overtake an angel?

She recovers herself, takes another furtive glance at the line of addicts, and continues. "I didn't have nowhere to go, nowhere but here. I thought about Basil, about what he said, that I could be safe here, and when I got here they took me in, gave me a job. I can't ever go back, now, Firoz. If I ever let CUSA know I'm here, CUSA will take me away, too." My angel's eyes widen. "You got to get out of here, Firoz! If they know I know you, they may start asking questions." She looks around, terrified. "Already somebody may see."

I stare at her wordlessly. I long for her to take me back to the line.

"No," the angel says, even more emphatically. "You got to go!"

"Where can I go?" I ask. "This is where I belong."

"You got to leave CUSA."

My heart aches. The angel knows my thoughts. "I can't," I reply. "Not unless I can get back to Noke. They're the only ones that can get me back to Clear Point."

"Noke?" the angel asks. "You want to go to *Noke?* Why?"

"I was—" I falter. Can I bear to admit this to my angel? "I used to...work for Noke. They'll...they'll take me back...away from all this."

The angel looks deep in my eyes, holds my scarred hands. "If I can get you to Noke, will you promise never to come back here? Never to tell nobody?"

Another promise. I nod.

I am riding on the train to DC Proper. I see a Uniform in the next car. He takes no notice of me.

There is a drug party at Noke this evening, the same sort of party where I first sampled the Blood. I am dressed as a Padre. My angel has given me a dummy drug-bag and a head start on the true Padre, who has no idea I am going, and who will arrive a little later with the real drugs. It is enough of a subterfuge to get me through the door.

Just before sundown the train stops at the entrance to Noke Washington. The building is much like its cousin in the Atlanta Hub, a large black pyramid with a clear glass point. The receptionist is happy to let me in with hardly a word. I know exactly where to go, have been through this building many times over the years.

They take me straight to the top, of course. They ask me to wait by the holo-statue of John Maynard Keynes until they are ready for me. When they give me the go-ahead, I begin roaming the offices looking for a familiar face. All the executives are hiding, it seems. Only low-level flunkies are out and about tonight. But the higher-ups must be here somewhere.

I stroll past doors with names on them—Smit, Shapiro, Dasani—names I know but have not thought about for so long. The doors are closed, locked. They are hiding inside, or they have gone somewhere else to make themselves numb.

Then, in a public lounge, I see the hunched, stooped shoulders of Mr. Tran. He is lazing on a couch in the middle of his green halo, talking with another, younger executive with whom I am unfamiliar. The younger executive sees me and energetically signals for me to enter.

I pass through the doorway and walk up to Mr. Tran.

"I'm going to spin tonight," he says to his superior. "Do you want to go double?"

Tran looks up at me. There is no recognition in his face. Even though I stare at him rudely, my face unchanged, even though I was his colleague for thirty years, he evinces not a shred of recognition.

"Yes," Tran says to me, nodding. "A double spin, please."

"Tran," I mutter to him.

He squints, insulted. "May I help you?" he asks, looking very offended.

"It's me," I say. "Sattari."

He rises to his feet, suddenly very angry. "What kind of a server are you? Do you think that's some kind of joke?"

"Tran—"

"I should have you removed. Ren," he says to the younger executive, who is looking equally surprised and very uncomfortable. "Call security."

The younger executive waves his hand, and a call matrix appears before him in the air.

"Tran," I say, "It's *me*. It's Sattari."

"No doubt you saw his face on the AVE, know about his crime," Tran rages. "It disgusts me that your kind would stoop so low in the name of hallucinatory entertainment. Did you think I'd already ingested?"

I pull my shirt up over my head. My shoulder is bare, my tattoo revealed. "Look," I tell him. "No joke. It's me."

He stares at the brand, caught between his indignation and his inability to decide what to do. At last he chews his lip into a decision. He whispers to the younger man, whose expression changes into one of angst as he rises and quickly leaves the room.

As soon as the door closes, Tran is upon me. "Sattari," he says, gripping me by my shoulders. "What in the *hell* are you doing?"

"I'm applying for my old job back," I say, fliply.

"Do you have any idea what an embarrassment this is?" he rages, hurling his words into my face. "We have you locked up!"

"What are you talking about?"

"We couldn't just let one of the most powerful men in CUSA disgrace Our President and walk away! That would have destroyed consumer confidence! We had to transfer your identity to a nobody, a rickshaw driver or something, so we'd have someone to put away for your crimes."

"So take me out," I say reasonably. "Give me back my tattoo and let me go."

Tran shoves me with as much force as his weak little arms can manage. Gamely, I back away and watch him, pensive, take a seat by the window.

"Why are you here?" he demands, facing the glass.

"I need help," I tell him. "I've been in the US, out in the woods, Clear Point, near Richmond. I have to get back there immediately. There's a girl—"

"When you left," Tran says, as if I hadn't spoken at all, "it created an enormous mess. Don't you understand that by leaving before terminating the employment of the million, you put the portfolio in limbo?"

"What?"

"The order had to come from you," Tran says. "Your office knew who was to be expunged. We couldn't just kill any old one million!" He wipes his hand across his mouth. "Nobody wanted to give the order. No one was willing to take responsibility to ferret out which million were to die. By the time we started to get things in motion again, someone had begun selling tip-off information to people about their termination. Some of them got out, changed names. It's been chaos!" Tran turns towards me once more, spit flying. "We still haven't resolved it! We've had to float billions to support these people who should have been dead six months ago. All that number has to be *reconciled*."

"That's not the worst of your problems," I say. "You have to help me get back to the US."

"Why?" demands Tran from the window. "Why shouldn't I have you incinerated right now?"

"Because General Ahmad Khorasani has discovered that our National Defense is just an extremely expensive commercial."

You would think that someone had dropped an iron bar on Tran's foot. He stiffens. "What?"

"It's over, Tran! The Homefront Campaign is a failure! Khorasani came to see for himself what our defenses were like. He didn't trust the commercials. Now he knows."

"This is the end," Tran says melodramatically, chewing a fingernail on his right hand. "This is the end!"

"I can show you where he landed," I say. "It's not too late! I can take you to the spot where I saw the soldier. We can—"

The door dissolves, and in the frame stands a striking woman about six feet tall, unyielding in her chiseled glamour, sleek black hair flowing over her shoulders and overflowing her halo, a woman with whom I am far too familiar.

"I knew you'd come back," she says, smiling.

"And I should have known you'd hear about it," I reply. "Maria."

Maria DeCarvalho moves swiftly towards me. To Tran, she curtly says, "Leave us." Tran, still shaken by my news, tries to blurt out to her.

"They've—"

"Yes," she says. "I watched the whole conversation on the AVE coming up the elevator. I always thought the Campaign was a stupid idea."

"It worked for fifty years," I say.

"Oh, Firoz," Maria says, rolling her eyes. "As if fifty years meant anything in the life of a Corporation."

Again she says to Tran, "*Leave us.*" The executive, now turned lackey, hastens out the door of his own office to leave me in the company of my former partner. My wife.

She sits on the sofa and settles in. She's looking at me the way she used to, as if I hadn't changed a bit. "It's so good to see you, Firoz."

"Thanks, Maria" I reply.

"You were always such a good team player."

"Thanks," I grunt.

"Especially our team."

I take her meaning. I look away. "How's Felipe?" I ask her.

"He's all right. He already has his own ideas, but we're working on that. Anyway, you'd be pleased with him."

I get up to stare out the window. My view is to the south. I can see the top of the Reagan Monument from here, the white obelisk towering over the submerged Mall wetland. "I came to offer you a deal," I say.

"You want us to fly you down to wherever it is you've been for the last six months in return for telling us where General Khorasani will make his landing."

"Yes."

"That's not much of a deal," she says, her eyes twinkling. "I have a better one."

"What?"

"How about we reactivate you?"

"*What?*" Even though it's what I expected her to say, the idea still seems ludicrous. "Why would you want me back?"

"You're being far too modest," Maria croons. "You think *Siyos* as talented as you grow like weeds?"

"I wasn't that talented."

"Do you know what I loved about you, Firoz?" Maria says, getting up and moving towards me. She puts one of her hot hands on my neck, and I inadvertently feel my desire rise at the same time that my nausea threatens to send me running from those long, shiny fingernails. "What I *love* about you? Your *ruthlessness!*" Her voice is coming out as a deep purr, as if she were some kind of cat. "Suggesting we terminate one million of our citizens to balance the budget, that was *brilliant!* Do you think we get *Siyos* with that kind of chutzpah every day?"

"Not so brilliant," I mutter, my legs shaking. I want to run away. I want to stay right here. Which do I want?

"Well, the plan was brilliant. Its implementation? That *would* have been brilliant, if you'd carried it out. What happened?"

"I don't know," I admitted. "I guess I wanted a second opinion."

"From yourself? Is that why you joined the Drug Church? To hear voices in your head tell you what to do?"

She is terrifyingly spot on, and I nod involuntarily, lulled by the sinuous stroking of her fingernails.

"You could have asked *me*. I could have told you what would happen. Just like Tran says. No one at CUSA could take up that stone once you dropped it. Too many details lost in your personal records. Even if someone had been willing, the mess you left behind was beyond any of us to sort out. The only one who could repair it was you."

She is silent now. I hear the sound of my own heart pounding. I strain to hear her heart beat, too, but all I can make out is the whisper of the air conditioning coming from the vents. Suddenly I understand what she is saying.

"You don't just want me back," I say, turning to her. "You want me to pick up where I left off."

She is smiling at me, our faces just inches apart. Brusquely I shove past her and out of her grasp. Unfazed, she does not stop smiling.

"You expect me to submit to reactivation and take the punishment for all those lives I extended. You want me to hunt those people down and see to it that they're killed properly."

"You understand me perfectly," says Maria, her smile broadening.

"Yes, I do," I reply. "That's why I left you."

Maria's face goes hard as if it had become an iron mask. Her eyes retreat into cold dark sockets . "Let's get something straight," she says, her voice taut. "*I* left *you*. Your tiresome compassion was always nothing but disguised self pity." I have disrupted her momentum, gotten to her. "Felipe certainly didn't need that kind of role model. It would have been a death sentence."

"I should kill *myself!*" I snap. "That would be more pleasant. How could I even afford to take on—"

"Oh, Firoz!" Maria chides, moving towards me once again. "Don't be naive. Our President doesn't want a destitute *Siyo!* He'll take care of you. Apart from some public condemnation, some apologies on the AVE, no one will make you surrender your number to cover the Corporation's debt! Not when you're the only one with the mind to get us out of it in the first place. Of course, it might take more than a million lives to settle the balance now."

My head spins in horror. "Forget it!" I yell. "It's not worth it."

"Why do you want to go back to the US, Firoz?" Maria has always had a sixth sense for getting to someone. "Is it a girl?" I do not answer, but Maria has never been fazed by my silence. She stares fixedly at me. Then she nods like I've confirmed her suspicions and she smiles. "Do you *love her*, Firoz?" she asks. I make no reply. "Does she love *you?*" she presses. Shaking, I can no longer hold my head up. I gaze at the navy blue carpet. "So compassionate!" Maria says, trying not to laugh. "Why not save her, then? There's still time, you know."

I tremble involuntarily, unable to raise my gaze from the carpet. She has me where she wants me.

"I'm supposed to trade a million lives for one," I mutter, by way of arguing with her.

"Maybe you could find a way to save the million, Firoz," Maria suggests. "Did you ever think of that? Maybe we could find a way to do it *together*."

I look up at her. The corner of her mouth is curled up with amusement, as if I am a laboratory animal. I know her far too well.

"Look at it this way," she says reasonably, moving away from me to sit on Tran's desk, her legs crossing beneath her skirt. "You're here now. You can't imagine we'll let you go. Really, the choice is whether you want to cooperate or not. Be reinstated and do your best for Our President, or be stubborn and remain under arrest for the rest of your life. Either way, the million will die. It's only a matter of time. The question is, do you want to use your power to make a difference, or not?"

I gaze at her. I am tired, so tired and weak. My last reserves are failing under the onslaught of Maria's argument.

Smoothly, Maria gestures in the air. A holographic signing pad appears beneath her fingers, ready for my fingerprint. "We'll make it easy for you," she says. "Come over here and let Our President know you're back." She beckons with her fingernails. At first I do not move, but it's like pulling against a leash. "Come on, Firoz," she urges. "It's best."

Still, I hold out.

"Do you want your girl to *die*?" she asks, quietly.

No. Not for what I did. I fall towards the holograph as if it is a well of gravity. My fingers sink deep within it, and in an unjustly short moment I commit to the fate laid out for me and for one million others. Instantly my AVE is back. I am looking at the world through a green glow.

"Good boy!" says Maria DeCarvalho. "Now go sit in the stasis chair." She waves her arm over towards Tran's chair. Obediently I plod over and drop into it. Instantly the dull sensation of timelessness overwhelms me. Ah, stasis! How I've missed you.

I don't recover in the same place. They've taken the liberty of moving me. Instead of a chair, I regain consciousness in a white bed, in a sterile, cool room. Always disoriented from the nothingness of those chairs, it takes me a while even to realize I've been in stasis.

I'm curious to know the hour. I look around. I've been placed in some kind of mini-suite with a bed, a sofa, a refrigerator. My AVE is quietly humming a commercial to me. I am lying on the bed, dressed in a pair of white pajamas.

I check the AVE for the time and date, resisting the temptation to buy a personal timepiece it offers, but although I can determine that it's morning, I realize that I had no idea what day it was when I arrived. How long have I been out?

The door is locked and will not open from the inside. There is nothing to do. Finally someone comes in. "Mr.

Sattari?" says a young woman in a Young Gun's outfit. "Are you feeling rested?"

"Yes, I suppose!" I snarl. "How long have you had me in stasis?"

"They kept you under for thirty-six hours."

"Thirty-six hours?" I cry. "Whose order was that?"

"Ms. DeCarvalho said you needed a full medical examination before you could be fit for reinstatement. The traces of drugs in your system have been purged. You've been reconditioned and you should be feeling a lot—"

"Am I a *Siyo* again?" I demand, sweeping my feet off the bed and standing before her.

"Yes!" she replies. "Of course!"

"Then get me the hell out of here, *now!*"

She doesn't know how to respond. Obviously she's been given instructions to the contrary.

"I want a suit of clothes," I say, putting my finger in her face. "I want an aircopter ready to go as soon as possible, fueled for a trip to the Richmond area."

"Mr. Sattari..." She hesitates.

"Are you capable of making these things happen," I ask, "Or do I need to *fire* you?"

She doesn't argue again.

As I cross-reference the location of Virgilina and Steaksbury on the AVE, I wonder just how far I should take this. Do I have the power to muster a squadron of Young Guns? I could overpower the Elder, and take what I want. The thought of wiping the smug smile off his face would give me immense satisfaction.

But it's been thirty-six hours. The Elder may have given up on me, if he ever expected me to return at all. Glory could be long dead. What would be the point of taking the town? No, I need to get down there as quickly as possible and find out what's happened.

As I board the cop, I feel certain Maria will interrupt me any minute, appear in my halo, countermand my orders. But she doesn't. She is nowhere to be seen. Does she know I'm recovered? Is she too busy working on a solution to the MexIranian army?

A tiny holograph of the pilot appears by my right shoulder. "Mr. Sattari," it says, "I've got the coordinates from the information you gave me. We can be there in thirty minutes."

"Don't land us too close," I say. "There's an old highway about ten kilometers west of town. Set us down there so no one knows we're coming."

"Right, sir."

My escort is restless during the short flight. She doesn't seem to know what to do, who to obey. The closer the cop comes to its destination, the more unsure she appears.

"Stay here," I say, shutting off my AVE halo. "I'll contact you when it's time to come in."

"You can't do that, Mr. Sattari," she protests as the cop touches down. "Before you woke up, Ms. DeCarvalho told me—"

"It's all right," I reassure her. "I'll take a sprayer with me. That way you know I'll be safe."

The woman shakes her head reluctantly. "No," she says. "I'm afraid I have to go wherever you go."

"Suit yourself," I say, as the cop lands with a bump. She does: She puts on a jacket and takes the only sprayer, acting as my bodyguard and prison guard both. I deactivate my halo. Together we descend from the cop onto the old highway on which we have landed.

The old expressway west of Clear Point is broken in many places from rock-slides and the attacks of the vagabonds who live out here. As we work our way down a sloping hill towards the road leading to the woods we can see the remnants of an old settlement under the overpass. It looks as though it's been abandoned for months, but the occupants may simply have scattered when they heard the engine of the cop.

My escort and I travel along what used to be the main strip. It runs between a series of ransacked restaurants and hotels. Cars scattered here and there, some used as dwellings, others as barricades, litter the cracked roadway.

At last the strip narrows. and the road is covered by summer foliage. My companion hasn't spoken once.

It's beginning to grow dark, and the coverage of the branches deepens the effect. This far out of town, nobody lives in the houses on either side of the road. Some have been stripped of everything and retain only an aluminum shell or a fireplace. After a while, the street begins to vanish from beneath our feet. The Young Gun is clearly uncomfortable with all of this.

Suddenly the Young Gun's head is slapped back by the force of an explosion. Her body follows in a lurching arc, and she falls lifeless to the ground.

Several men emerge from behind the trees holding rifles and shotguns. One of them is Cob.

Cob's swollen face has more of a mix of emotions than anything I've ever seen from him before. He looks both disgusted and also somehow glad to see me, and he doesn't know which to feel. "What are you doing?" he asks, not knowing the right question for the situation.

"Escaping," I tell him, while I swallow my own revulsion at another life wasted for my own. "This uniform had me in her power, this CUSA garbage. She wanted me to show her the town. I think she wanted—" I run out of ideas, but I've said enough. The men look at the faceless body. "But there are more," I say.

"Spigger!" cries a voice from across the woods.

I look up to see Sheriff Lyman and seven of his men, their faces lit dimly by the remaining poor light from the west. They have surrounded me at a distance as though I'm some kind of radioactive element.

"What are you doing, Sheriff?" I ask wearily.

"Just shut your mouth!" he barks, making a jerky little movement in my direction with the muzzle of his gun.

"Did you think I wasn't coming back?"

In answer, he cocks his gun and raises it to his shoulder. "You men get on," he says to Cob and the others. "I'll deal with this."

Cob and his friends quickly disperse. Now it's just me and Lyman and his men. "Leave him to me," the Sheriff says to his men, putting his gun to his shoulder. My mind races.

"You know why the Elder let me go?" I ask the Sheriff quickly, almost before I can think.

"Shut up!" snaps Lyman, aiming the rifle at my head.

"Aren't you supposed to take me to him?" I ask quietly, reasonably.

"I said, shut up!" the Sheriff repeats. His trigger finger trembles.

"The Elder and I, we're partners now," I continue, smoothly. "I'm his new Sheriff. Didn't you know that?"

The Sheriff's hands fall a little. His mouth begins to work hard, in an obsessive, chewing motion. His men are looking at him, unsure.

"It's true. He sent me back to CUSA to bring him guns, and men, *real* men, men who can serve him. Not like you."

"That's a damned lie," snarls the Sheriff.

"If you don't believe me," I say casually, "Let's go see him. He'll tell you himself. But if you kill me, he'll be so angry, I'm sure you'll be the next one to die."

The Sheriff wavers, unsure. His men are frozen, not daring to make a move without their leader.

Finally, "Come on!" Sheriff Lyman snarls, gesturing up the path with his gun.

"Good boy," I say.

We head halfway up the path, with me in the lead. All of a sudden I notice how quiet it has become. I stop, and I hear the sound of a gun cocking once more. I turn around in surprise to look back up the muzzle of the Sheriff's rifle.

The Sheriff aims at the sky and shoots. The thunder shakes the treetops. It is just the two of us here in the darkness. He must have instructed his men to stay behind. Why?

Sheriff Lyman's eyes narrow wickedly. I have seen those eyes before. "I'd have taken you to the Elder of course, Seenyour. But then you tried to run. What else was I supposed to do?" The Sheriff grins. "Now it'll just be you and me, just like it was when you got here." Instinctively my body grows cold as the sound of the Sheriff's voice transforms itself. "We're gonna *string ya up, Spook!*"

I can't help myself. I run, just like he wants, my feet splaying panicked through the tree roots, my heart filling my throat with each pounding of blood that passes through it. Not like this, I think. Not like this!

His limping footsteps are just behind me, and other men are flanking me—men in white sheets made black by the night, holding torches high, surrounding me, distant but too close. It won't be long, I think. Not long now, at all.

Something wraps around my legs, and I hurtle headlong into black brambles. I tumble, trying to regain my balance, but I am quickly overcome and land on my stomach. I turn towards my attacker, ready to fight for my life.

But he is not attempting to restrain me. He sits across from me, his gentle fingers wrapped in my shirt. "Put on my clothes and give me yours. Stay down."

"Pastor?" I am incredulous.

"In the dark they'll never know the difference," he mutters reassuringly.

"What are you talking about?"

"You have to live," he says.

"You can't do this!" I shove him away, but his hands are on me vengefully. He is far stronger than I would have suspected.

"Please," the Pastor says, imploring me. "Please. It's all I have left." His face is far away as he contemplates all he has ruined, all he has lost.

"To die?"

"To be redeemed. I don't know another way. Please."

The men are getting closer now, triangulating upon us.

"I'll take your place and lead them away," the Pastor says.

"No!"

"Firoz!" insists the Pastor. "You must believe me. I never meant to harm Glory. I never would have...I loved her more than life."

"Is she your daughter?"

He winces, looks around. "Her mother died for the sin we committed. I thought by taking Glory, I could atone. But the Lord brings things back around for us to face from a different direction." He looks down. "I tried to change the circumstances of my life. I thought I wasn't really capable of what I had done...that it wasn't me. I thought, if I did good...then...in that way...that my sin would be cancelled out."

My heart begins pounding. I understand him perfectly.

"*Señor!*" he cries. Have they heard his voice? Do they know the Pastor is lying here? "Please!"

Will his black outfit protect me?

Hastily, my eyes burning from the torch smoke all around us, I throw off my white pajamas and take the Pastor's clothes. Triumphant, the Pastor leaps to his feet wearing my CUSA clothes. Bending down, he suddenly seizes my face in his hands which are dough-warm and soft. "Whatever you've done," he says, gazing into my eyes with compassion and joy. "You've got to *forgive* yourself. Do you understand? You can't do the right thing until..."

"Get him! This way!" they shout, spotting the moving figure that has now become me. The Pastor looks up with alarm, then hurtles into the woods, pulling them away from me. I lie still on the cold ground, horribly ashamed with my head down, as a shot rings out.

When the last sounds have faded into the distance, I rise feeling cowardly, ragged, unworthy in the Pastor's robes. I lope along, searching half-heartedly for the road, still terrified of every distant sound, even though all I can hear is the laugh of the crickets.

Then I hear something else.

As I get closer I increase my pace, knowing full well that I may be too late, that Glory's body may already be draped over the courthouse steps, and I wonder, is there anything I can do, really, to stop what I have started?

The sound I heard grows louder, an insistent thrumming, a ragged, hoarse, self-satisfied insistence of a voice. It talks on and on, loving to hear itself speak, the way it did at the Thanksgiving supper, the way it did in front of me. The words begin to come clear, righteous words, arrogant, yet compelling in a way that only leaders' words are. "Transgression," "sin," "God."

The first sentences are clear as the sparks of the torches become apparent through the dense branches. The only thing that keeps me going is the fact that this voice would not be speaking if Glory were dead. By the time I emerge from the woods into the outskirts of the downtown, I can hear the owner of the voice, Elder Oughta, as he gives his customary lecture before another one of his trust is murdered in the name of the Law.

Glory is standing in a simple grey dress, staring sideways at the ground, her hands bound behind her. She is meant to see the townspeople standing before her with rocks in their hands, hefting them for weight, itching for the signal to throw, for the release of the terrible anticipation, the permission to enact the ritual. But in her mind she is far away from this scene.

I want to call to her, bring her back from Heaven or Wheeling or wherever she is, as if I could will myself into spirit form and float to her, make her insubstantial, untouchable by this mob.

But it isn't Glory who sees me first. It's one of Mrs. Bell's kids.

"Firoz!" he cries, rushing over, a rock in his hand. "Firoz! Did you come for the stoning?" Other children follow, tied to one another by the giddiness of the evening entertainment. Before I can stop them, I am surrounded by them, waist high in innocent delight. Each one tries to hand me a rock.

Now all the townspeople have turned. Now the Elder's voice has stopped, and his eyebrows go up. Is he surprised to see me? Or is he simply surprised to see me alone, in the Pastor's robes, with no army of Young Guns, no sprayers, no retinue?

"And what can we do for you this evening, *señor?*" he asks obsequiously.

"Glory!" I shout, now free to seize her attention.

Glory's head jerks up, but she is not delighted to see me. I can't read her expression at all. Is it dread? Would that be possible? Have I caused her nothing but misery?

"Firoz..." Mrs. Bell says, coming up behind her children. Her face is very sad. "You shouldn't have come. You shouldn't have come back."

"You've got to stop this, Charlotte," I cry. "You can stop this!"

She looks so forlorn, but not because of what she is about to witness, not because of the stone in her own hand.

"You're not part of this," she says, shaking her head.

"You're wrong!" I protest. "You're all wrong! It's *my* sin! Not hers!"

"Your sin was being born with a black skin," says Mrs. Bell. "Not your fault. No one expects anything of you."

"This girl, on the other hand," exclaims the Elder. He makes a motion towards Glory with his head. "This girl is one of God's children, and she has let her God down. "

"You said you'd let her go!" I scream.

The Elder looks suddenly uncomfortable. The people of the town turn their heads uncertainly from one to the other of us. "I never said any such thing!" he curses. "Some of you men seize this gorilla."

But nobody moves on me. They are still afraid of me, of something I represent, their own darkness. I take advantage of the moment to move towards Glory. Perhaps the hesitancy of these people will save us in the end. But the children slow me down. They are like a sea, uncomprehending, but an obstacle nonetheless. I have to wade through them. I don't want to knock any of them over.

In the time it takes me to break free, some of the adults have come between me and Glory. I look up to see Whitaker standing before me, chewing his lip, holding a gun. He intends to ward me off, but he looks none too sure of himself.

"Whitaker!" I cry. "What are you doing?"

"Seenyour?" he mutters under his breath.

"Do you love her?" I demand to know.

He doesn't answer.

"Do you *love her?*" I shout at him.

He looks up at me, and I know that this is his answer. "Then redeem yourself," I whisper into his face.

With a startled blink, Whitaker pauses. A light goes on in his head. Then he turns. He holds the gun to his shoulder and points it at the Elder.

Only the fire breathes. Everyone else has gone stock still. They could be an old oil painting, the skeleton of death peering over the edge of the hill.

"Let 'er go, Elder," Whitaker utters.

The Elder is clearly shocked. Slowly, he finds his voice. "You've been living with that Pastor too long," he remarks. "Don't you know you'll go to Hell for disobeying me like this?"

"So be it," answers Whitaker, "but you'll let her go."

The Elder remains calm. "Didn't you ever wonder why I gave her to you, Whitaker?"

Whitaker's arms shake just the tiniest bit as he continues to point the gun at the Elder.

"Why I sent you to live with that wretch of a Pastor in the first place?"

"Sure," Whitaker says quietly. "I used to wonder. But I think I know, now." He swallows once. "You're my pop, aren't you?"

The Elder smiles widely, nodding several times. "That's my boy! Figured it out. Smarter than I thought. I underestimated you. I never should have sent you off with your mother and that troupe."

Whitaker's face crumples. "You knew my mama?" he asks, as if the obvious is only now occurring to him.

But the Elder does not want to continue this conversation in front of his people. "Put the gun down, son," he implores, putting out a hammy hand. I notice his own stone, the black heart of rock, held in that manicured palm.

Whitaker has frozen now. The gun is still in place, still aimed at its target, but Whitaker has chosen not to move rather than to give way to the uncertainty that is surely racing through his mind.

"Put it down!" orders the Elder. "Act like a man for once!"

The insult strikes home, and again Whitaker trembles.

Glory has been watching the whole scene from her perch on the steps of the courthouse. Oblivious to me, she nonetheless seems to want to know her own fate.

Now, as Whitaker's resolve begins to waver, her eyes open wide.

But Whitaker has not dropped the rifle. He continues to point it, though now it is aimed for the Elder's chest rather than his head. The Elder is studying Whitaker carefully, looking for an entrance, for the right words to seize the strings of this man who threatens his life.

Finally, the Elder's face softens, and he speaks quietly to Whitaker across the space. "I'll find you someone worthy of you," he says.

Whitaker's eyes open wide. His mouth opens soundlessly. Then he finds the words. "To Hell with you," he says.

A terrible shot rings out across the still woods, splitting the crackle of the torches and echoing across the hills.

Whitaker's gun leaps from his arms in a rusty arc and clatters to the ground. Whitaker seizes his right shoulder and lets loose a stream of curses. The Elder has crouched unceremoniously at the sound, looking undignified in the face of his own death. But realizing he is unharmed, he turns and quickly stands up, his expression of triumph returned.

I follow his gaze and see the Sheriff, still pointing his own gun at Whitaker from the edge of the woods.

"That's enough," says the Elder quickly, gesturing at the Sheriff with his hand. "Don't kill him. Not now." Disregarding his son and disregarding me, he swings his head towards Glory. "It's time!" he cries. "Who will cast the first stone?"

The children surge forward, each of them without sin. They rush to the edge of the courthouse stairs and cock their arms back, ready to hurl their missiles at their target.

"Wait for my word!" instructs the Elder. They pause, though they are obviously hard to contain. Behind them, the adults prepare their own rocks for the assault while Whitaker stands helpless, gripping his bloody arm in his other hand.

"On three, then," says the Elder, shaking off the last effects of his own near-death. "One..."

"No!" I cry.

"Two!"

"Wait!" I protest. "Doesn't she get to speak before you kill her?"

"Stop this!" cries a woman's voice.

My legs sag at the sound of Glory's reprieve.

She steps out into the clearing, tall, dignified, and the Elder is transfixed by the vision.

"I order you to halt this idiocy or we'll shoot everyone in the square," says my wife, Maria DeCarvalho.

"No," I moan. "No."

Maria takes no notice of me. Like a hostess at a magnificent party, her green halo winking around her head, she struts around the small torchlit area while Young Guns fill in behind her, each with a sprayer pointed at a different citizen. As they come into view, one by one, lit up like Ex-mas ornaments in the torchlight, the townfolk gape, awe-struck.

The Elder turns towards me. "What is this, spigger?" he demands.

"The end of you," I mutter, barely audible.

"Is this some kind of joke? Are these the guns you promised me?"

"If you want guns, that can be arranged," says Maria. "Are you the owner of this town?" The Elder has to think about that one. He's not used to defining himself in those terms. "I am," he finally says.

I look up at my wife through the tops of my eyes, barely able to lift my head. I'm fairly certain I know what she's about to do.

"It's the most expedient solution," she answers me, smiling, her eyes sparkling in the firelight. Even the bugs seem in awe of her. They fly around her head, but they refuse to land.

"Maria," I begin. "You can't..."

"Don't talk to him, talk to *me*," says the Elder, taking his black stone and thumping it against his chest.

"I'll talk to whomever I please," retorts Ms. DeCarvalho, looking the Elder square in the face. "You, on the other hand, will keep your mouth shut."

The Elder is flabbergasted and almost drops his stone, huffing and puffing. As satisfying as the spectacle is, I find I am just the tiniest bit sorry for him in that moment. He has no way of dealing with someone like Maria. He has no experience to tell him what she is. Only the guns pointed in his face give him some notion of his true place in the new scheme of things.

"Maria, they're *people*," I begin again. "They can't be bought and sold like cattle."

"Don't be sentimental," Maria says coolly, cutting me off with a wave of her hand.

"Look here," says the Elder, interrupting again, though a little more contrite. "What's this about buying people?"

"As a representative of CUSA I'm here to make a legal purchase of this town from its agent or title-holder. Is that you, because if it isn't, stand down and send the right person over here."

"No, it's me, it's me," the Elder hastily replies. He catches on quick.

Maria smiles. "That's what I thought. What currency are you using here?"

"Some gold...we mostly trade..." fumbles the Elder.

Maria tries unsuccessfully to hide her disdain. "All right," she says. "The easiest way would be to make you a citizen of CUSA and provide you with the requisite number."

"Number?" the Elder repeats.

"Elder," I try to intercede.

"Enough credit with the Corporation to provide you with a comfortable existence for the rest of your life, a fashionable dwelling..."

"What about my people?" Elder wants to know, looking around, gesturing at everyone including the woman still bound with her hands behind her, standing in the clearing center.

"They'll be well-ta..."

"They'll be herded like..." I try to intercede.

"Firoz!" cries Maria, her voice snapping across the clearing like a rifle retort, bringing me up short. "What good will it do to say things like that?"

I know she's right. Though I am reeling, though my very bones are writhing beneath my skin, her reasoned voice continues in my head. It would do no good. It would frighten them when they really have no choice. At this point, they can either believe something good will happen to them, or they can live out the rest of their brief lives in terror.

"We'll take good care of all your people," Maria reassures the Elder. "In the meantime, we want to take good care of you." She gestures in the air. Instantly a signature pad appears before her, precisely like the one I stuck my hand through two days ago. The Elder jumps back when he sees it. Standing on his toes, he peers at it from a safer distance.

Nauseated I turn and run, escape towards the darkness of the woods. No one tries to stop me, no warnings issue forth. I am allowed to penetrate the blackness and sink into it.

I've done this. Everything that's happening here started when I failed to make a choice.

I have little conception of where I'm going, but I find myself at the door of the Elder's house nonetheless. The gate is wide open. No guards remain to ward it. Everyone is in town for the stoning. I stumble through, not knowing where I want to be.

My feet take me down the familiar hallway, my nose following the path of stale tobacco smoke towards the study, where a constellation of ship and plane models are arrayed carefully around various tables and counters. I walk up to them and gingerly touch them with my palm, almost afraid to dislodge them. The little pieces stick to my clammy hand, then drop to the tabletop, bouncing haphazardly in a different order than they were.

I turn towards the door by which I entered.

The blond-haired boy is there. He stands in the doorway watching me silently.

"This is the end isn't it?" I ask. "There's nowhere to run this time."

He stares at me with no emotion.

"What do I do?" I ask him.

The boy moves towards me. He reaches out to take my hand and he pulls. I follow him where he goes, around the desk in the Elder's office. Silently, the boy opens the desk drawer and pulls my hand down so that it touches the cold, black metal of the revolver.

Now I have a gun in my hand.

"What?" I ask him, though I know exactly what he's saying. "What do you want me to do?" But I know. I know the choice he's giving me.

The boy stands before me, studying my face carefully with his pale blue eyes.

"I know I deserve this," I say, "But I can't do it alone. Help me."

The boy does not move, shows no interest in relieving my discomfort.

"Please help me," I beg. "Tell me to do it." He does not respond does not react at all, but patiently watches.

I point the gun directly at him. "You have to help me."

The boy shows no concern. He just simply stares.

"Tell me to do it," I say, "Or I'll do it to you."

No response. No answer at all.

"Answer!" I yell. "Me, or you?"

I am sweating, now, the moisture dripping out of the sides of my head. He refuses to reply. Just stares and blinks, waiting for me.

Slowly I raise the gun so it points to my head.

The barrel is cool against my beaded temple. The hole fits neatly into the gap behind my eyebrow. How long will it take the bullet to glide through its pathway, slide into my head, betray me with its kiss?

The gun seems heavy, impossibly weighty. My wrist aches, my hand trembles. If I don't act soon, I won't be able to hold it up. It may drop and shoot me uselessly in the leg. I cock it with my thumb.

I feel the cold steel thumping against my sweaty forehead. I'll do it in just a few seconds. In just a few seconds it will be over. I'll be unable to make any more bad decisions.

I pause. I breathe.

I imagine a little girl who decided to run away.

I pause, I breathe.

I have a vision of a common man deciding to become something greater than he is.

My hand shakes, and shakes, and my heart thumps louder, louder and louder.

I remember the decision the little boy had to make, the one that gave me the body and the blood.

Are my eyes closed? Someone is walking in my direction whose face I can't see, but she glides towards me ghostly, tall and slender on feet that make no sound. Even as she approaches I can't bear to look up at her, but I think I know what expression would be on her face if I did. Compassion, pity. Sadness. She reaches up to my gun hand with her own two hands and embraces it in them. Long, cool fingers. They touch the sinews between my digits, say hello to my ridges.

Gently they urge the gun away from my head. I protest inwardly. It's me or him, I think. Me, or *him*. But the downward pull is insistent, not defiant but compelling. I feel her touch and I want to do what she says.

The barrel moves down, down, until it is pointing towards the floor.

I love you...

I expel a trembling breath, still shaking terribly in my insides.

"You know, I wasn't sure if you were going to do it." A woman's voice. Is it her? No, this is farther away. I open my eyes.

Watching me the whole time while she leaned against the doorframe, watching me decide whether or not to kill myself, Maria's eyes are fixed upon me. Under that cool, calculating gaze, I sweated and squirmed. I'm some kind of show for her.

"Would you have cared?" I ask, my voice betraying the tremors.

She smiles and doesn't answer me. "You've decided to live after all?"

My eyes lose their focus. My arm lowers. "If you can call it that."

"Oh, don't be silly, Firoz," she chides me, and she stands. "What do *you* have to die for?"

"For them."

"They don't need that!" she scoffs.

"How would you know what they need?" I hiss.

"We all need the same thing, Firoz," she says, walking slowly into the room. "To feel like what we do matters."

She is right, as always. Infuriated, I gaze around at the room, the room full of models. They are useless now, deprived of their maker. "Where's that boy," I ask.

"What boy?"

"The little boy, the blond-haired boy. The one who handed me the gun."

Maria shakes her head. "I never saw a boy." She frowns. "You pulled the gun out yourself. I thought we detoxified you."

"Don't make fun of me!"

She is perplexed, but she turns it into her habitual mocking smile.

I hear the silence. With the boy gone, vanished completely and forever, silence sounds like a thing I could hold. No longer just the absence of sound. It signifies something new.

"Your girl is going to be all right," she says, moving towards me listlessly. Her fingers curl over my gun-hand so that we are both holding it. "Does that please you?"

I throw off her hot, confining hand with an irritated flick of my slippery wrist. "Glory?"

"Whatever," she shrugs. "The man she was with, they're getting on a cop now. Do you want me to do anything special with them?"

They left together. They are together now. Whatever happens, I've done one thing right.

"No," I reply. "It...it doesn't matter anymore."

"That's what I say," she says, seeming glad of my answer. "Are you ready to go?"

"I'll stay here."

"Don't be ridiculous!" she replies with a patronizing grin. "There's going to be a war here!" Beckoning with her red manicured nails, she says "Come on."

I blink a couple of times, and again soak in the silent air. It is soothing, forgiving. I place the gun on the desk, hear the sound it makes as it comes in contact with the wooden surface, how loud a sound like that can be.

Stepping away from the gun, from the bureau and the dusty models, I move beyond my wife. I step out the door and into the unlit woods. It is difficult to make my way for fear I'll trip and fall on my face in front of her. Maria has a little flashlight, but I want to get as much distance between us as I can, even if it means falling.

I think about the space between me and my wife. As I ran into the darkness, I threw others out behind me to create a buffer between my actions and their ramifications. But nothing remains between us now.

Each time I have come into the light, it has only been a respite. Darkness is inevitable, even necessary, my salvation all along. Love is in the darkness. It is felt when not seen, making some things more apparent: horror, despair, and self-deception. Through darkness I have seen more than the light would bear.

When I resurface, take a gasp in the light, I may choose to do something about what I have seen.

The torches will be out. Nothing will guide me back to the town.

What should I do? I don't know. More than nothing, more than run. Something that speaks to the light, that answers the absence of love. Something that points to the darkness.

It has begun to rain once more. Soon the rain will be violent.

About the Author

Adam Cole is the author of five novels and numerous short stories. A music educator, he is the author of two nonfiction books on music: *Solfege Town* and *Ballet Music for the Dance Accompanist.* In addition, he maintains a certification in the <u>Feldenkrais Method (R)</u> which he uses to teach music in a unique way.

As a composer, Adam has written for a variety of ensembles and instruments. His orchestral piece, *Themes Off A Variation*, a tribute to Robert Schumann, is archived at the Schumann House in Zwickau, Germany. His music can be heard at <u>www.mymusicfriend.net</u>.

CPSIA information can be obtained at www.ICGtesting.com
Printed in the USA
LVOW121204121212

311246LV00001B/24/P